...and the Nocturne City novels

"*Pure Blood* pounds along hard on the heels of *Night Life*, and is every bit as much fun as the first in the series. With a gutsy, likable protagonist and a well-made fantasy world, *Pure Blood* is real enough to make you think twice about locking your doors at night. A swiftly-paced plot, a growing cast of solid supporting characters, and a lead character you can actually care about—Kittredge is a winner."
—Jim Butcher

"I loved the mystery and the smart, gutsy heroine."
—Karen Chance, *New York Times* bestselling author of *Claimed by Shadow*

"A nonstop thriller laced with a ferociously deadly menace. Count on Kittredge's heroine to never say die!"
—*RT Book Reviews*

"Kittredge takes readers on a dark adventure complete with thrills, chills, and a touch of romance. Well written...and impossible to set down."
—*Darque Reviews*

"Fast-paced, sexy, and witty with many more interesting characters than I have time to mention. I'm looking forward to reading more stories in the exciting Nocturne City series."
—*Fresh Fiction*

"Wow, I am still thinking about this book. The last time I reacted to a book this way, it was the first

Mercy Thompson book by Patricia Briggs. If you are looking for a book that seamlessly blends a police procedural with a paranormal, go out and get this book." —*Night Owl Romance*

"A tense, gritty urban fantasy that grips the audience from the onset." —*Mystery Gazette*

"Caitlin Kittredge just keeps honing her craft with each new book. *Second Skin* has some pretty creepy elements and page-turning action. Readers who enjoy good solid urban fantasy will enjoy this installment." —*A Romance Review*

"*Night Life* dived right into the action, and carried me along for the ride...If the following books are written with the same care and interest as *Night Life*, they will be a welcome addition to this fantasy genre." —*Armchair Interviews*

"Hot, hip, and fast-paced, I couldn't put [*Night Life*] down. Don't go to bed with this book—it will keep you up all night. It's that good."
—Lilith Saintcrow, national bestselling author of *Working for the Devil*

"Luna is tough, smart, and fierce, hiding a conflicted and insecure nature behind her drive for justice and independence, without falling into cliché...a lot of fun to read."
—Kat Richardson, national bestselling author of *Poltergeist*

DEVIL'S BUSINESS

CAITLIN KITTREDGE

St. Martin's Paperbacks

This is a work of fiction. All of the characters, organizations, and events portrayed in this novel are either products of the author's imagination or are used fictitiously.

DEVIL'S BUSINESS

Copyright © 2011 by Caitlin Kittredge.

For information address St. Martin's Press, 175 Fifth Avenue, New York, NY 10010.

ISBN: 978-0-312-38823-2

Printed in the United States of America

St. Martin's Paperbacks edition / September 2011

St. Martin's Paperbacks are published by St. Martin's Press, 175 Fifth Avenue, New York, NY 10010.

10 9 8 7 6 5 4 3 2 1

PART ONE

LEGION

"I am the devil, and I'm here to do the devil's business."

— Charles "Tex" Watson,
member of the Manson Family

CHAPTER 1

When the checkout girl at Sainsbury's tried to murder him with her bare hands, Jack Winter decided he should probably get out of London for a while.

He'd joined her queue with a fistful of crisp packets, chocolate, and a few wrapped sandwiches. The woman ahead of him wanted to argue about her change, and Jack simply wanted to get outside so he could smoke.

The Sainsbury's on Fenchurch Street was crammed into a dingy granite shopfront above a 1960s brick box that tried to blend in with the older, more ornate row buildings around it and did a piss-poor job. The two front windows were planked over with plywood and caution tape, and Jack still detected the sandy crunch of glass fragments under his boots.

The area around Aldgate had gotten a hard hit from the rioting and general chaos of the weeks before, and the Sainsbury's was one of the few shops within striking distance of his flat that was open late, or open at all.

He shoved his food onto the belt and felt in his pockets for spare coins, few and far between these days. Any residual jobs he might have had as an exorcist or clearing homes and workplaces of the dead, or the undead, dried up with the chaos. When you're responsible for releasing an old god like Nergal from his prison to devour the psyches of London's inhabitants, people tended to hold it against you.

Even if you'd promptly helped put him back again.

Jack supposed that was fair. If he were a hearth witch, ghost finder, or anyone else who knew what'd really happened to cause half of London to lose their minds and take to the streets, he'd tell him to fuck off right along with them.

The checkout girl ran his food listlessly over the scanner, staring directly at a buzzing light tube behind Jack's head. His total popped up, and she just kept staring.

" 'Scuse me, luv," he said, thrusting his mess of lint-encrusted coins and a crumpled fiver at her. "I don't mean to be that bloke, but I wasn't planning on spending the entire night in your shop, edgy and deconstructed as it is in its present state."

He expected a sneer, or possibly a muttered curse—she looked the type, riot of blue hair and chain necklaces under her uniform shirt, in sharp contrast to most of her colleagues, who ran more along the lines of *hijabs* and sensible shoes.

She turned her dull gaze from the light fixture to his face, and Jack took a step back. Her eyes were entirely blank, and filmed over with the first stages of decomposition.

"You did this," she said, before she launched herself over the till at him.

His step back wasn't enough, and her fingernails caught Jack's neck. He fell into a display of tea mugs and digestive biscuits and slammed the floor hard. The checkout girl couldn't have weighed more than fifty kilos, but she wrapped her hands around Jack's throat with the strength and rage of a much larger and more predatory creature.

She was screaming, and black blood-infused spittle flecked her lips and chin and landed on his cheeks. She slammed Jack's head into the vinyl floor in time with each cry.

It wasn't the most alarming situation Jack had found himself in by a long shot, but it was worrisome enough. Deranged types were the worst—there was no reasoning with them, and usually the only way to end the scuffle was to knock them out or chop off their heads, depending on their level of deadness.

He gathered his legs under him and tried to buck the girl off, which worked in the sense that she flopped to one side but didn't detach her fingers from his throat. Hitting her with a paralysis hex at this range would be dangerous—the thing could bounce back and smack him in the nose, and then he'd be easy pickings for this crazy twat.

Jack decided on the next best thing—he balled up his fist and punched the girl under the eye, glancing the blow off her cheekbone. He'd more intended to startle than hurt her, but she hissed as if his fist were made of hot iron, falling back on her arse and scuttling through the broken glass. She paid no more mind to her cuts than if she were crawling through a bed of custard cake.

Hauling himself to his feet, Jack got out two breaths before the checkout girl was back up. "You did this," she repeated in a guttural, ragged snarl. Her movements weren't her own, her next attempt to tackle him resulting in Jack sidestepping and the girl falling into the sandwich case, more glass slicing at her skinny arms as it shattered.

Not a zombie—she was breathing like a chainsaw, pulse throbbing in her neck, plus she wasn't sewed up with red thread and encased in hoodoo magic. Not a demonic possession, either—his psychic sight wasn't pinging off the charts trying to tell him something from Hell was wearing a nice punk girl's skin.

Human magic then. That narrowed his options to fight back considerably.

Jack grabbed a mop from where the janitor had abandoned it and snapped the head off, holding the pointy end in front of him. "*Stop,*" he ordered when the girl came at him again. She was fading rapidly, blood flowing freely from her nose and mouth, black stuff oozing out of her tear ducts as her brain strained to contend with the violation of a compulsion spell.

Whoever was running the spell had to be nearby—and that was who interested Jack.

The girl ignored his ultimatum and sprang again. She was as agile as a shapeshifter with the accuracy of a predator. Whoever had hit her with the compulsion had juiced her with a few enhancements. No wonder her body was shutting down one system at a time. Soon her brain would pop and she'd be a blue-topped carrot on the floor of Sainsbury's.

Jack gripped the mop handle like a nightstick and whipped it up and across her temple as she came. He'd gotten hit by enough members of London's finest to know it was the quickest way to put someone down.

The girl dropped straight down, knees folding up. A thin line of blood ran across the tiles from her nose, and Jack swiped it onto his palm as he joined the exodus of panicking customers into the street.

He stopped, tried to catch more than a lungful of air, and cast his eyes up and down the pools of light illuminating Fenchurch Street. Most of the nearby cars were parked and empty, but a Peugeot sitting in a loading zone contained a passenger. Said passenger was trying to turn over the engine as the whoop of police klaxons closed in.

Jack darted into traffic, causing the driver of a small hybrid to swerve up onto the pavement. He ignored the cursing and horns, reaching the Peugeot just as the engine caught at last. There wasn't time to be delicate and ask leading questions, so he drew back his elbow and drove it through the driver's window.

The man inside started to shift into gear to run him over, but Jack grabbed him by the jaw with his blood-stained hand. "Shut it off."

His victim squirmed and twisted, but he didn't scream for help or shout for the police, like a normal person should when a crazed man covered in blood smashed into their car on a public street. Jack gave the driver a shake. "Shut it off or I'll lay a blood hex on you that'll have your eyeballs dripping out your arse."

The man considered him for a few seconds more, and then took his hand off the gearshift and foot off the clutch. The car stalled out, but Jack didn't relax his grip. "Why are you after me?"

The man glared, trying to swallow under Jack's grip. "If you're going to kill me, just do it. My soul is right with my gods."

Jack wiped his hand clean on the man's wrinkled yellow shirt and opened the door. "Get out."

He did, and stood with his hands dangling at his sides, lip poking out like a sullen teenager. "What's the matter, Winter? Never thought you'd be the type who needed to look someone in the eye before you topped them. Way I heard, you're more the kind to creep up with a knife in the dark and put it in a bloke's kidney."

"What the fuck are you on about, me killing you?" Jack demanded. He had a reputation as a wanker, certainly—shifty, disreputable, untrustworthy. Americans would probably sum it all up with *asshole*. But going about East London doing people in wasn't usually in his repertoire, even by reputation.

"You almost killed every single person this side of the Black and the other," the man spat. "Wouldn't think one more would matter."

It all made sense then. "Ah, you're miffed I almost let Nergal out to play," Jack said. "Well, I've got news. You're not the first and you're miles from the last. You want a shot at me? Take a fucking number, mate, and join the queue."

The driver drew himself up. Balding and barrel-chested, he wouldn't have rated a second glance if Jack had passed him on the street, but the fury in his eyes belonged to a much younger, angrier man. "You don't get to nearly destroy the world as we know it and laugh it off, Winter." He jabbed his finger into Jack's chest. "You've seen it now. We can find you anywhere, at any time, outside the Black or in it. The Stygian Brothers remember their enemies, and the mark will never fade."

Jack felt the point between his eyes begin to throb. "Seriously, mate? You expect me to believe you're a Stygian? Somebody's creepy uncle, maybe, but that's as far as I'd go."

The Brother rolled up his sleeve in response, and exposed the many-lined tattoo all initiates received after they'd had what the Brotherhood called the Dream—the prophetic vision, brought on by hallucinogenic compounds rubbed into the skin—of the Stygian's many-eyed, tentacled Nameless Ones that stood as an excuse for their adventures in flesh-crafting, self-mutilation rituals, and mind-control spells. A Stygian's idea of a fun night out.

"Fuck," Jack muttered. He'd been hoping the bloke was a lone outlier, a nutter who'd gotten a flowerpot smashed during the riots and taken it out on him at the expense of the poor checkout girl, but he was a Stygian, true enough.

"It's not just us," said the Brother. "It's everyone, Winter." He smirked, revealing a mouthful of missing molars. Jack couldn't be sure if they were a result of ritual mutilation or NHS dentistry. "Our bounty will never expire. The sorcerers, the white magic cabals, even the fucking kitchen witches—they know what you did. It doesn't matter that you decided you'd rather play hero at the eleventh hour. What's to stop you from changing your mind, the next time that pea-sized brain of yours decides to go Hulk smash? You destroyed half the city, and you ripped holes in the Black, and nobody is safe while you're about." He stabbed Jack in the chest again. "I may not be able to toe up to you one on one, but soon enough somebody will. And that'll solve the problem."

The man got back into his car and slammed the door. More glass fell to the pavement while he revved the engine. "You want to stay breathing, stay out of London. You are no longer welcome."

He pulled away into traffic, and Jack cut through an alley when he saw the blue lights of a police car swing around the corner.

The Stygian Brothers. And more, from the sound of it. Nobody could keep track of every sect and small-time group of magic users that proliferated around London like a particularly stubborn venereal disease, but if the Stygians had marked Jack as an undesirable, he was in enough trouble.

He kept to side streets until he came out at the Aldgate East tube station, and waited in the shadows for another ten minutes, until he was sure with both his eyes and his second sight that he hadn't been followed. Nobody and nothing was watching him.

The cuts on his neck and all of the assorted bruises had begun to ache and sting while he'd been walking. Not to mention his fucking midnight snack was lying crushed on the floor of Sainsbury's.

Nobody followed him on the tube, and nobody followed him down the Mile End Road to his flat, but Jack didn't allow himself to relax until the door was shut and locked behind him. The flat was layered in hexes, cobwebs of spellcraft that floated in front of his sight and then flickered and disappeared. He'd shored them up nearly every other day since the riots had died down—not because he was afraid of looters or marauding packs of hoodie teenagers, but because of the exact thing that had just happened at the shop. It hadn't done one fucking bit of good, though—they'd just waited until he'd left the safety of his flat, like properly smart vengeful psychopaths.

He couldn't stay shut up in Whitechapel for the rest of his life, and he couldn't risk another incident like tonight. If the Stygian Brothers had made a move on him in public, outside the Black, then it'd only be a matter of time before somebody with their shit together and their brain clear of low-grade peyote finished the job. It could be necromancers (although the ones who'd tried to wake up Nergal were mostly little bits of flesh and bone in a London mortuary) or it could be the light side—druids or

Wiccans or just a pack of particularly slagged-off hippies. And how humiliating would that be?

"Jack?" Pete Caldecott appeared in the hallway from the bedroom, rubbing her eyes. They fell on his empty hands. "Where's the food?"

"About that," Jack said. "Anyone been by while I was out? Anything unusual?"

Pete's gazed closed up and became calculating. "What did you do now?"

"Me? I'll have you know I'm the victim here," Jack muttered. "For once." He got his bottle of Jameson from the old record cabinet that served as a liquor stash, because all at once that seemed like an excellent idea.

"You're bleeding." Pete came into the light and tilted his head with a finger, examining the scratches on his neck.

"Not the first time, likely not the last," Jack said. He tried to keep it lighthearted, but Pete just sighed and went into the kitchen to fetch her first-aid kit. She was silent while she disinfected the scratches and put a large plaster over the spot on his neck. She was silent entirely too much since they'd put Nergal back where he belonged.

"What's my diagnosis, doctor?" he tried.

Pete shut the metal lid of the kit. "You're an idiot, but you'll live."

She got up and went back into the bedroom without another word. Jack spread out on the sofa, after swallowing a handful of aspirin with his whiskey. It was easier than going to bed and listening to more of the silence.

It hadn't happened all at once—after the rioting had mostly died down and it was safe for Jack to leave the hospital, where he'd checked himself into the psychiatric unit to set up a psychic buffer between himself and various types who wanted inside his head—things had been rather normal.

No, they hadn't. That was a comfortable lie, as was the fact that he'd only committed himself to use the psychic static of the other nutters in the place to block out both Nicholas Naughton, necromancer and cunt of the first order, and other, darker, less human things that wanted him. Wanted him to awaken Nergal, wanted him to order the oldest of the old gods to wash the world clean, and leave it slick and bloody for her advance.

Jack mashed his thumbs into the center of his forehead, massaging the point between his eyes. He hadn't seen her, or dreamed of her, since he'd refused to do what she asked. But it was only a matter of time—she couldn't die, and she wouldn't be put off forever. She was the maiden of death, the bride of war, and the hag of the ashes and dust that came after. The Morrigan had marked him when he was only a teenager, and eventually, she'd get her pound of flesh. The fact he'd disobeyed her and her mad plan to cleanse the Black of all but her faithful would only make it a far longer and more painful carving.

But he had more important things to worry about than some bitch and her army of the dead, so he drained the whiskey and shut the light off. Pete had gone quiet by degrees, first about the baby and then about everything else. She was only a few months along, but Jack could already see the endgame. She was realizing that despite her own talents, she couldn't raise a kid in their lifestyle. Would be mad to try.

Jack agreed—nobody deserved to grow up in the sort of life he'd found himself in. Pete was being practical, letting him down by degrees, slowly cutting off circulation to each part of them rather than throwing crockery in a spectacular breakup. She'd move out in another month or two, go live with her sister, and that would be that. Weekends, alternate bank holidays, and carefully e-mailed pictures to mark each waypoint of the spawn's growing up. If he was lucky. If he wasn't, he'd be exactly like his own father—ignorant and happy to stay that way.

Maybe happy wasn't the word. But he wasn't fit to be a father, and any daydreams of trying were just his conscience poking him. He didn't even have to be an actual deadbeat—once Pete made up her mind, that was that. She was immovable as a standing stone. The kid would be better off without him. The world would be, really. But until Pete actually threw him out, he'd be damned if some Universal horror mob bent on revenge was going to do anything to her or the kid to get at him.

The Stygian Brother had been right about that much—he needed out of London. And he needed to convince Pete to come with him.

CHAPTER 2

"I don't understand," Pete said at breakfast. She insisted on cooking for them unless she was vomiting so much from morning sickness she couldn't lift her head off the loo tiles. It was as if she was insistent that Jack would find no fault with her, when she finally broke it off officially, and for good. He wouldn't have anything to recriminate with. Not that he would have, even if she'd lain about all day shouting at him to bring her chocolate. He was the one at fault here, not Pete.

"Not much to understand, is there?" Jack said. "Pretty much everyone in the greater London area who can sling a spell is clamoring for me blood, and we need to lie low until they find something else shiny to hold their attention."

"No," Pete said, "I mean I don't understand why *I* have to go."

"Because like it or not, they think you and I are in this together," Jack said. "A matched pair."

Pete's fingers twitched as she picked up their plates, but that was all she betrayed. Jack hopped up from his chair. "Let me. Need a smoke anyway."

He carried the plates into the kitchen, dumping them in the sink with soap and hot water. He slid open the window and blew his smoke in that general direction.

"I don't want to do it," Pete said, so quietly he nearly didn't hear her over traffic. She stood at the arched entryway to the kitchen, hands folded protectively over her stomach. "It'd be one thing if it was just me, but the little one isn't paying for your mistakes, Jack. I think this is enough."

When he thought about Pete chucking him, Jack felt nothing—just the same numbness that cropped up when most people decided they'd had enough of him. Non-feeling. It didn't matter one way or the other, because it was always going to be this way. But now, he felt something, and it wasn't a feeling he enjoyed. It was all the things he didn't let in—anger, because Pete, in his eyes, wouldn't even give him a chance, and disgust because she was right not to, and the big nasty monster, guilt, because as usual Pete was right. She'd been paying for his mistakes, in one manner or another, for over a decade. He'd already decided to let her go. These feelings cropping up like weeds would die back eventually. He was just doing the decent thing, that was all—keeping an innocent kid and its mother safe.

"Please," he said, flicking the fag out the window

and coming to Pete. She flinched when he took her by the shoulders, but didn't let herself lean away. Pete was tough. Tougher, in a lot of ways, than he'd ever be. "Look, Pete, I know that you didn't want this, and that it was a stupid thing for both of us to get into, but it happened. You can think whatever you want of me and when this blows over you can light out and never look back, but until then I'm not letting anything happen to you. Or the kid. It's my mess, and for once I'm cleaning it the fuck up." He realized he was squeezing her hard enough to feel bone. "Sorry," he said. "I'm sorry."

Pete stared at the stained vinyl, pocked with clusters of yellow flowers and cigarette burns, rather than look at him. "Are we really in danger?" she said.

"Believe it," Jack said. "Fucking Stygian Brothers almost took me head off last night, and they're far from the most organized outfit I've slagged off."

Pete tightened her jaw, and then pulled a piece of paper from her back pocket. "I was planning to do this on my own," she said. "I wasn't going to tell you until my flight had lifted off from Heathrow."

Jack took the scrap, tried to summon the non-feeling again and not let Pete's words sting him. The paper bore Pete's neat, round Catholic school handwriting. *Benjamin Mayhew Investigations, Venice Beach Blvd., Los Angeles.* An American phone number was scribbled beneath.

"Who's this?" he said.

"Used to be a cop in Los Angeles," Pete said. "We met at a seminar a while back. He's gone private, now, and I guess he was always in the life, because he heard about me from someone around a month ago and e-mailed our business address. Said he had a problem only I could help with."

"Wait." Jack waved the scrap, not believing that Pete of all people could fall for such shit. "You were going to fuck off without telling anyone, never mind me, and wander into an obvious trap?" He felt a throb start at his temples that could be from the bottle he'd killed last night, or from pure irritation.

Pete put her hands on her hips. "I'm quite capable of getting into and out of my own trouble, Jack. I managed it nicely before I met you, and after, too. Besides, Mayhew is an all-right bloke. American, but, you know. Not one of *those* types."

"Even his name makes him sound like a git," Jack said. "And what's this problem only *you* can help him with?"

Pete snatched the paper back. "First of all, *you're* far more of a git than Mayhew ever was, and I don't know. I figured I'd ask when I got to Los Angeles."

"No," Jack said. "Over my dead, cold, and possibly violated corpse. This is just more shite drummed up by somebody who wants to explain to me the error of my ways, and use your dead body to do it."

"You're not in charge of me, Jack," Pete said. "Just because you managed to reproduce with me doesn't automatically make you smarter. So fuck you, stay here and play your little revenge games with your ridiculous friends. I'm leaving."

Well, he'd handled that brilliantly. Pete wriggled

free of him and slammed into the closet, emerging with her battered Samsonite.

"Pete . . ." he started, but she held up a finger.

"It won't work, Jack. I tried, but it won't. I'm not pointing blame—this is as much me as it is you, but I will say that if you didn't have the pathological need to be the hero, and to protect me when I don't fucking need it, none of this would've ever happened."

He tried to keep his mouth shut, but self-control had never been one of his strong points. Hell, if he was honest, it'd never even been a point at all. "Your getting knocked up has very little to do with me being a hero," he snapped. Pete stopped short, boring holes in him with her glare.

"You're right about *that*," she said. "But I wasn't talking about *that*, was I? The fact that you happen to be my sperm donor has very little to do with what's happening now."

He picked up the whiskey bottle and threw it. Not at Pete, because he didn't want to hurt her. He just needed to break something, to hear the crash and feel the glass fragments bite into the soles of his boots when he crossed the room to the front door. Break something or break himself, and he couldn't allow himself that luxury right now.

At least it was out in the open. She'd never even considered that they'd do it together. And that was fine by him. Like he needed a brat on top of all the other problems in his life. Maybe if he said that line enough times he'd start to believe it.

Jack almost missed the BMW idling across from his flat. His pulse was throbbing, and his lungs were constricted down to fist size. She wanted a fucking absent father, he'd show her one. He could be on a boat to Ireland in forty minutes, cadge a passport from a bloke he knew in Belfast, and from there make his way anywhere he pleased. Sooner or later someone would come looking for him via Pete, and she'd wish she'd listened to him then, wouldn't she? But you couldn't tell Pete anything, and Jack almost wished he'd be there to see her face when necromancers showed up on the front stoop.

He tried to let the anger flow, and the lies with it. Hoped they would eventually be true too, because the alternative was that he was alone again, and it was remarkable how quickly that had become the worst fate imaginable.

"Mr. Winter." The car window rolled down and with it, out rolled black magic, rendolent and velvety against his senses. Jack nearly flipped the occupant of the car the bird and kept walking, but then he saw the face, craggy and nearly the same color as stone, topped by a wide-brimmed hat.

"Oh, fuck me," he said.

Ethan Morningstar egressed his poncey ride with surprising grace for a man of his size and bulk, and gave Jack a smile that held all the warmth of a tombstone in January. "You're more eloquent than usual, Jack. Been taking your vitamins? Men of your age need to start considering these things, you know."

Jack set his feet and let a tendril of power uncurl

inside his head. Morningstar was a dangerous, unpredictable snake of a man, and it wouldn't surprise Jack if he tried to open him like a Christmas pudding just for the fun of it. "Get the hell out of my patch, Ethan," he said. "We don't want what you're selling."

"I'm here informally," Morningstar said. "A friendly gesture, if you will."

That made Jack laugh. The Order of the Malleus was never friendly, not to people like him. With mages, they tended more to thumbscrews and waterboards. "Whatever you say, Ethan. I'm still telling you to fuck off."

Morningstar leaned against the fender of his motor, which creaked and shifted under his weight. He might look like somebody's surly headmaster, but every bit of his bulk was muscle—muscle he knew how to use. Jack had to admit, so far the witchfinder was being remarkably civil. That in and of itself bothered him.

"I was hoping after you failed to set Nergal on the waking world like a hungry dog, somebody would do my job for me," Morningstar said. "One of the other mud-grazers would creep up on you in the dark and put a knife in your ribs, and that'd be the end of it. But like the man says, we can't always get what we want."

"I've got another one," Jack said. "'Oh bondage, up yours.'"

Ethan sucked his teeth, then folded his arms. "This can't go on, Jack."

Here it was. The nightstick, the Taser, the needle

full of dream-time. Waking up in a dank basement tied to a chair whose wood was already soaked with other men's blood. Tortured and prodded until the Malleus had extracted all of his useful information, then fed into a crematory furnace by a discreet and sympathetic mortuary worker. Fascists, magical or not, didn't employ a lot of variety.

Jack braced himself. "I'm not going to go quietly."

"I don't care how you go," Ethan said. "Just that you do. Get out of my sight, get out of my city, and don't come back." He stood up and moved into Jack's space, so that they could've kissed if Jack had been remotely interested. "How did you put it? If I see you on my patch again, I will kill you. You're spreading chaos, making the other spell-dabblers nervous, and somebody innocent is going to be hurt. I won't allow that."

Jack felt his heartbeat peak and recede, like a tide smashing on a rock. "That's it?"

"What did you think I was going to do, stuff you in the boot and take you away to a secret prison?" Morningstar chuffed. "Not hardly. Maybe I'm soft in my old age. Maybe I just remember that your little girlfriend did give us Nergal's reliquary when it was all said and done. Maybe I think you're not worth the time it'll take to clean the blood off my boots." Morningstar opened his door and got back into his car. "You'll just have to wonder, won't you?"

He started to pull away from the curb, then tapped the brakes. "Speaking of Petunia, take her with you. The same rules apply, and she's a lot more dangerous than you. She comes back here and sows more trouble for London, the Malleus will be forced to take steps." He tipped his head, grinning wide for the first time, then gunned the engine. The BMW roared away into Mile End traffic like a black shark, but not half as beastlike as the driver.

Pete was standing on the stoop of their flat, watching him with folded arms while he crossed the road again. "Was that who I think it is?"

"None other," Jack said. "And it looks like I'm coming with you, whether you want it or not." He held up a hand when Pete started to object. "Look, I'll stay out of this thing with your friend Mayhew. But I can't stay in London and I'd just as soon go someplace that's not pissing down rain." Los Angeles was as good a place as any. He could look up some old mates from his band days, have a laugh, and get away from London and all of the memories it implied. And if he was closer to Pete until she had the kid, so much the better. She'd made her feelings clear, but Jack wasn't prepared to be that much of a shit father. Letting your kid and its mother get murdered because you two had a spat wasn't parent of the year material in anyone's book.

Pete flapped her hands. "Fine. But it's not a bloody comic book team-up. You'll let me conduct my business with Mayhew and you'll stop dragging me into this ridiculous feud of yours."

"Fine," Jack agreed. "Consider me a ghost, luv. You won't even know I exist." Pete went inside without another word.

It took Jack remarkably little time to pack up

what he needed from the flat. He'd have thought
that after nearly twenty years, he'd have more essen-
tials. But the books, aside from a few rare grimoires
that he could hock for cash if he needed it, the vinyl, the odds and ends that one collected after
twenty years of living half in and half out of the
Black . . . they suddenly seemed like so much junk,
piled up in all the corners and crevices. Whoever
eventually broke in here wouldn't find anything
worth salvaging, unless they were into moldy takeaway or vintage porn.

Jack packed up a few changes of clothes, his
leather, his least disreputable pair of boots, and the
master reel of his band's first and only album. The
Poor Dead Bastards had something of a cult following, and maybe he could trade it for something, if
he needed to. He hadn't been to Los Angeles since
the early 1990s and what he remembered didn't
exactly inspire fits of joy. He'd need money, and
he'd need to make a good impression on the locals.
American mages tended toward pompous and ter-
ritorial, instilled with the idea that they were special, as if there weren't tens of thousands just like
them the world over.

Pete had allowed them to get on their flight together, since it was her charge card that was financ-
ing the venture. They took the fast train to Heathrow,
found the Virgin flight to LAX, and Pete proceeded
to ignore him again. She took the window seat and
fell asleep, or at least pretended to, as soon as they
were in the air.

Jack decided the only antidote for his hatred of

being locked inside a large metal lipstick tube suspended above the earth was to get as drunk as the
twenty quid in his wallet would allow, and flagged
down a flight attendant.

He drifted in and out, and when he woke for
good, the plane had touched down and they were
on the tarmac at LAX.

Pete climbed over him and got her carry-on bag.
"Been fun," she said, and got ahead of him, cutting
herself off with a herd of slow-moving passengers.

"Yeah," Jack muttered, shouldering his own bag.
"Like getting teeth pulled in the middle ages."

CHAPTER 3

LAX was interminable, moving walkways shunting along herds of people, most of whom were wearing sunglasses. Coming from a place where the sun was a luxury, if not an outright oddity, and if you wore shades you never wore them indoors, Jack decided they were all cunts.

He got through customs, got out to the curb, and found himself facing a wasteland that went on as far as the eye could see. Palm trees poked above the landscape here and there, and the roar of jets competed with the drone of the nearby freeway.

"Christ," Pete said at his elbow. "It's a bit *1984*, isn't it?"

"I think you'd need a few more government billboards and few less birds in midriff tops for that," Jack said. He looked down at her. "You ditching me, then?"

Pete kicked the dirty concrete. "Look, Jack. I was

really angry, and I still am, but . . ." She drew a deep breath, and then made a face. "Even the air here tastes dirty. Anyway, I think the thing to do is stick together. At least until great swaths of the UK don't want us dead any longer."

"I really am sorry," he said quietly. He was, too. He wasn't sorry often. Sorry was for people who lived their lives looking for something to regret, and when you'd gotten as many friends killed as he had, you could be sorry straight down to the bottom of a whiskey bottle or the point of a needle full of smack. There was no future in being sorry for every fucking thing.

But this was Pete. And he was sorry, for both of them.

"Save it," she said. "I don't want you to pity me. I just want you to stop walking around like a kicked puppy."

"Then stop kicking me," Jack snapped. "I know your life plan didn't include a kid, Pete. I know it didn't include me, and I know you're slagged off that you have to put up with either of us. I know you blame me. Fuck it, *I* blame me. I know it all, that you're done with me soon as the sprog makes an appearance. So until then, can we just agree that's how it is and leave off kicking a dead horse in the balls?"

Pete blinked, and Jack let himself imagine that for a moment, she'd wanted to deny what he was saying, but then she nodded. "Sounds good. We're colleagues, nothing more."

"Fantastic," Jack agreed. He'd protect Pete until the baby came, and then he'd go his way and she'd go hers. And that would be that. No need for crying or hair-pulling on either end.

He knew he'd never believe that one, but Pete wasn't leaving him much of a choice.

A long, low convertible, in a shade of yellow Jack would describe as "violent sunshine," pulled up in front of them, and Pete took up her bag. "That'll be Mayhew," she said. "I told him to meet us here."

"Christ," Jack said. "If I'd've known he was bringing a boat, I would've worn a life vest."

"Behave," Pete muttered, moving to shake hands with the car's driver. Mayhew was short, but not too short; fat, but not too fat; with a smile that was sincere, but only just. Completely average and utterly unremarkable. He must've made a hell of a cop.

"Pete, great to see you," he said, although the words didn't match his face, which was sweaty and pinched.

"Yes, same," she said. "Shall we?"

"Oh, yeah," Mayhew said. He chugged around the car and picked up Pete's bag, noticing Jack for the first time. "Hey, man," he said. "Thanks for coming, both of you."

"Wouldn't miss it," Jack said. He held out his rucksack until Mayhew took it. "Cheers," Jack said, and slid into the back seat. Pete shot him the look, the one that meant he was being a cunt, but Jack ignored it.

The interior of the car smelled slightly sour, whether from Mayhew's sweat or the plethora of fast food wrappers crushed under Jack's boots, he didn't care to speculate. Plush dice dangled from the rearview mirror and a small plastic hula dancer undulated her hips from the dash when Mayhew pulled away from the curb.

"So," he said to Pete, "first time in LA?"

"For me," Pete said. "Jack's been."

"Oh yeah?" Mayhew hooked a look back at him in the mirror. "You like it?"

"Not particularly," Jack said, and fished a cigarette out of his pocket.

"Oh, sorry," Mayhew said. "Can't have you smoking in Lucille. The upholstery is original."

"You can't be serious," Jack said, and got the look from Pete again.

"'Fraid so," Mayhew said. "Believe me, I understand. I polished off a pack a day when I was LAPD. Quit a year ago and I've never felt better."

As they drove past warehouses, used car lots, and cheap airport motels and merged onto a freeway roughly the width of the Thames, Jack felt a marked urge to reach over the seat and bang Mayhew's head against the steering wheel.

He stabbed his fag out against the car's door panel instead, then rubbed the sooty mark in with his finger. Small and petty, yes, but Mayhew was already up his nose and he'd barely spent ten minutes with the man. Jack bet with himself that Mayhew's "problem" would involve teenage Satanists in store-bought robes and missing neighborhood pets.

"You named your car?" Pete said, sliding closer to Mayhew on the sofa-sized front seat. Mayhew immediately forgot about Jack's existence.

"Sure did. This is my baby Lucille. Sixty-five

LeSabre—restored her myself." He ran his hand across the dash in the proprietary manner with which most men touch women's thighs.

"Really," Jack said. "You pick out the color?"

"Hey, this is LA," Mayhew said. "Land of big tits, good teeth, and primary colors. Takes some getting used to if you're from a place like London."

Pete twitched but she jumped in front of the bullet again. "It take long? Fixing this thing up?"

Mayhew shrugged, an aw-shucks gesture that clearly implied yes, normally, but not when you were a special sort like him. "A while. Supposed to do it when I retired in twenty years, but what the hell? Being a PI is a lot of waiting around, and I like to keep busy."

Jack slid down on Lucille's slippery plastic seat and shut his eyes. Mayhew was trying to do the civilized equivalent of pissing a circle—his car, his city, his eyes all over Pete's tits. Jack wished him good luck with the last one. Pete didn't need white knighting—Mayhew would find out soon enough, with a knee in his balls if he was especially unlucky.

As to LA, he could have it. The sun penetrated Jack's eyelids and made his head throb, and he threw his arm up as Lucille crested a rise and revealed a glimpse of the downtown before Mayhew veered off onto another freeway. Who needed a concrete-covered, haze-choked hellhole full of women with silicone sacks in their chests and men like Mayhew, whose biggest concern was his motor and getting into a dick-measuring contest with everyone he met?

"You'll need a car," Mayhew said to Pete. "I set it up with a friend of mine who runs a garage—you can drive American-style, right?"

"I'll manage," Pete said.

"Great," Mayhew said. "We'll go back to my office and talk business. I really am glad you're here."

There it was, the hook. Jack had no doubt that Mayhew's real reason for gladness was that whoever was pulling his strings wouldn't immediately peel his skin off his fat form and put it on toast. He'd actually gotten Pete to show up and proven himself a useful underling. Jack could put up with the git just as long as it took to see the big picture, the puppeteer rather than the puppet, and then he was going to give Mayhew a real reason to be glad for American dentistry.

He dozed on the drive, the rank air doing little to replace his need for a fag. When they finally bumped to a stop, he realized he'd been somewhere else, the freeway turning into a long, black road made of smooth obsidian, and the smog cloud becoming the ashes of things burnt alive, drifting down to catch in his hair and eyelashes like charnel snow.

Jack didn't have many memories of his time in Hell. When the Morrigan had led him back from the Bleak Gates, she'd smoothed his mind over, picked out with her beak all of the time that Jack had lost when he went down to the Pit, and left plain gray nothing in its place.

He'd seen a few flashes in dreams, which was par for the course for a psychic who couldn't shut out the feed on his best days. But nothing concrete. No flashbacks, no coming awake and screaming.

He still didn't know the extent of what the Morrigan had done to him, besides the markings. He felt better than he had before he went to the Pit, but that wasn't saying much. He'd been sick, using whiskey as a food group, and battered by his sight. It wasn't as if he could suddenly lift cars and run five kilometers without hacking.

Pete stuck her head in his window. "You coming?"

Jack shook off the dream. That was what you did with dreams—his weren't prophetic, as Pete's had a tendency to be, and they certainly weren't worth remembering. "Yeah," he said. "Right along the yellow brick road."

CHAPTER 4

Mayhew lived in Venice, so named by its city fathers in a startling fit of originality because Venice, California, also had canals. "You know, just like Italian Venice. Was a big tourist spot in the fifties."

Jack could hear the swish of the ocean when he stepped out of the car, and the air was sticky with salt and carbon monoxide. Mayhew had parked in an alley, and he let them in a side door. "One of the guys on the force owned this pad and let it go for a song," he said, flicking a light to life. "Got the hell out of the city, moved to Montana. I guess he's a sheriff now or something." Mayhew shrugged. "Miserable fucking existence, if you ask me, but some people can't hack LA."

Not feeling any hexes or other sort of protection on the place, Jack stepped in after Mayhew. The "pad" ended in a T-shaped hall, one end leading to an office that looked out onto a street full of similar small

bungalows and semi-detached flats, the other leading back into a living room done up in rattan with
bright cushions, tiki idols on most surfaces, and a
sort of 1950s clock above a bubble-shaped telly
with rabbit ears. A small fireplace was crowned with
a glamor shot of Jayne Mansfield and an array of
framed movie posters for flicks like *The Hellcats*
and *Faster, Pussycat! Kill! Kill!*

"Fuck me," Jack muttered. "Did Dean Martin's
corpse projectile vomit this shit into his sitting
room?"

Mayhew continued through a kitchen done entirely in powder blue, including appliances, and
showed them into a small back bedroom.

"You can crash here," he said. "Sorry about the
one bed situation. Maybe Jack would be more comfortable on the sofa?"

"Being stared at by a headless movie star and
fifteen tiki idols?" Jack said. "Yeah, don't think so."

Mayhew's neck swelled a little, but he wouldn't
take it up with him. Not in front of Pete. "You're
not a fan of kitsch, I take it."

Jack dumped out his rucksack on the bed. "What
gave me away?"

"Anyway," Pete said. "I think we're both interested to hear what's got you in such a lather, Benjamin."

"Call me Ben." Smile, smile, smile. "Everyone
does."

Pete did not call him Ben, just went into his office
space and plopped herself in the visitor's chair. Jack
made sure Benjamin-now-Ben walked ahead of

him. There was more than the obvious convenience of Mayhew's timing. He stank of flop sweat, and he kept shooting nervous glances at all the doors and windows. It could be that whoever had convinced him to set Pete up wasn't the type to take tea and biscuits, or it could be something else. It was the off chance of "something else" that had Jack's teeth grinding.

Mayhew's office was a far cry from his frenetic tribute to tacky acid trips of a flat. The furniture was from the same vintage, but it was dull metal painted in varying colors of Piss, Vomit, and Hairball. Papers crowded every surface and the blinds were broken over a painted front window. *Mayhew & Co. Investigations,* Jack read backward. The letters were bisected by spider cracks where somebody had chucked a small, heavy object at the glass.

"'And Co.'?" Jack said, taking the second client seat. The vinyl was sticky with some long-ago spill. Dust motes flew up in a flock when he sat.

"Yeah, that's just to make me sound more trustworthy," Mayhew said.

Jack rubbed the dust from the arm of his chair between thumb and forefinger. "Does it work?"

Mayhew kept that slightly nauseous smile on his face. "Most of the time."

"Your problem," Pete reminded Mayhew. "The sooner you tell us, the sooner we can get to solving it."

Mayhew got up and dug through a file cabinet, dislodging a stack of duplicate forms and old gun magazines from the top.

Jack sat and rubbed the grit between his fingers. You could learn a lot from dust. Places picked up the psychic leak of whoever'd stood in them, glass and iron and stone and wood. Mayhew's dust stank of magic. Not a human, not the kind of residue left by a talent or even by black magic. It was dry and harsh and tasted of ash and hot wind in the back of his throat.

He rubbed his hand on the leg of his jeans. The dust scattered, and the sensation faded.

"I was a homicide cop for ten years," Mayhew said, dumping a bulging file of photocopies and blurry photographs onto his desk. He nudged a container of takeaway into the trash and spread the photos out. "This was my last case."

Pete obligingly drew the photos closer, handed them to Jack one by one. They were gruesome, he supposed, but nothing that garden-variety humans couldn't do to one another. Four people, in various stages of defenestration, lay on a tile floor. A door stood open to the outside, and blood dribbled over walls and various other surfaces.

"Somebody decided to redecorate?" Jack said, holding up a close shot of a woman who'd been opened from sternum to pelvis, her blood feathering across the tile under her in a spidery, winglike halo.

"That was Mary Kay Case, the homeowner," Mayhew said. "She was eight and a half months pregnant." He sat back, and waited for Jack's scrabbling apology.

Jack tossed the photo back on the desk. "Yeah?

Unless the baby was a flesh-chewing mutant Hell-spawn that ate its way out, grew tentacles, and joined a traveling circus, what's this got to do with the Black?"

"Jesus, man," Mayhew said. "You really are a block of ice, aren't you?"

"Look," Jack said. "You were a cop. You know that perfectly plain human beings are capable of doing this and worse to each other. So I can sit here and wring me hands, or you can stop wasting our time with the suspenseful fucking buildup."

Mayhew pointed at the photo in Pete's hands. "Recognize that?"

Pete displayed a close-up of the door. The word PIG had been scrawled with a fingertip, in blood. "Copycat?" she asked Mayhew.

"I wish," Mayhew said. "Manson family fanboys would've been a lot easier to close up than whatever I've got."

"Manson's people murdered a pregnant woman, too," Pete said. "This one—her baby didn't make it, did it?" She shifted in her seat, and Jack reached out without thinking and put his hand over hers.

"Honestly, we don't know," Mayhew said. He rubbed his thumb across his forehead, drawing beads of sweat. It was claustraphobically hot in the little office, and Jack itched to get up and throw open a window.

Pete laced her fingers with his, though, so he stayed where he was. "How can you not know?" she said. "It's not as if you can lose an infant down the cracks in your sofa cushions."

"We don't know because when the first respond-
ers came on the scene, the Case baby was gone,"
Mayhew said. He sat back, digging in an overflow-
ing drawer and bringing out a bottle of bourbon.
"Snort?" he said, dashing a bit into a glass.

"None for me," Pete said. Mayhew tossed the
drink back without offering Jack.

"The medical examiner said the kid could have
survived," he murmured. "You know, if they cut it
out instead of just cutting. But I could never think
that. Why take a baby and murder its parents and
their dinner guests? What the hell would the point
be of keeping that baby alive?"

"And you think they were involved in the Black?"
Jack cut in. "The doers, I mean?"

Mayhew collected the photos, keeping his hand
on top of the one of Mary Kay Case's dead body.
"We found evidence that the Cases were in the life,
yes," he said. "More than that, they didn't have a
single enemy on the daylight side. Larry Case was a
tax accountant and Mary Kay was a real estate
agent. Good people. Good people don't deserve this
shit."

"So naturally you assume it's some baby-stealing
nutter from beyond the beyond," Pete said.

"It's not that," Mayhew said. "I could never close
this one. It's not easy to tell your captain that you
can find the murderer based on a load of horseshit
that most people think went out with the Salem
trials, if they believe it at all. But the Case murders
aren't why you're here."

He pulled a fax off the machine and thrust it at

Pete. "My buddy in the ME's office sent this to me. They caught the bodies last night."

Pete shared the fax with Jack. The photo was of bad quality, but he could make out the same rough outline as the Case bird. A pregnant woman, missing the center of herself, on a steel table under harsh light.

"Almost identical to the Case murders," Mayhew said. He poured himself another shaky measure of bourbon. "It's been ten years, and whoever did this is back in LA."

CHAPTER 5

Jack excused himself to smoke. The street Mayhew's bungalow occupied ended at a cement embankment, and from there it was just beach and ocean. The sun had set, and the memory of it was crimson contrails streaked across the sickly yellow sky.

Pete joined him after a few drags. "What do you think?" she said, looking at his cigarette longingly before Jack stubbed it out.

"I think it's a sad story, but there's nothing here to do with you, or us, or the Black at all," Jack said. Sure, it was awful that some nutter was ripping babies out of their mothers. But no more awful than the usual sort of awful people could be.

"Oh, come on," Pete said. "At the very least, somebody *thinks* they're doing black magic with those bodies."

"Thinking and doing aren't the same thing," Jack said. "Also, Mayhew's about as twitchy as a rat on an electric fence. For all we know that case could not even be his. Just a lure to get you where he wants you."

Pete folded her arms. "Just because you don't like him, you're saying there's nothing to this. That's a shit way to conduct business."

"What business?" Jack demanded. He should know better by now than to try and fool Pete. "Pete, at the very least he's a sad old lush who can't let go of his big failure. At the worst he's setting us up to be a snack for something we've pissed off that's been biding its time."

"Fine," Pete said. "You can go on, then. I'm going to look into it."

Jack blinked. "You can't be serious."

"I think by now you know the answer to that," Pete said. "You want to stick your head under a rock until you can crawl back to London, go right ahead. No skin off of me."

"Well, luv, if we're shouting uncomfortable truths: You want to take on this stupid errand for Mayhew because you're pregnant," Jack said. "I saw your face when that picture came up."

"Oh, *fuck* you," Pete snarled. "Just because I'm knocked up, I suddenly have a deeper understanding of the feminine mysteries of motherhood?" She shoved Mayhew's file at Jack, hard enough to knock him off balance. "Wanting to catch some depraved bastard who preys on helpless kids is *not* some flighty side effect of my owning a vagina, Jack. *Not* wanting to says a hell of a lot more about you than my having a baby bump says about me."

"Wait!" Jack said when Pete turned to storm inside. The file fell between them and Mayhew's slaughter porn scattered across his stoop.

Pete threw up her hands. "Why should I? You're not going to be one bit of help. As usual."

Stupid. He was stupid, and why couldn't he have just kept his mouth shut? Now Pete was looking at him like he was less than dog shit on her boot, and he deserved it. "It's not that I'm unwilling to look into this," Jack said. "I mean, I still don't think we should be here, but you can't run on back to Mayhew on your own."

"Why not?" Pete snapped. "You afraid I might get used to a man with a job who doesn't constantly have childish fits at me?"

"He's a liar, for one," Jack said. Pete laughed, short and sharp.

"If being a liar was a disqualification, I'd've chucked you out years ago."

"I know you're angry at me now," Jack said. "But Mayhew is not on the level, Pete. His office stank of demon."

Pete stopped with her hand on the door. "You wouldn't just be saying that to sway me into leaving, would you? Because then I'd have to hit you in the balls."

"I'm not going to lie about something like that," Jack said. Lying about demons was just inviting them to show up and make a truth-teller out of you. Anyone who said Hellspawn didn't have a sense of humor had never met one.

"Why would Mayhew be having anything to do with demons?" Pete said.

"That," said Jack, "is an excellent fucking question."

"I still think he's got something with these dead folks," Pete said. "Assuming he didn't just make it up out of whole cloth."

Jack shrugged. "Easy enough to find out. We can go ask somebody who's not arse-deep in black magic, for a start."

"So you're staying?" Pete said.

Also an excellent question. Pete didn't want his help, and Mayhew sure as shit didn't want him around. He practically puffed his chest out like a frog whenever Jack was within ten feet. He should do exactly as Pete expected—go hide somewhere until it was safe to go home. But separating made them both vulnerable. He'd stay—and keep up the line that he was only there until the kid was out, which Pete seemed to have no problem believing. She could take care of herself, then, and the baby, and he wouldn't be a danger to anyone except himself.

"Yeah," Jack said aloud. "Wouldn't miss it."

CHAPTER 6

In the morning, Jack found Pete and Mayhew drinking orange juice on his small balcony. Mayhew offered him a glass. "Sorry, man. Pete said to let you sleep. Jet lag and all that."

Jack ignored his offer and pulled up a chair. "Got any food?"

"Yeah, I called out for some breakfast," Mayhew said. "Didn't think Pete here would feel like going out."

He brought Jack a bowl of cereal, sickly sweet with bits of pink marshmallow floating in milk that had just turned. Jack ignored the civilized bachelor's version of a Fuck You and took the time to size up Mayhew while the detective chattered at Pete about what an absolutely tip-top sort of place Venice was.

If Mayhew was a practitioner, he wasn't much of one. His talent was barely a flutter, and he didn't seem to realize that a mage could size him up and ferret out his demon-soaked aura like smelling a dead mouse in your vents.

Aside from his questionable grasp on magic, Mayhew was a sad sight. He'd probably been a big, strong man around ten years ago, but now his ridiculous Hawaiian shirt was taxed to capacity with a round stomach, and his hair was starting to get more salt than pepper, like dirty snow covering dirtier ground. His jowls hung heavy, and when he talked to Pete he stared at her intently with his slightly too-small eyes, a look that Jack recognized well enough. Most straight men looked at Pete that way.

Altogether, Mayhew didn't inspire any more confidence in Jack that he wasn't out to bugger them thoroughly and completely, without the benefit of Astroglide.

"My buddy called and said you can pick up your car," Mayhew told Pete. "Any ideas about the case?"

Pete shoved back from the table. "None I'd care to share. Come on, Jack."

Mayhew blinked, clearly having expected that their little duo of Bogart and Bacall would continue for as long as he kept grinning and pouring orange juice. "But you'll need a ride."

"You said it was nearby," Pete said. "We'll manage. People in London walk."

"Nobody walks in LA," Mayhew said, and then barked a laugh at his own questionable cleverness in quoting an old-as-the-hills pop song.

Jack followed Pete. "You should try it sometime,"

he said. "Your shirt landscape might get a little less hilly."

"I wish you'd stop that," Pete said, when they were walking up the hill away from the beach, the address of Mayhew's mechanic friend tucked into Pete's pocket.

"What?" He was shit at playing innocent, but he could always try.

"Your life would be much easier if you just quit taking the piss for no good reason," Pete told him.

"I have a good reason," Jack said. "Mayhew's a slimy git. If that's not a reason I don't know what is."

The mechanic's shop was tucked into a side street a few blocks beyond the top of the hill. Here, the ocean was a sound, not a sight, and the glaring green-yellow sunlight was even more revealing, giving unfavorable clarity to the faded boards and the sad, sagging sign proclaiming SAL'S AUTO R PAIR.

The garage door was open to emit exhaust fumes, Black Sabbath playing on a tinny radio propped on top of a toolbox, and the shriek of metal on metal. Sal was bent over a fender, sanding off blue paint to reveal the primer beneath.

Jack didn't care much about cars—they got you from point A to point B and beyond that, blokes used them as a way to extend their cocks, or to fuss over them incessantly, the way people more in line with his way of thinking obsessed over original pressings of the Sex Pistols' EMI release.

"Oi!" he shouted, and Sal shut off the sander, raising his goggles.

"Hey," he said. "You Benji's buddy?"

"Wouldn't go that far," Jack said. Sal grinned. His teeth were even and startlingly white, considering how ugly the rest of his face was. Sal looked as if his features had been dumped into a sack, and then his maker had slammed the sack sharply against a cement wall a few times before letting things settle. His nose was a monument to how not to take a punch, and his cheekbones were uneven. A slick black pompadour, dented by the band of his goggles, topped off the look and added a touch of absurdity.

"Benji doesn't have a lot of interpersonal skills," Sal said. "Probably why he's shit broke most of the time." He winked at Pete. "Only giving you the car because he did me a favor a few months back. Some fuck rented one of my gals and returned her with the grill and bumper banged all to hell. Come to find out, asshole was in a hit and run out on Hollywood Boulevard, put some wannabe actress slash hooker in the hospital, all kinds of crap. I could've been liable."

"Sounds like he's a veritable superhero," Pete said.

Sal's grin widened until it was practically pornographic. "Love your accent, doll." The grin abruptly ceased. "You do know what side of the road we drive on in the USA, right?"

"I'll manage, although being a woman, the very idea of a combustion-operated vehicle frightens and confuses me," Pete said. Sal laughed, and then coughed, and then pulled a Marlboro from a pack and lit it.

Jack took it out of his mouth. "Not in front of the lady," he said. Sal sized him up for a second, and Jack stared right back. Sal considered for a minute longer, then shrugged.

"Sorry. Anyway, she's out back."

He led them down a narrow hall lit by a single bulb, and back into the hard-hitting sun, which now gleamed on a host of finned, chromed, detailed beasts that looked like nothing so much as a flight of especially decorative UFOs.

"Wow," Pete said. Jack had to admit, the collection was impressive. Cherry red, powder blue, wasp yellow, the cars were all perfect, and all different. He recognized a few that aped famous sorts from films—James Bond's Aston Martin, Steve McQueen's Mustang, and the white Challenger from *Vanishing Point*, which was one of his friend Lawrence's favorite films.

"I was going to sling you into whatever I didn't have rented out today," Sal said. "Paramount is eating up most of the fleet for this period movie they're shooting over by the boardwalk. But you two need something special." He considered, tapping one sausage finger against his troll jaw. His hands could have easily palmed Jack's head, and Jack was glad he hadn't pressed the cigarette issue. Too early in the day to get his face broken. You needed to at least have lunch and a proper drink first.

Sal led them between the rows until he came to the far back corner of the lot. "This one's my baby," he said. "Great gal, she'll do whatever you need her to do. She's famous, too—she was in *Christine*."

"Great," Jack said to Pete. "Fucking demon car

to find a nonexistent demon spree killer." That sounded about right.

Sal handed Pete a keyring with a grinning Dia de Los Muertos skull for a fob. "Be nice to her, and she'll be nice to you," he told Pete.

Jack looked at the crimson Plymouth Fury. "Fuck me," he muttered, sliding into the leather bench seat.

Pete took it slowly until they were headed away from the beach. "It's not so bad," she said. "Handles nicely. It's not the Mini Cooper but it'll do." Jack saw the huge grin on her face, and even though the windows were open and the LA air made him even more short of breath than inhaling an actual lungful of smoke, he had to return it.

"So, what's your mad plan?" he said.

"Mayhew's old partner from the LAPD agreed to meet with me and show me the crime scene," Pete said. Jack whistled.

"How'd you manage that?"

"I think it's my accent," Pete said. "People around here listen to it and practically fall over their own feet."

"I don't think it's just your accent," Jack told her. Pete stopped smiling.

"You have anything to add? Anything you thought of?"

"I think this is all bullshit and that there's nothing spooky going on," Jack said. He tilted his head back and shut his eyes against the sun. "I'm just along for the ride, luv. Go where you will."

CHAPTER 7

The hot wind was back, reaching right down his throat and clawing away all the good air. Replacing it bit by bit with tinders and ash. What he'd taken to be the howling of the air was in fact screams, his own and others. Screams as the vast plain before them shifted and changed, the red sands shifting and forming faces, which stared at him with lidless eyes before vanishing under the next gust.

He tried to shut his eyes and shut out the grit, close his mouth and gulp down a breath, but his eyes and lips were pinned back, fine hooks through his flesh. His blood turned to crystal the moment it hit the air, and all he could do was scream until he suffocated.

This was the first part of his time in Hell, the torture before the demon who'd pulled him into the Pit got down to the real business.

He was dead, and in Hell, and never going free.

"Jack." Something poked him hard in his biceps. "I swear, you could sleep through a missile raid," Pete muttered. The Fury sat at the foot of a driveway that snaked up a landscaped hill and ended at a small imitation castle.

"We here?" Jack stretched and consciously did not run his hands over his face. His old face, needing a shave, broken bottle–induced scar down his cheek, no flayed flesh or flowing blood.

"No, I liked the view and thought I'd sit a while." Pete withered him with a glance and got out, slamming the door. Jack took his time.

If he was starting to remember Hell, that would just be one more *fuck you* from the Morrigan. One more bit of shit to heap onto his psyche. Well, he already had a mountain of it. What were a few more bad dreams?

That's all they were. Dreams or, at the worst, faded memories he couldn't be sure were ever real, or had happened at all.

Pete had made it halfway up the drive, and he followed. The house was, up close, even more of a horror. They were up in the hills now, looking down at the bowl of smog shot through with the tops of skyscrapers populating downtown LA. Plaster gargoyles glared down at Jack from every available flat surface, and the door had been made to look like the entrance to a particularly upscale sex dungeon. The knocker was a demon head, and you grabbed the tongue to shove the door to and fro.

A flash black car, the kind favored by plainclothes policemen, was parked in the circle drive, nose pointing toward the hillside. The demon door opened, and the selfsame policeman stepped out. His suit was cheap and his eyes were hard as the rock that made up the facade of the fake Gothic mansion.

"Ms. Caldecott?" he said.

"One and the same," Pete told him, accepting his handshake.

"Detective Shavers," he said. "Ben's partner. Well. Used to be."

He ignored Jack, and Jack mentally subtracted *good detective* from his mental checklist of Shavers. If he were a copper, he'd be all over shifty gits like himself.

"So Ben's told you about his pet serial killer theory?" Shavers asked.

"He certainly has," Pete said. "With visual aids and everything."

Shavers flinched. "Sorry about that. You know, I don't normally allow civilians to just wander around an active crime scene, but I want to make something clear to you, Ms. Caldecott." He stood aside and gestured them inside.

The front hall was done in black tile, inlaid with the head of Bahopmet. The goat's heads, except for horns, had been covered with a cheery rug, and paintings and photographs covered the burgundy walls, in stark contrast to the aggressively dark décor. Evil Chic, Jack thought. Early Gothic Trying Too Hard.

"House belonged to some cult rocker in the 80s," Shavers said. "Been a rental since, with the condition that nobody change the decoration. They shoot movies in here sometimes—that's a real good way to make some cash in this town."

"Never would have guessed," Pete said, but Shavers didn't pick up on her attitude. "What did you want to make clear to me?"

"That Ben is retired for a reason," Shavers said. "That there's nothing to this case to connect it to his old murders. Yes, they're similar. But that's it."

"They're a little more than similar, if Mayhew's photos are to be believed," Pete told him.

Jack caught sight of a stairway leading to an upper level, a loft ringed in ornate iron railings. He slid down the hall, Shaver's and Pete's voices echoing off the two-story cathedral ceiling. His sight screamed the moment he mounted the stairs, vibrating and red-rimmed. Shavers was giving Pete the brush off, but there had, at the very least, been a real murder here.

"Listen," Shavers was saying. "You have to understand something about this town—it's almost as obsessed with death as it is with movie stars doing each other up the ass. You know how much James Dean's Ferrari wreckage went for at auction? Point is, every tabloid and sleazy blog has sources in the ME's office and in the LAPD. The details could've gotten out through a dozen pinholes. At worst, we've got a very dedicated copycat. But not a serial. Not ten years apart, with no activity anywhere in VICAP in between."

"You seem very sure," Pete said.

"I am sure," Shavers rumbled. "I'm sorry you came all this way, but this is just going to be another cold case. Only difference is it's in my file instead of Ben's this time, and I'm a lot better at letting things go."

"I understand, believe me," Pete said. "I used to be on the job. Can you just walk me through the scene, so I can tell Ben *something*?"

"Yeah, sure," Shavers said. "Not like I got anything better to do, like pursue cases I can actually close, right?"

Jack pushed open the first door, keeping his ear tuned to Shavers and Pete. An office, done in bloodred wallpaper and black carpet, a layer of dust thick enough to draw in over it all. Not here.

"There was no forced entry," Shavers said. "But we didn't think too much of it at the time. Rental properties, the gate code never changes and a dozen staff have it, plus the family that lived here. The Herreras," he added. "Mom, dad, son, and unborn daughter. Just in town for a few months while he produced a film."

Jack tried the next door. A kid's room, baseball memorabilia pasted up over the rock 'n' roll walls, toys scattered across the floor.

"They killed the boy first." Shaver's voice echoed. "I say they, because we decided there had to be at least two. One to subdue the parents and one to go after the kid."

The tile floor of the bedroom was stained, old blood trickling along the grout like vines breaking through stone.

"Cut his throat," said Shavers. "Quick and clean. He bled out in a matter of minutes."

"And the parents?" Pete's boots clacked on the tile.

The last door was really just an iron lattice with more of the demon head motif. The pulse of his sight got worse when he pushed it open, and Jack ground his teeth against the sensation of a spike being driven through his skull sideways.

"They killed and mutilated the father in their bed," Shavers said. "Knocked the mother over the head and dragged her down here."

The mattress was bare, and marks of a crime scene team were still in place. There was much more blood this time—almost all the blood that a person's body held, Jack wagered.

The psychic feedback was strong and bloody, but it wasn't anything unusual for a murder scene. He backed out and looked down at the top of Shaver's bald head as he bent over the Bahopmet rug. "She was here. They, uh . . . they did the final mutilation here on the tiles."

"And the fact that her unborn baby was cut out of her on an image that's been widely co-opted by Satanists the world over didn't trigger any alarms?" Pete said.

"Come on, Ms. Caldecott," Shavers said. "You were on the job. You know the shadowy Satanic cabal is just a myth fundamentalists and shrinks looking to make a buck conjured up to amuse themselves. Satanic Panic in this country is not something the LAPD is ever going to buy into."

"Yeah, fine, the Satanist angle is bollocks," Pete said. "But there was no sign of the child?"

"No," Shavers said. "The baby was gone, along with whoever did this."

"And nothing about two unborn babies being stolen, ten years apart, strikes you as a little strange?" Pete said.

Jack looked down at the bloody tiles. It was almost too trite to be believed. Home invasion mutilation inside a house that would give any weekend Satanist a hard-on, missing baby, all the hallmarks of a ritual murder—if all you knew about ritual murder came from television.

"Strange?" Shavers said. "No. Depraved, yeah. But not that strange. People are capable of sick shit, Ms. Caldecott. We get copycat murders all the time." He opened the front door. "Now if you don't mind, please ask your buddy to come downstairs, and go on back to England. There's nothing for you here."

"I think Ben would be a lot more willing to let it go if I could take a look around myself," Pete said.

Shavers threw up his hands. "Fine. You got five minutes, and then I have real police work to get back to."

Pete joined Jack on the landing. "This is weird, yeah?" she murmured. Shaver's mobile rang, and he stepped outside.

"Maybe if I couldn't see ghosts and demons, yeah," Jack said. "As it is, no. Not really. Kind of cliché, actually."

"I meant Shavers," Pete said. "He seems very happy to write this off."

"Suppose it could be just what he says," Jack said. "Two blokes, ten years apart, decide it'd be a laugh to hack up a pregnant lady and her family."

"Or Shavers could be giving us the broom," Pete said. "Trust me—no copper wants a case like this. Messy and unsolvable, drives your whole average down. Never mind that if it's a serial job, you're seen as lazy as well as incompetent."

Jack leaned on the rail. "I hate to say I told you so . . ."

"Oh, please," Pete snorted. "You *love* saying it."

Jack massaged his forehead. His sight heralded a headache that would only be knocked out with a lot of booze or a little bit of something stronger. Time was, he'd have his shooting kit in his pocket, but that time wasn't now. The cravings had gone along with all of his scars and tattoos, as if the Morrigan had remade the fire in his blood into glass. "Still," he said. "There's not actually anything supernatural afoot, unless you count the supernaturally horrible state of this place."

"Then I guess we're done here," Pete said. "I'll tell Mayhew what we found and we can go our separate ways."

Jack nodded. "Yup. Have fun disappointing Mayhew." *Just walk away,* he told himself. *Let her think you're the one to leave.*

He'd put his foot on the first stair when he felt the wind. The ashes choked his throat and his sight spiked, and blood trickled out of his nose.

He wasn't in Hell. He was here, in this hideous

death-rock palace, and he was alive. For better or worse.

"Glad I caught you," the demon said from behind him. "You are a slippery one these days, Jack."

He swallowed the taste of blood and ashes. "You can put aside the dramatic entrances, Belial. I've seen all your tricks."

Belial grinned at Jack. "Oh, you haven't seen my best ones, boy. You haven't even peeked up my sleeve."

"What do you want?" Pete appeared at his side. She was never one to engage in small talk with spawn of the Pit.

"For you to pull your heads out of each other's arses and do what I sent you here to do," Belial said. He favored a small form, natty black suits, narrow ties, and flashy ruby jewelry. Aside from his lava-glass eyes, he could've been any ponce in a throwback getup on the street.

"The fuck are you on about?" Pete demanded. "You didn't do a bloody thing."

"Getting knocked up's made you downright unobservant," Belial told her. "I've been with you all along, my dear, along your winding trail to this spot."

Jack massaged his forehead. "You were the demon in Mayhew's office."

"'Course I was," Belial said. "You think a stain like Ben Mayhew's capable of getting in touch with your caliber of mage and . . ." he flicked a black nail at Pete, "whatever you are?"

"I'll ask once more before I stop being nice," Pete told him. "What do you want?"

"The same thing you do, I expect," Belial said. "To find the villains who hacked up this nice little family. I may be a demon, but I do have feelings. All right, not feelings, but desires. And I desire them caught and delivered to me."

This was rotten. Demons didn't just pop up and start demanding favors. They hung back until you were bloody and desperate, and then they showed up to listen to your screams for mercy. That was how it had worked last time, between Belial and him.

"Forget it," Jack said. "If this whole trip was your doing, then piss off. We're done, and I'm not your rent boy any longer."

"You're not," Belial said when he turned his back. "But your little woman is."

Pete grimaced when he turned on her. "It happened when you were . . . away," Pete muttered. "I needed his help to get you out of the nuthouse and shut down Nergal."

"For fuck's sake, Pete!" Jack shouted, because shouting was the only thing he could do. He couldn't very well haul off and punch Belial in the face, not unless he wanted his limbs in new and different configurations.

"Don't scold her," Belial purred. "She did right to cut the bargain she did. Saved the world, properly, because of it. And she—and you—do this for me, and we'll be square."

"I know what you are," Jack snarled. He didn't know who to rage at—Pete for being so monumentally stupid or Belial for the smug look on his face. "I know demons. She'll never be free of you."

Belial moved like ink through water—one fluid second and his hand was around Jack's throat, Jack's skull making a dent in the dark wall. "I honor my bargains," Belial snarled. His teeth were pointed, each filed to a perfect razor point, and a little blood trickled from the corner of his mouth as he bit his own tongue. "I am a Named demon of Hell and I do not deceive, lie, or employ trickery."

Jack's feet were off the floor, and a black border encroached rapidly on his vision. A smug demon was bad enough. A slagged-off demon was lights out for all humans concerned. He should just learn to keep his trap shut, but it was never a life lesson that had sunk in.

"Yeah," he choked. "You're just a warm fuzzy life coach, ain't you?"

"I am something much, much higher in the food chain than you," Belial said. "And you'll live a lot longer if you learn to show me a little fucking respect."

He dropped Jack, and Jack didn't bother to try and stay upright. He sucked in air, tile digging into his knees.

"Supposing we do pretend to trust you at face value," Pete said. "What the fuck is going on here?"

"Excellent question," Belial said. "Suffice to say that you're the hunting dog, and your man here is holding the leash." He nudged Jack's side with the toe of his shoe. "Come on, Winter. Where's that fighting spirit I saw in Hell?"

Pete took a step. "Don't touch him."

"Be a luv and give us a moment alone," Belia

told her. Pete started to protest, but Jack waved her off.

"Go. Nothing he can do to me he hasn't already."

"Wrong again," Belial said, crouching next to Jack. "Now, I'd hoped you'd cling to your dignity, but I can see I was setting my hopes much too high."

Pete clearly wanted to stand over him, but Shavers shouted at her from the front hall, and she worried her lip. "I'll deal with him. If you hurt Jack . . ."

"I assure you," Belial said. "I only hurt Jack for the fun of it. This is serious."

Her footsteps retreated and Belial stared after her, shaking his head. "Going to be a crying shame when she bulks up and loses that rear bumper." He hauled Jack up by the front of his shirt. "So, you picked out names and wee little booties yet?"

"You say another word about my fucking kid and I don't care who you are or how many Named demons you hobnob with," Jack said. "I'll send you back to the fucking Pit in a shoebox." Pete could shove him off and tell him she wanted him out of the baby's life, but a demon didn't get to talk about any offspring of his. The kid would be raised to know that Hell was never the answer, and demons were never your friends. If somebody had drummed that into Jack a bit harder, he wouldn't be here.

Belial held up his hands. "All right, then, Papa Bear. Calm yourself." He walked through the blood-spattered master bedroom and out onto the balcony, which looked down the back side of a canyon, scrub and loose dirt fading back to green on the upswing. Across the canyon, another miniature replica of a mansion from some other sort of place stared back at them with blank, shuttered windows.

Belial breathed in and leaned on the railing. "Air's good up here. The rich swim in their infinity pools and the masses suffocate." He tapped his pointed nail against the iron. "Remind you of anywhere, Jackie?"

Hot wind, sand, and glass in the bleeding cuts and patches of missing skin. Watching carrion demons creep among the dead, their red stone nails pricking distended abdomens.

Jack lit a cigarette. "Nope."

"You know this place is neutral ground?" Belial said. "The City of fucking Angels. No demon of the city, no Named putting his feet up. A cesspit built on top of a faultline, rimmed with mountains and eroded by a poison sea. If I could never go home again, I'd go here. Fucking paradise, this is." He held out his hand. "Let's have one, then. Don't be greedy."

Jack handed the demon a fag and offered him his lighter. Belial inhaled and studied him through the resulting cloud. "You're looking fit. Not cutting back on vice, are you? That'd make me cry."

"Never felt better," Jack said. "Been eating my spinach."

Belial blew smoke from his nose. "Nice ink," he said, before flicking his fag into the dry scrub below the deck. "You know in sixty-nine the fires in Malibu burned so close to the beach the rock stars and big-titted third-rate actresses were standing in the fucking ocean, praying their condominiums didn't go up? And then a few weeks later, Charlie Manson creeps down from the hills and hacks up their friends. Must've been a run on mother's little helpers that summer."

"Manson didn't actually hack anyone," Jack muttered. "What are you, some kind of groupie? You and he going to be best friends when he goes down the stairs?"

"Oh, Charlie's not one of ours," Belial said. "What demon would deal with a deranged midget who can't carry a tune? Useless."

"I'll be sure to keep that under my hat for the next pub quiz," Jack said. "Did you really come here to give me the dirty history of Los Angeles?"

Belial jerked his thumb in the direction of the bedroom. "This was one of ours. Well, I'm simplifying. More than one. Not really ours."

"Jesus, could you dance around a bit more?" Jack muttered. "Put on some tap shoes. They'd suit you."

Belial tugged his tie loose and ran a nail under his collar. Jack didn't think demons could sweat, but if they could, Belial would be damp. If he didn't know it was a ridiculous notion, on par with thinking a turnip had feelings, he'd say that Belial was scared. Demons understood fear, but they didn't feel it. They didn't feel anything. They worshiped bargains and they fed on the fear and blood of other things.

"I made a fair deal, you know," Belial told him. "You agreed to it."

"Yeah, I agreed to the Pit in exchange for not bleeding to death on a cold floor," Jack said. "Some fucking choice."

"You're a coward, Jack," Belial said. "Not my fault you took the coward's deal rather than going into the light."

"I am this close to chucking you over this fucking railing," Jack said, holding his fingers apart. "I'm beginning to think you crawled up out of that living sewer you call a home just to chat."

"Demons aren't the only things in Hell," Belial said. "We're not even the first things." He looked back out over the canyon. A helicopter puttered across the white-blue sky, and Jack could hear Pete and Shavers talking downstairs. And still, the murder house screamed at him, sight knifing his head.

"Is this going to be a long story?" Jack asked. "Because if it is, 'm going to need a drink and a sit-down."

"When Nergal cracked open his prison," Belial murmured, as if he hadn't heard, "it sent shocks through all of the Pit. Through the Underworld, through the Black, even through the daylight world. You saw it."

"Painfully close up," Jack agreed. This wasn't the Belial he knew—the smirking, insufferable cunt who delighted in pulling the legs off of human flies. Belial looked almost human. Even his form was tired and rumpled. Whatever could make a demon this nervous was firmly in the realm of Not Fucking Good.

"You ever think about what else might have slipped the locks?" Belial said. Jack folded his arms.

"You can't be serious."

"Before there were demons, there were other

things," Belial told him. "Things that crawled in the dark, things that made us what we are. Spawned us out of mud and shit and blood. Things that we realized we could never let free of the Pit."

"And I'm guessing I wouldn't be here if you didn't fall down on the job," Jack said.

Belial twitched inside his human skin. "This isn't my mess, but I'm cleaning it sure enough."

"Ten years isn't exactly a weekend in time outside the Pit," Jack said. "One of these bastards has been free a while, hasn't he?"

"One, we could manage," Belial said. "Hunt him with our own blokes. But the tears Nergal caused gave him the chance to let loose all of his little friends."

"And what do they hope to accomplish by running around up here, slashing families to death?" Jack said.

"That'd be your job to figure out, wouldn't it?" Belial said. "LA is a safe haven for things like that, but outside we could track them. You bring them to me, and I'll be done with you and your little bit of sunshine."

Jack pushed back from the rail. "I still don't trust you."

"Can't imagine why," Belial said as Jack walked away. "You know I'm a demon of my word."

CHAPTER 8

Pete stayed silent until they were nearly back to Venice. "You hate me?" she said finally, pulling the Fury to the curb by Mayhew's office.

Jack lit a cigarette and sat on the Fury's fender. Did he? Have to be the world's largest hypocrite if he did, one for the record books. "No."

"I think you can understand why I didn't tell you," Pete said.

"It's all a bit moot now," Jack told her. "Belial always has a way of getting what he wants, and apparently he wants us to do his little errand."

Pete plucked a note from Mayhew's door. "Says he's down the road in a bar."

"Shocking, that." Jack dropped his butt and stamped out the ember. "We're going to have a little chat."

"Be nice," Pete called after him.

Jack thought about the likelihood of that, considering the whopper Mayhew had told to get them into this morass of Hell politics. " 'M always nice," he told Pete.

The bar fronted the beach—not the tony bit near the boardwalk, which wafted pot smoke down the sand all hours of the day and night and called out with bright lights, frying food, and pretty girls with tan lines, but the bit where all the buildings turned into cinderblock boxes. The Shanty, the place was called, and somebody had tacked driftwood and net to the front in an attempt to disguise the fact that the place was a hovel in practice as well as name.

Peanut shells and other crunchy bits crushed under his boots as he came in, giving his eyes a moment to adjust. The usual sad bastards had bellied up to the bar—a pair of old men in Bermuda shorts, the bleary-eyed, Rudolph-nosed drunk working on his glass of whatever was cheap and plentiful, and a couple of hungover gits sporting Wayfarers, even in the near-subterranean dark of the bar. Musicians, Jack guessed, although not decent ones. If they were, they would've known to keep hair of the dog on hand, roll out of bed, and go back to practice with a bottle of whiskey and a fistful of aspirin. Who had time to be pissing about in old man pubs?

Mayhew was at the end of the bar, the short leg, where he could keep an eye on the gents and the front door simultaneously. It'd be a good vantage if he wasn't piss-drunk, head dipping over his glass, which was clear and slippery with ice cubes. Jack could smell the juniper when he got within a few feet.

"Hello again, Ben," he said, sliding onto the stool next to Mayhew, blocking the view of the rest of the patrons while appearing to simply be having a friendly drink.

Mayhew looked up at him, eyes sliding blearily in and out of focus. "Oh," he said. "Back already?"

"Too right," Jack said. He leaned in, keeping one elbow on the sticky vinyl of the bar top and snaking his other hand out to grab Mayhew's balls. It wasn't the most delicate or dignified way to get somebody's attention, but it had the bonus effect of sobering Mayhew up while inflicting the kind of tight, hot pain that inclined the subject to the truth. "What exactly," Jack growled, leaning close enough to lick Mayhew's ear, "did you think was going to happen when Belial showed up in your tacky little horror of an office?"

"I didn't know," Mayhew gasped. "A demon asks you to do something, you do it."

"Now, I can feel you've got balls," Jack said. "So unless he owns your arse, why're you helping a Hellspawn reel me in?"

"He came to me and he said he needed to get you here," Mayhew said. "Said if I did, I'd find out who killed the Case family. It was a good deal." Beads of moisture worked their way down Mayhew's glass, and down his face, and the stench of his breath enveloped Jack in a furnace of fear and desperation. "I'm not like you," Mayhew whispered. "I'm just a scryer—I find things, people, and I'm not even very good at it. I can't find out who killed those people and I . . ." He gulped. "I promised Mrs. Case I would."

"Here's a tip," Jack said. "Don't make promises to the dead. It never ends well for the living."

"I swear I didn't think he'd hurt you," Mayhew said. "Did he? Hurt you?"

Jack released Mayhew's crotch. "You're a fucking idiot," he said. "What do you know about the things Belial has me looking for?"

"Nothing," Mayhew muttered, dipping back into his gin. "Less than nothing. If I knew, don't you think I would've gone after them myself by now?" He gave Jack a grin, loose and pink with gums. "I wasn't always a lush who calls himself a PI, you know. I used to be a good cop."

"I used to be a dead man," Jack said. "We all used to be something, Ben."

"And now you're the demon's bitch." Mayhew chuckled to himself. "Better you than me, that's all I've got to say."

Jack told himself Mayhew was a drunk, a washout, and a fringe practitioner who didn't have the sense of a gnat, but he still found himself standing up, fisting a handful of Mayhew's Hawaiian shirt, and shoving him against the nearest wall. "You have no bloody idea who you're talking to," Jack snarled. "Or what you're talking about."

"You're some big-shot badass where you come from," Mayhew muttered. "I get that. But this isn't London, and I'm not fucking impressed. I did what I had to do to get you here and put a stop to these murders. You don't scare me."

That was the problem with losing your temper—you didn't think beyond the violence, and now Jack had the choice of propping Mayhew back on his bar stool or beating the shit out of him, neither of which particularly filled him with joy.

"Hey, man." One of the hungover hipsters tapped him on the arm. "Gonna have to ask you to cut that out."

"Fuck off," Jack said. "This ain't your business."

"Actually, I think it is," the git said. He flicked his sunglasses down, and Jack caught a flash of pure white eye.

"Ah, shit," he muttered.

"You can leave now, or you can go through the wall," the creature said. "Either way, let go of Ben."

Jack let Mayhew drop. He hadn't clocked the creature coming through the door. Not human, not dead. That didn't narrow it down a whole hell of a lot.

"You let any sloppy drunkard who'll deal with a demon into your pub?" Jack asked it. "Bad for business."

"I wouldn't know anything about that." The creature gripped Jack's forearm. "I do know strangers busting in and starting fights isn't something we allow. Now are you going to move, or do I move you?"

The touch spread cold through his entire body, and Jack placed the sightless eyes and the pale corpse-colored skin. "All right, all right," he told the wraith. "'M not here to cause you trouble."

He knocked open the door to the alley behind the bar, and stepped out, patting himself down for a cigarette.

The wraith came after him, shutting the door. "Sorry about that. For what it's worth, Mayhew had that coming, but nobody causes trouble in my bar."

"Your bar? Monsters Incorporated, is it?"

The wraith shrugged its narrow shoulders. "Not a lot of safe havens for us. Even in this city."

"Might have something to do with the whole draining people of their blood and leaving them frozen to death bit," Jack said. "Humans tend to get upset about that."

The wraith grinned. "You don't seem to be afraid of me, Mr. Winter."

"Ah, my reputation precedes me," Jack said. "Tell me, did it piss on the carpet or just pass out in the corner?"

"Somebody like Jack Winter, the man who nearly ripped Europe in half over a pissing contest with necromancers," the wraith said. "He lands in your city, you hear about it."

"Seems unfair," Jack said. "You know me, but I don't know you."

"People call me Sliver," the wraith said. "I don't have a name where I come from."

"Sliver." Jack held out his hand. He didn't relish touching the inhuman thing, but he also didn't relish Sliver thinking he was some kind of racist prick. "Pleased to meet you, I suppose."

"Not surprised Mayhew's mixed up with demons now," Sliver said. "He always had his head up his ass in one way or another."

"Yeah, well," Jack said. "My problem now, isn't it?" Not that Belial had been any help at all. The demon loved being cryptic almost as much as he loved his poncey black suits.

"You looking for his phantom killer?" Sliver chuckled. "I've heard that sad story so many times I could tell it myself."

"The demon thinks there's something to it," Jack muttered.

"Yeah, well," Sliver said. "That's a demon for you."

CHAPTER 9

"So you went 'round the pub, tried to beat seven colors of shit out of Mayhew, and wonder why this whole thing isn't working in your favor?" Pete said. She sat crosslegged on the bed in Mayhew's spare room, the photos from the case file spread around her.

"It's not my favor," Jack muttered. "It's not working at all."

"It's a good thing I'm here," Pete said. "Because you're hopeless." She held out a photo to him. "Look at this."

Jack took the photo, showing a back door bookended by blood spatter. A small dark rectangle in one corner was marked with a yellow ruler. "What am I looking at?" he said.

"It's a pet door," Pete said. "The Cases had a dog, which was also never found."

Jack tossed the photo back into the pile. "The

dog did it. Mystery solved in time for tea. Agatha Christie's ghost should tongue-kiss me."

"You are such a bloody idiot, it's amazing you can walk and talk at the same time," Pete said. "Whatever came into those houses had a physical form, yeah?"

Jack shrugged. "A poltergeist doesn't usually hack women open." Or steal their babies. Or get a Named demon of Hell in such a lather he was recruiting human mages to go after his mistakes, contract-killer style.

"So, both of the houses had security systems," Pete said. "On, and not compromised. Neither alarm company reported any pings the night of the murders." She waved the photo. "This is the only way into the house that's not alarmed."

Jack took the photo again. The door was small, undoubtedly for one of those miniscule, hairy yapping things that rich women carried in purses. "You'd have to be a fucking midget to get through that thing," Jack said. "And I've seen a lot of strange shite in my time, but murderous demonic dwarves is stretching even my credulity."

"It's a start," Pete said. "There *was* a way in, and that means at some point, whoever did this had a body." She gathered the photos into a stack. "If they have a body, somebody saw them."

Jack doubted that Belial's boogeymen would let themselves be seen unless they wanted it, but Pete's idea was better than any he'd managed to come up with. How he'd hunt these things—well, he wouldn't. He'd leave them the fuck alone, like any sensible person. Something bad enough to spook

Belial wasn't anything he wanted to meet face to face. He couldn't tell the demon to go fuck himself, for Pete's sake, but neither did he have to toe the line like a good boy. Chances were, whatever Belial was after could be convinced to move along from Los Angeles if Jack offered not to snitch to the demon. Belial wasn't the only one who could make deals.

"The old crime scene's address," Pete said, waving one of Mayhew's files. "Have a look around, talk to any neighbors that are still about—what do you say?"

"Haven't got a better idea." Jack shrugged. "Let's go to it."

CHAPTER 10

The Cases' home was in Westwood, a tony spot populated by shiny, beetlelike cars and nice-looking white people. The UCLA campus kept the bars along the main drag hopping, even at the late hour. Pete rolled slowly with the ever-present molasses-like slog of traffic, guiding the Fury onto side streets, along a row of gates and low-hanging trees. Each home was more brightly spotlit than the last, security systems gleaming like the metal teeth of cybernetic dogs. *Look,* the neighborhood whispered, *but don't think you can ever be a part of what's behind these gates.*

The Cases' home was dark, and an estate agent's sign sat crookedly on the fence, faded by sun and wind.

Jack wasn't surprised—even if you weren't psychic, who wanted to live in a murder house? The Black had an effect on mundane sorts, too, except they wrote it off to "intuition," or bad dreams, or Jesus appearing in their cereal.

Pete eased the Fury to the curb and shut off the lights. Jack got out and examined the gate. The alarm was a good one, but the estate agent's key box gave him an in. He passed his fingers across the slot and whispered a few words of persuasion he'd picked up long ago, when his talent was primarily aimed at breaking into places and nicking things. The box popped, and he found the alarm code and a front door key in his palm.

Locks were his faithful lady—he and locks understood one another, and they understood his talent. Now if he could just get his sight to mind, he'd be ahead of the game. But you were never really ahead—look over your shoulder and you'd see the hounds snapping at your heels.

Sprinklers hissed on as he and Pete crested the walk, wafting the scent of something sweet and earthbound through the air. The Case house wasn't a screaming void like the Herreras', but there was a dome of oppressive air over the low, rambling stucco palace, a prick of chill in the warm night that warned anyone with a modicum of talent to turn the fuck around and run.

Pete wriggled her shoulders inside her cotton jacket. "Spooky, isn't it?" she said.

"That's one word for it," Jack said. He tried the key, and after a bit of a struggle the door popped open. The air inside was stale, recycled by central air. The crime scene cleaners had done a good job of scrubbing blood out of the marble entry, but it wavered as silver film on Jack's sight, luminous over the walls and floors.

He let the silver streaks guide them, through a media room with a giant blank screen taking up an entire wall, and into a kitchen roughly the size of two of his flat back to back. The pain and misery were much more ingrained here, in the walls and wood and bones of the house. Nobody who lived here would ever feel truly settled again.

The largest streak of psychic residue lay across the counters and floor, a great swath where Mrs. Case had met her end.

"There's the pet door," Pete said. The door led to a patio, which ended at a swimming pool lit from beneath the water. With Jack's sight, the water turned black and bottomless, the light shading to orange and then red. A trail wandered from the back fence, across the patio, to the door, and when he looked it was gone.

Jack blinked. Something that could erase its psychic trail—that sounded like the sort of thing Belial was after. He took a breath in, and let his sight open up, and allowed the oppressive atmosphere of the murder house to overwhelm him.

He saw the blood, saw the wavering lines of pain from where the Case woman and her child had lain in their last moments, but he shoved it aside like cobwebs. The trail wavered, through the pet door and across the tiles, stopping over the silvery pool of spectral blood.

It blinked in and out, a line of white little more

than smoke, curling and wavering back on itself. Jack tried to focus his eyes, but doing so produced the familiar spike between his eyes. Look too hard, and the sight would pulverize the parts of his brain that he cared about, leaving him a turnip with interesting dreams.

Just a little more, he begged. The smoke wafted over the back wall of the Case house, down into the light-studded blackness of a canyon. Jack heard a faint whisper, nothing he could make out, and then his sight flared, the smoke twirling into a spiral, swirling around him and down his throat, choking him.

He came back to himself to find that his nose was dripping blood, gleaming black droplets on the Cases' countertop. Pete sighed and wiped it up with her sleeve. "You think you could manage not to leave your DNA all over everything, genius?"

"Sorry," he muttered. For the moment, he left aside thinking about what could set a trap for any psychic who might try to follow it, keep it on for years after the fact, and burn out every trace of its presence. Right then, breathing was enough of a headache. "You were right," he told Pete.

"What is it?" Pete said. Jack thought about the smoke, trailing through his sinuses, burning with that ashes-and-dust scent that he recognized from his dreams. The scent of the wind in Hell. Belial's missing nightmare was definitely the nasty git who'd hacked up the Case family.

Jack rubbed his forehead. His headache in the

morning was going to be a thing of epics. "Something that doesn't appreciate me sniffing after it, that much is certain."

The creature had done a good job—it had left only a burn scar on the Black around the Case house. Nothing Jack could probe further, unless he relished his brain leaking out. But it hadn't disappeared into thin air. It was a thing, with a form and a body, a thing that *had* to hide its passage, because otherwise any psychic worth his bad dreams would know it for what it was.

Pete tensed as a car passed on the street, headlights sweeping down the hall from the foyer. "Our luck's probably up," she said. "We should get out of here."

Jack waited until he was back in the Fury to punch the dash, leaving a crack in the veneer.

"Oi!" Pete said. "I have to return this in pristine condition, you know."

"Yeah, yeah, my fault," Jack muttered. "You can tell Sal that Christine did it."

"What's your problem all of a sudden?" Pete demanded. "Throwing a tantrum isn't going to get anything done."

His knuckles were bleeding, and Jack swiped them against his jeans. Pete made a fair point. "With a ghost or a demon, I can track it or summon it, find its true name and compel it to appear. But all I've got now is ashes." Belial's boogeyman thought it was smarter than him, and Jack didn't like creatures that thought that.

"I'm just a little frustrated, and I very much

want to nail this bastard to the wall and be free to be on my way," he told Pete.

"We, you mean," Pete said. "Belial can act like I'm some shrinking flower, but I made that deal and this is as much my mess as yours." She started the Fury with a rumble and pulled away. "*We'll* nail him, and then you can go right back to your sordid little magic lifestyle and *we'll* no longer be a bother for you."

"You know it won't matter if I give it all up," Jack said quietly. "Something will still come knocking." He wished he could force Pete to believe him, by screaming or shaking her or any other way, but he couldn't, and trying to do so now was just burning daylight he could be using to finish Belial's latest exercise in ant-farm sadism.

So he stayed quiet, and she stayed quiet, and things went on exactly as they'd been for months. Pete drove for a bit, until Jack couldn't take the confined space and the wanting of a cigarette any longer. "Let me out here, yeah?" he asked Pete. She braked and gave him a stare.

"Why?"

"Need to walk a bit," Jack said.

"Right," Pete said, but she let him get out of the car without anything further. "See you back at Mayhew's?" she called.

"Maybe," Jack said. Dealing with Mayhew again was somewhere on his list of activities after letting a ferret chew on his balls, but he didn't want to give Pete more problems.

She followed him for a few feet before pulling

back into traffic. Jack stopped on a corner and lit a cigarette. He was on Hollywood Boulevard, near an on-ramp to the 101 freeway. At night, the low cinderblock buildings were mostly dark and gated. A pair of hobos dozed in a doorway, cradling their paper-wrapped bottles close. "Hey, brother," one said. "How about a few bucks?"

"Sorry," Jack told him. "Not from around here."

"Then how 'bout a smoke?" the other said. Jack sighed and handed over the rest of his pack.

"God bless you," the hobo said, snaking the fags inside his jacket faster than a stage magician.

"He's got fuck-all to do with this, hasn't he?" Jack said, walking on. He clocked the shadow half a block down, along a dark section of unoccupied storefront. Cars swooped past, but the streetlamp above was burnt out, creating a slice of dark perfect to pull someone close and stick a knife in their kidney.

Jack slowed his steps a little at a time, then stopped and dropped his cigarette, crushing it under the toe of his boot.

The shadow was silent, just a ripple in the psychic airflow, but it was there, hanging back and taking its time. Jack spread his arms. "I haven't got all night," he said. "Come on out, then."

Sliver melted from the shadow of the storefront. "They said you were good. That's just spooky, though."

"Says the shadow-walking wraith to the mage with bad knees," Jack said. " 'M not that good.

Maybe you're just crap at this spy gig, you ever think of that?"

Sliver looked at his feet. "I wasn't going to actually kill you."

"What a comfort," Jack said. He didn't try to throw a curse on the wraith. That would only slag Sliver off. He could turn tail and run, or cut down the alley to the next street, but if a wraith really wanted to catch up with you, it could have a hand inside your ribcage before you could draw your last breath.

"This is all Mayhew's fault," Sliver said. "He brought you here."

"Yeah, it was pretty fucking convenient that you wanted to be my best friend back at your bar," Jack said. "But I thought maybe you just fancied me."

Sliver looked up and down Hollywood Boulevard, studying each pool of light and neon sign, silver eyes reflecting like pools of oil. "I don't know who wants you dead, Jack, but they reached out."

"Lots of folks want that," Jack said. "Too many to list."

"Nobody has that kind of influence in this city," Sliver said. "Not anyone who followed you. But these people do. They're tossing around threats and cash like it's Mardi Gras."

"How mysterious," Jack said. Sliver fell into step beside him when he started walking again.

"I was just keeping an eye on you," the wraith said. "There's a lot of mean and hungry bastards in this city who wouldn't think twice about erasing you for the kind of things these dudes are offering."

"Wouldn't be the first time I banged a stick against somebody's cage," Jack shrugged.

Sliver blended with the shadows for a moment, then reemerged. "You need to watch your ass," he said. "This isn't merry England. The Black here, this is the Wild fucking West. And you're stomping around in those big boots of yours across the top of everyone's bridge."

Jack thought about what Pete's father, a detective inspector with bad lungs and a worse temper, had once told her. "When somebody tries to kill you, means you're getting somewhere," Jack said to Sliver.

"And are you?" the wraith said. "Getting anywhere?"

"No, not really," Jack said. The missing trail of the thing that had murdered the Cases dogged at him, though he tried to ignore the obvious solution. That would open him up to all kinds of nasty things, lay his mind bare and at the mercy of his sight. He could go catatonic and never come back if he did what most psychics would do in this situation. But he wasn't most. A mage with the sight was a time bomb as it was, without inviting the entire world of the dead inside his skull.

"Then what?" the wraith asked. "You're going to wander around Hollywood waiting to get offed?"

Jack shook his head. "No, I do have one idea." A stupid idea, but the only one, as was usually the

way with him. "You know where I can find somebody who deals esoterica around here?" he said.

"Yeah," Shiver said. "There's a shop on Cahuenga
that I'd trust to sell, and not drop a dime on you
after you leave."

"You want to get off me bad side, take me there,"
Jack said, and tried to ignore the prickle on the
back of his neck while Sliver walked them to his
car. The feeling that he might have just had his last
stupid idea, and the fear of what he was going to
have to see. When he'd been shooting heroin, it had
kept the fear at bay, along with everything else. Now
there was nothing—a few tattoos to keep him from
going completely around the bend when his visions
kicked in, but beyond that, there was his sight and
the void it looked into.

Sliver's car was roughly the same vintage as Pete's
loaner, but dented on every sharp edge and pocked
with rusted continents floating in a primer-colored
sea. "It's a piece of shit, I know," Sliver said, "but
who'd steal it?"

"Fair enough," Jack said. A spring poked out
from the upholstery and into the small of his back.
They drove east, and Shiver pointed out a bridge
across a concrete trough. "That's the LA river,"
he said. "Site of one million movie car chases."
He jerked his thumb at the ironworks lamps flash-
ing by. "The bridge is famous too. Fourth Street
Bridge. Look it up."

"What is this city's obsession with the movies?"
Jack demanded. "Every bloody person I've met

had some precious anecdote about the silver fuck-ing screen."

"Before the movies, this place was mostly orange groves, train tracks, and a few shitty apartment build-ings," Sliver said. "Not a lot of real history, so we take ours from films." The shadows under the bridge rippled as they passed, and Sliver pointed ahead. "This is East LA. Badass neighborhood, my girl lives in, too. Don't wander around here on your own."

A few more turns, and Sliver pulled up in front of a bodega, saints' candles lining the window. "Just tell the old lady I sent you," he said.

"Cheers," Jack said. The shop wasn't anything special—graffiti covered one of the front windows and the door was bright red, but he could feel the protection hexes vibrating from the sidewalk. Some-body who knew what they were doing had put a tight net over the whole building, and Jack got the distinct feeling he wasn't welcome. Not that it had ever stopped him. He pushed open the door and a bell jangled to announce him.

The front of the shop was crammed with dusty junk, rosaries and bundles of sage, more candles, prayer cards, and plaques of the Virgin and the cru-cifixion dangling from the ceiling. Most esoterica dealers had this sort of window dressing, to discour-age the daylight world in general from looking too closely. What was true in porn shops was also true for magic shops—the good stuff was behind the curtain.

Jack pushed the red glass beads aside, setting up a clatter, and found himself in an even more claustrophobic back room. A small circle on the floor was painted with a *veve*, to a *loa* Jack wasn't familiar with, but the white paint was far less engaging than the woman behind the pile of wooden crates serving as a counter.

"Well," she said, setting down her magazine. "Look at you."

Jack flashed her a smile. Charming women wasn't any harder than picking a recalcitrant lock—it just took a little time and a light touch. And working on the assumption that his mark went for scars, leather, and tattoos. The girl behind the counter returned his smile.

"Don't get offended, but how the fuck did you get in here? This shop is reserved for select customers."

"Didn't see a doorman," Jack said. He leaned on the counter, pulling her into the radius of his smile while skimming the surface of her talent. It was there, strong and bloodred. "So explain something to me," he said, gesturing around the room. "Your select customers, they all *vaudaun*, into Santeria, and advocates of Santa Muerte at the same time? Because that'd get a touch confusing, speaking for myself."

"We specialize," said the girl. "We don't discriminate."

"Brilliant," Jack said. He stuck out his hand. "And you are?"

She looked at his hand, looked at him, smiled with an expression that could razor flesh. "Out of your league."

Jack retracted the hand. "My favorite kind." She wasn't touching him, so she was either being smart or really did think she was too gorgeous to be believed. She was, at that—long dark hair twisted in a rope with red ribbon, gleaming skin. She could be one of the saints pasted onto the sides of the candle holders, lit from within by a flame.

"Bloke who sent me here said you'd be old," Jack said. "Glad to see he was wrong."

"Maybe I am old," the girl said. "Maybe I'm a wicked witch, sent to lure you into my candy house before I show you my true face."

Jack shrugged. "There are worse ways to go."

"Well, you're not Santeria or *vaudaun*," said the girl, abruptly shifting from smiling shopkeeper to sharp-eyed avatar. "Death worshipper? Following the saint of killers?"

"Death more sticks out its foot and trips me if I try and follow it," Jack said. The girl tilted her head, and then she reached across the counter and snatched his hand in a parody of their aborted handshake.

Jack got a strong, dark pulse, from his throat down to his cock—bodies piled in trenches, blood running through dirty gutters while wild dogs fought over meat, hollow-eyed men walking dusty streets with guns in their hands and speed in their blood. Skinless corpses dangling from balcony rails while the crows gathered on the roofline. Always the crows, their caws echoing in his skull.

"You don't worship death," the girl said. "But it sticks to you all the same. It's under your skin."

Jack yanked his hand away. His heart and his head both throbbed. "I'm spoken for, luv," he said. "Death already has her claws in me, so get in line."

The girl laughed. "I don't want you, crow-mage. I'm Death from the dirt and the desert, not some rainy little shithole of an island." She settled back on her stool. "Now, what can I do for you?"

Jack decided not to ask why a death avatar was running a shitty bodega in a bad part of LA. He'd seen stranger things—and in the last day, at that. "I need to read a crime scene," he said. "Psychically. I suppose I need a censer, and the stuff to put me under."

"Trancing out at a murder site," said the girl, and grinned. "All you psychics decide to live on the edge lately?"

"All?" Jack said. She hopped off her stool and hurried around the room, getting an iron pot and tossing packets of herbs into it, along with a few candles, a bindle of red thread, and a packet of children's blackboard chalk.

"There was another *pendejo* in here about a week ago, wanted to trance at a crime scene." She set the pot on the counter and rang Jack up on a cash register so old it had a crank handle.

"This wouldn't happen to be a fat bastard in a Hawaiian shirt, would it?" Jack said.

"Nah," said the girl. "We don't get many white boys in here. I'd remember that." She shoved the pot at him. "Six bucks for the candles and the chalk. Consider the rest a gift."

Jack narrowed his eyes. The one thing he wanted

even less than to owe a demon was to owe one of the Morrigan's sisters in death and blood debts. "I'll pay."

"Oh, you will," she agreed. "Just not today."

Jack handed her a ten dollar bill—American money all looked like scraps of dishrag to him—and she made change. "Have fun," the dead girl told him, before picking her magazine back up.

CHAPTER 11

Pete thought he was insane, and told him so, and he didn't disagree with her. Jack told her she didn't have to go back to the Case house, and didn't have to be a part of it at all.

"Don't be a fucking idiot," Pete snapped. "You swallow your tongue, who's there to roll you on your side?"

The street was the same when they returned the next evening—quiet shadows broken up with barking dogs and hissing sprinklers. Jack set himself up in the kitchen, in the center of the bloodstain where Mrs. Case had kicked it. If he was going to be mad, he might as well go straight over the top.

"Need me for anything?" Pete said.

"Not unless I start choking on my own fluids," Jack said. Pete peered out the windows.

"I see a private security car," Pete said, as head-lamps swept the room. "Haven't seen any cops."

Jack wasn't worried about the police—all they could do was arrest you, whack you a few times in the skull with a stick, and send you on your way. He wasn't at all worried about anything human that might happen.

He touched his lighter to the candles and drew a chalk sigil on the tiles—a sort of all-purpose *Hey, let's have a look* sigil that psychics and seers used to boost the signal.

A trance reading wasn't dangerous to a run-of-the-mill ghost-peeper. A psychic went under, they witnessed the murder via the psychic echoes, saw the dead's sonar picture recorded for posterity on the site of their passing. They were just an observer and when they came up they were able to tell the family that Aunt Mabel loved them and had skipped merrily into the light. Except his sight didn't let him be only a observer. The dead were a tide, determined to suck him under and make him one of them, sooner or later. His gift from the Morrigan showed him death in vivid, screaming reality, and this would be no different.

He'd done a few trance readings when he was much younger and stupider, one of which had cumulated in the dead girl he'd called up sitting in the corner of a cheap hotel room in Dublin, watching him slice his wrists to finally, once and for all, make the visions and the whispers stop.

Permanently trapped in the replay of the Case murders, or Pete, and by extension the kid, on the wrong end of a deal with Belial? It wasn't a har-

fucking choice. Jack figured he was already half-crazy anyway.

"Find some matches." he told Pete. He dumped the herbs into the iron pot and sat in front of them, rolling his jacket for his head in case he keeled over.

Pete handed him a blue box, and Jack lit a pair of matches, dropping them into the dry herbs. They lit with a crackle, curling into blackened ash, and smoke curled up, fragrant and overpowering. The back of Jack's throat went sticky, but he forced himself to breathe the cloying stuff and let it fill his lungs.

Trances felt like a shitty high at first—none of the warm pool of smack, not even the pleasant fuzziness of pot. You floated, dizzy and sick to your stomach, and then out of the corner of your eyes, you noticed that you were no longer part of the world.

Jack's head throbbed once as the smoke filtered into his brain, his sight opening wide and straining to all corners of the Cases' kitchen.

It was night, but not the same kind of soft night he'd come from. This was dark, lights glittering through the darkened door higher on the hill. One by one, the faraway lights blinked out, until only the glow of the pool and the digital clock on the Cases' oven gave light.

Jack stood up, although the small, remote part of his mind that wasn't fucked up beyond recognition knew that he was likely sprawled on the tile floor.

The darkness became absolute, rolling through the crystal water of the pool like a cloud of blood.

Jack kept his eyes on the back wall, where the trail had been, the erasure of something ripping through the Black that floated over the Case house like a bleak fog. Even before the murders, this hadn't been a happy home.

After a time, a figure appeared at the back wall. It was human, Jack supposed, if you were loose about the definition. The limbs were long, ragged with extra skin, sores popping out all over wrinkled skin. A pair of tattered suit pants were barely holding on to starved hip bones. The thing had a beard, long and hiding a hollow-cheeked face, and burning eyes fixed on the pet door.

The thing wriggled through like a worm, bones rippling under the sagging skin. It turned and stared directly at him, but Jack held his ground. It wasn't real, just an echo, replaying for his sight like a tattoo needle going over and over a piece of skin.

He watched as the man—it had been a man, once, before whatever was inside the skin had hollowed it out—went to the knife block sitting on the kitchen island. It pulled out the largest blade, silver-handled and gleaming in the low light, and then reached out and grabbed a bowl of oranges and lemons with a hand ragged and bleeding, nails cracked and brown. It flung the bowl at the tiles, and then it stood, ragged chest rising and falling, until a light flared from the hallway and Mrs. Case appeared.

In the trance, she flickered, almost transparent. Her echo was much fainter, and with a few decades or a good cleansing of the house by a practitioner, it'd be gone entirely.

She didn't see the thing waiting for her. Never saw Death spread its wings and dive. She waddled into the kitchen and saw the bowl. "Oh, for fuck's sake." Underwater whispers, barely a voice. "Badger, did you get on the counter again?"

Badger must be the mutt. Jack hoped for the furry rat's own sake he'd clocked the thing waiting for his mistress as something not to be fucked with, and stayed away.

"Badger?" Mrs. Case bent her knees with difficulty, pregnant belly swelling under her robe, and started picking up the glass shards. "Goddamn dog," she muttered.

The thing moved then, behind her, pressing the knife against her neck and wrapping its free arm across her breasts. It whispered something to her that Jack didn't catch, but Mrs. Case went limp, and the thing laid her out in the spot that Jack's body occupied in real time.

It pointed the knife at Mrs. Case. "Tape."

She was shaking, eyes filling with tears. "Drawer by the sink. Please don't . . ."

"Shut up, bitch." The thing had an ancient smoker's rasp for a voice, gravel and phlegm rattling in its chest. It hacked and spat a gob of something on the tiles.

Mrs. Case's eyes roved around the dark kitchen, lighting on the glass shards. While the thing turned its back, she reached for one, but it lay out of her grasp. She clasped her hands over her stomach again, shaking uncontrollably. "What do you want?"

The thing turned back with a roll of packing

tape. It bound her wrists and slapped a piece over her mouth. "I told you to shut up."

It finished taping up Mrs. Case and then turned, nostrils flaring and burning eyes widening.

"Honey?" It'd be Mr. Case, coming to save the day.

Jack watched, following in the wake of the thing, as it met Mr. Case just over the threshold. Quick, brutal jabs, knife angled up, piercing vital things like lungs and heart and stomach. Mr. Case gurgled, and the thing stepped back and drew the knife across his throat in a slash. Blood hit the walls and floor, and pooled with startling speed.

The thing's bare, knobby feet slicked in Mr. Case's blood as it turned and focused its attention back on Mrs. Case. Her wide, marble-like eyes watched its every move. Jack did too. This was a predator wearing human skin. Belial's vague scary story aside, Jack could see when something was not of the daylight world, when it crawled from the shadows to hunt and feed.

It crouched above Mrs. Case, and pulled her robe away with its half-rotted hands. She mewled under the tape, and thrashed as best she could, and Jack wanted to tell her not to bother. Mrs. Case was dead. She just hadn't caught on yet.

Pushing up her pale blue nightgown, the thing let its palm rest on Mrs. Case's belly. It grinned, and Jack saw teeth that were black and gums that oozed rot. He couldn't begin to guess what shape the body had been in before the passenger had climbed inside, but it was falling apart faster than an imitation handbag.

"You had to know it would be this way," the thing told Mrs. Case. "You had to know you don't turn your back on something like this once you've agreed to it." He peeled back the tape and cocked his head. "Got anything to say for yourself, you lying whore?"

"I didn't agree to *this*," Mrs. Case gasped. "I didn't agree to . . . you . . ." She trailed off, sobbing too hard to get any words out. The thing slapped the tape back over her mouth, and even though he was less than a ghost here, Jack crouched by her head. He needed to look into the thing's face, try to see what was behind the eyes.

Mrs. Case jerked as the thing placed the knife against her stomach, screaming behind the tape, strangled and animal-like. She sounded like a pig hanging in a slaughterhouse rather than a person, and the thing laughed. "We all pay our debts, kiddo," it said. "One way or another, blood or money, we all pay. You, me, everyone."

Mrs. Case tried to speak through the tape, but the knife went in, and the thing drew the blade across the curve of her belly in one economical motion. Jack watched, not wanting to blink, as the thing went about its work, cutting the child from Mrs. Case and holding the slick, still body in its palms.

Mrs. Case's eyelids fluttered, but her fingers flexed as she reached for the child. Jack gave her full credit—even hacked to bits, she was a tough bird.

The thing wiped the blood and amniotic fluids away from the baby's mouth and nose with a ragged fingertip, and then breathed into the tiny mouth until the child wailed.

Jack reached out reflexively, but it was like being stuck in one of those dreams where you couldn't move your own limbs. The Case baby wasn't dead— the thing had cut it out of its mother and breathed life into it. "Why?" Jack said. "What could you possibly want with a fucking baby?"

The thing wrapped the baby in Mrs. Case's bathrobe while it squalled, setting it almost gently on the tile floor, and then stood over Mrs. Case while she stared at it, her eyes glassy and fixed.

"Consider us squared," it said, and then leaned down and jabbed the knife into the hollow of Mrs. Case's throat, twisting until blood flowed in small rivers down her neck. Her body was a ruin, and she lasted not even one more sucking breath before she went still.

The thing picked up the baby, and Jack waited. He'd been prepared for a dead kid, something small that could be left in a canyon for coyotes and other scavengers to devour. He'd been prepared for the sort of thing that considered child-flesh a rarified taste, or your basic sick human bastard who got his rocks off on killing a mother and her unborn baby.

But if it was keeping the child alive, that opened up a host of worse things. There were far blacker fates for children who stayed alive in the grasp of something like this creature. Jack felt his stomach knot, even though he didn't really have a stomach in the vision. He was at the end—the smoke was wearing off and soon he'd be back, vomiting his guts into the Cases' kitchen sink.

He tried to follow the thing, but the cold-water feeling was still there, and every step was agony.

At the door, the thing turned back to Jack, and locked eyes with him for the first time. "I see you," it rasped. "But you don't see me. Not really. You don't have any idea what I am." It laughed, and Jack couldn't do a damn thing. He watched the creature, with the Cases' child, disappear back over the wall. It laughed the entire time.

The eyes were bottomless. Demons riding human bodies had glassy, flat eyes—dead man's eyes. These were alive, horribly so, a forest fire ravaging its human shell.

I see you.

A tremor went through Jack, unbidden, as he started to back himself off the vision, shut down the ebb and flow of the Black that washed across his mind, and try and make reentry into the real world.

They were just echoes, a memory that lived and breathed. The creature couldn't see Jack any more than he could reach out and touch it, ten years past. Couldn't. But had.

"Jack?"

Pete helped him sit up, and Jack tried to push down the wave of nausea. He'd managed to shoot smack for close to a dozen years without puking on everything. He could handle one bad trip.

"Fuck," he said. His head was throbbing like a skinhead had taken a brick to it, and his upper lip was slick with cooled blood. The echos still vibrated in the Case house, like listening to faraway klaxons.

"You all right?" Pete handed him a wad of paper towels, and Jack shoved it under his nose.

" 'M fine." It came out muffled. His tongue was thick and dry from inhaling the smoke, and his chest felt like he had sucked down a tongue of flame.

"You're a blood-coated mess, is what you are," Pete said. She dumped the herbs from the pot into the sink and ran water on them.

"I'm a blood-coated mess who saw some real interesting stuff while he was under," Jack said. The sky outside was creeping toward pink-gray, and he rubbed his face. "How long was I under?"

"A while," Pete said. "I think we should go. Been here long enough to make people suspicious."

Jack collected his kit and shoved it back into his sack, then followed Pete out the front door. On the sidewalk, a female jogger wearing tight hot pink leggings slowed down to stare at them. Jack nodded and flashed her a smile. "Morning, luv."

She didn't return it, but she sped up again and didn't reach for her mobile to call the police down on the freakish British axe murderer squatting in the vacant mansion next door.

Jack watched her pert pink ass bounce away around the corner, and then tossed his kit into the back seat of the Fury. "Can we get some breakfast? I'm knackered."

"Yeah, and I'm constantly starved," Pete said.

"Always thought that eating for two was crap, but I'd lick the paint off the bloody car, at the moment."

They drove south along the 405 freeway. Traffic was already packed in, but it moved, and Pete jumped off near Venice. Jack saw the black sport utility vehicle come behind them, neither too close nor too far away, lights off even though it was barely light enough to read street signs.

"Pete," he said, and pointed into his side mirror.

"Yeah," she said after a moment. "I see 'em."

The van followed them through a pair of turns and onto Venice Beach Boulevard, the only light coming from a coffee stand. Nobody was on the street except for dozing bums. No witnesses to bother whoever was following them around.

"All right," Pete said. "Hold on." She jerked the wheel and the Fury fishtailed onto a side street, laying a thick strip of rubber.

Jack slammed against the passenger door. The handle caught him sharply in the ribs, and he grabbed it to avoid being tossed around like a doll.

The SUV came screeching after them, and Pete cursed. "They know what they're doing. And I don't know these fucking streets."

In London, Pete would be able to lose a tail, either in the maze of pre-automobile streets in the city center or in the myriad one-way roads of Hampstead. Here, though, she wasn't able to shake the black car. Jack winced as the Fury nipped a curb, undercarriage scraping.

"Slow down up here," he said, as Pete steered

them into a back alley behind a row of bungalows. She gripped the wheel, knuckles pale.

"What are you going to do?"

"Just don't worry about me," Jack told her. "I'll be fine."

"Jack . . ." she started, but he shoved open the door and dropped out, pavement rushing up.

The trick was to let yourself fall—ball up your head to protect it, and let yourself go limp. Your body will absorb the impact. You tense up, you try to fight the falling, and you'll break, smash your bones against the pavement, and end up roadkill.

Jack tucked his head down, gravel and shards of broken bottles raking his arms, and rolled to a stop amid a collection of bins. The SUV jerked to a stop, and a pair of legs emerged. Jack stayed where he was, letting his heart slow down and feeling himself over to make sure nothing vital had broken in the fall. He could still wiggle all his fingers and toes. The road rash would heal. All in all, not the worst landing he'd experienced.

One pair of legs was clad in black denim and boots with flat, rounded toes, the kind specifically made for kicking seven kinds of shit out of a person. A second joined them, sporting a pair of alligator shoes and blue slacks that came to a stop above knobby ankles.

"Nice tuck and roll, brother," said Alligator. "Didn't need it, though. Just wanted to talk at you for a minute."

"You always chase down blokes you want to speak with in a spook car?" Jack asked.

Shitkicker drew back his foot and drove it once into Jack's abdomen. It was a strong, enthusiastic kick delivered by a man who enjoyed his work. Jack jerked, folding around the knot of bruise, and fought hard not to vomit. He had a feeling Alligator wouldn't appreciate him redecorating his shoes.

"He said he talks, not you," said Shitkicker, and drew back.

"Jesus, Parker," said Alligator. "We need him not pissing his own blood, you stupid piece a' shit. Slow your roll, all right?"

There was a click as Parker lit a cigarette, and Alligator leaned down into Jack's vision. "Howdy," he said. "Sorry about that."

"Piss off." Jack sat up. His guts rolled back and forth. The seasick throbbing in his skull would fade, eventually, but it wasn't helping him any.

" 'Fraid not, partner," said Alligator. "We all need to have a chat."

Jack tried sitting up, which wasn't a day at the park, but he managed it. Standing was a little easier. "I don't talk to flash gits who chase me down and knock me around," he said. "Sorry to disappoint, but you'll be deprived of my sparkling wit and charm."

Parker, the big one, snorted. He blew smoke from his butt into Jack's face and looked at Alligator. "We gotta listen to him yap?"

"We're not kidnapping him, for fuck's sake," Alligator said. "He's a guest."

"A guest of what?" Jack calculated that there was no way he could break for the end of the alley, not unless he wanted the bulge under Parker's leather jacket to materialize into a pistol. For now, he'd have to have Alligator's little chat.

"Come on, now," Alligator said. "Get in the car."

"Sure," Jack said. "Got nothing better to do than run off with strangers on mysterious errands."

Jack had to admit he was curious—the person who'd bought the trance herbs from the dead girl in the bodega would be the one wanting to talk, he'd wager, and he wanted to see exactly what they were about. He wouldn't put it past Belial to use competing mages to get his job done, not one bit. And if Jack failed, Belial would have an excuse to void his bargain with Pete, and keep his claws in her for who knew how long. These two didn't seem to want to bash his skull in just yet, so he could play their game and see what they really had in store for him.

"You ain't what I expected," Alligator said, sliding into the back seat of the idling SUV after Jack and boxing him against the door. "Heard you was a USDA Grade-A choice badass, and look at you. You couldn't hardly swat a fly."

Parker gunned the engine into a U-turn and Jack watched the morning, tinted by the SUV's black glass, roll past. "So now that I've disappointed you, where are we going?"

Alligator grinned, displaying one front tooth rimmed in gold, and the rest a startling shade of two-pack-a-day brown. "Now, Jackie. If I told you that, it wouldn't be a surprise."

PART TWO

JUDGMENT

*"We are your fathers, brothers and sons,
and there will be more of your children
dead tomorrow."*

—Ted Bundy,
American serial killer

CHAPTER 12

On the freeway, Alligator pulled out a black canvas sack. "You understand," he said. "Our boss is pretty privacy conscious."

"Fuck off," Jack said. "He wants me so bad, he can bloody well take me without a sack on me head."

Alligator sighed. "Figured you might say that."

Jack felt a prick in the side of his neck, and whipped his head around to see Alligator holding a disposable syringe. "Nothin' to worry about," he told Jack. "Just a little shot of dream-time. You'll be right as rain by the time we get where we're goin'."

Jack tried to reach for the man's thick, sweaty neck, or even merely curse at him, but his mouth was stuffed with cotton wool and his brain was flying out the window, lifting up and then falling into crushing depths.

He tasted the hot wind and felt embers land on

his exposed skin, face and chest and arms. Belial stood with him at the lip of a chasm, smooth sides made from riveted iron plunging into blackness his eyes couldn't fathom. Far away, the fires of Hell burned, keeping the souls of the damned hot and aware of every second of their torture as they powered the great city that shredded the horizon like the claws of a beast in the tender pink flesh of the sky.

"You're not supposed to be here," Belial told him, but Jack couldn't step away, couldn't stop staring at the blackness below.

"This is an old place," Belial said. "A damned place. Nobody should be here. How did you slip away and find it?" His face in Hell was different, reptilian and slit-eyed, two sets of lids blinking against the hot wind. A forked tongue raked over his pointed teeth. He put his hand on Jack's shoulder, black nails digging bloody half moons. "I'm not finished with you yet," he said. "It'll be a long time before I put you down there, Jack. You don't need to start making friends just yet."

The blackness rippled gently far below, the slightest echo across his sight. Just a match flare in the endless dark, and then it was gone. At the time, panic and fear had overridden his senses. He'd managed to slip from his cell, cross acres of bone and ash, turning to glassy sand and finally to foot-shredding rocks, before he'd fetched up here. Now Belial was leading him back toward the fires and the cities of Hell, to start his sentence all over again, and the next time escape wouldn't be simply a matter of physical pain.

But now that he was remembering, he heard a whisper drift up from the ravine, from that ripple across his sight.

Hello, Jack.

Jack came awake when the SUV guttered through a rut, and slit his eyes open to get his bearings before Alligator caught on. Another mansion, another gated drive—but this wasn't the cookie-cutter glass-and-rock type that the Herreras had been murdered in. This was an actual mansion, a pile of rocks that looked like William Randolph Hearst could have put his feet up and felt at home.

"Wakey wakey, eggs and bakey," said Alligator, jabbing Jack in the tender side of his ribs.

The drugs left him thickheaded and slow, but Jack shook off Alligator's fat, gold-encrusted hand and walked under his own power. The mansion had double doors, banded in iron, a giant Mission-style statement that whoever lived there was better than you.

Iron bands could mean other things, too, and Jack looked up as Alligator and Parker skirted him through the door. A protection hex hung above. A magic user, then, and somebody who either knew what he was doing or knew somebody he could pay to do the job right. The hex was strong, and Jack felt it examine and discard him as he crossed the threshold.

"This way," Alligator said. Parker broke off for parts unknown, and Jack found himself escorted through a high-ceilinged sitting room where dust filled his nose, and out to the ubiquitous pool. This one was surrounded by statues, pitted and chipped from wind and sun to be faceless and in many cases limbless. A thin scrim of algae floated on top of the pool and a dead squirrel bumped against the filter.

A single figure stood with his back to them, looking out over the water and to the drop into the canyon beyond.

"Mr. Winter," he said, and turned. "Thanks so much for agreeing to meet me."

"He didn't exactly agree, boss," said Alligator. "Had to dose him up."

"That's unfortunate." The man approached Jack and turned his head this way and that with a strong, tanned hand. "You five by five, Winter?"

"I've felt a lot worse," Jack said. Nothing sparked when they touched. So far nobody except Parker had pinged his radar as talented in any way besides paying people to do dirty errands for them.

"Good to hear," said the man. "Give us a minute."

Alligator glared at Jack from under his thick eyebrows, but he drew back into the sitting room, watching Jack from behind the stained-glass French doors.

"Sorry about my man," Jack's host said. He went to a poolside bar and dropped two ice cubes into a glass, covering them with scotch. "Drink?"

"You'll forgive me if I don't want to go any further down the rabbit hole," Jack said. He was still slow and sounded as if he were shouting at himself from down a long tunnel, but he could at least move and speak under his own power. Running and screaming might soon have to follow, so he was counting the small favors.

"That wasn't my intention," the man said. He sipped the scotch, nodded as if it had said all the right things, and gestured Jack into a high-backed wicker chair poolside. It creaked under his weight and smelled of mold. "I have to say," his host said, "it really is a thrill to have you sitting here."

"Your life's not very exciting then, is it?" Jack asked. "Who the fuck are you, mate? What do you want with me?"

"My name's Harlan Sanford," the man said. "I'm what's called a money man, or a silent partner—I finance films, but I don't need to get jerked off by having my name scroll up the screen."

"Nice for you," Jack said. He shoved his chair back and stood up. "I'll just be finding my way home now."

"Oh, I don't think you're going home any time soon," Sanford said. "There's a cash bounty on your head over there in the UK—not to mention bragging rights as the one who offed Jack Winter." He held out his hand. "Sit. I promise we have things in common and a lot to talk about."

Standing wasn't working out very well, so Jack sat back down. Vertigo rippled at the edges of his vision.

"The film business is just a job for me," Sanford said. "I reinvest, and I'm a collector. I think under different circumstances you and I could have had a nice afternoon chatting about magic."

Jack tipped his head back. The sun was coming up, and it sent jets of sickly green light refracting from the pool into his face. "What are we chatting about instead?"

Sanford tossed back the rest of his scotch. "I know that Belial's been in contact with you. Slippery bastard, isn't he?"

Jack lifted one eyebrow. "You and he pals, then?"

"Oh, not at all," Sanford said. "Hate fucking demons. Never had a transaction with one that didn't end in a big hassle for me and some fork-tongued son of a bitch trying to screw me out of what I was owed. Like dealing with studio execs, except demons have better manners." He took a pack of gum from his pocket and shoved a wad into his mouth. "Quitting smoking," he explained. "Belial is a moron," Sanford continued. "A power-grubbing, shortsighted moron, and greedy even for a demon, which should tell you something."

Jack laughed. Sanford was either insane or stupid, and he'd find out soon enough that demons had a way of finding out when humans mocked them.

"I know why he's here," Sanford said. "He wants what I want, and that means you and I want the same thing, and we can help each other."

Jack rubbed his forehead. "No offense, mate, but when somebody offers me an out that's too good to be true, it usually means something worse is just out of sight."

Sanford laughed. "Cynical bastard, aren't you?" He stood up. "Come with me, Jack."

He led Jack back inside, past Alligator, who

grinned and nodded at him. Despite the stuffy air of the house, Alligator was wrapped in a ribbed, shiny turtleneck that stretched nearly transparent over his pot belly.

"Again, sorry about them," Sanford said. "But in my line, good security is worth its weight."

"And what is your line, exactly?" Jack said.

Sanford stopped at a door with a keypad and punched in a long sequence. "I told you," he said. "I'm a collector."

The door revealed a set of stairs leading down, cut directly into the stone beneath the mansion. "Wine cellar," Sanford said. "This house was one of the first built on this stretch of Sunset. Doug Fairbanks lived here at one point. Very nice address."

"If you want a round of applause," Jack said, "I'll try to muster it up."

Sanford flipped a big old-fashioned circuit, the kind used to fry a bloke in an electric chair. "I started collecting when I was twelve," he said. "I was a dumb kid from Ohio, and a neighbor down the street died. My friends and I went poking around the yard sale, and I found a little box, a box full of bones.

"She was a witch," Sanford continued, as lights flickered on, bulbs strung along the length of the stairs, "and they were children's knucklebones."

Another door was set into the rock at the bottom of the stairs, brand new brushed steel, locked with a keypad and a submarine-hatch wheel. "I don't have much in the way of my own talents," Sanford said. "But I knew those bones had power, and I wanted it.

I started looking for more, going out for weeks at a time in this old rusted-out pickup, all over the Midwest, poking through barns, pawing through junk shops, talking my way into dying men's bedrooms and dark secrets."

Sanford punched in another code and spun the hatch open. "This is my life's work. Not many people ever see it."

The small room under the rock was crammed stiflingly full, wooden shelves running floor to ceiling, with a glass display case filling the center. A small reading table, chair, and lamp were shoved into a corner. Rather than the somber atmosphere of a museum, or the crammed comfort of Jack's own flat, this place was full and filthy, dust piled inches thick on top of the cases, the scent of closed-up air and human sweat wafting in Jack's face. He'd never been so reminded of a troll cave in his life.

Sanford hit another switch and lights bloomed from hidden alcoves. "What do you think?"

Jack sneezed. "Your maid's not doing a bang-up job, is she?"

Sanford spread his hands. "Los Angeles is a nexus of power, Jack. It's why when the lines were drawn, neither side claimed it. Nobody wanted to constantly defend their territory, so it became neutral ground. It draws these objects in like a tornado, and people, too. Los Angeles has serial killers and mass murderers like some cities have coffee shops and sports teams. I find them where I can, the relics and the memorabilia, and I keep them safe." He sat at the desk and pulled a red cloth book to him. "Do you know the name Basil Locke?"

Jack examined the crammed shelves. Most of the objects whispered against his sight, and a few screamed. Sanford might be full of shit, but he was right about his collection. There was power here, bad mojo, enough of it to light up the Sunset Strip. "No," he said. "Should I?"

"Movie star in the 1930s, mostly B pictures, crime stuff and screwball comedies," said Sanford. "He never caught on the way Grant and Gable did. Birth name was Brian Chernik. Russian Jew, raised in England, fell in with a bad crowd." Sanford shoved the book across the table. "Our old boy Basil kept a grimoire, detailing all his attempts to summon and control the forces of Hell."

"Demons," Jack said. Many of the things Sanford had collected seemed innocuous—costume jewelry, photographs of crime scenes and autopsies, one bloodstained woman's pump—but they all vibrated, malignancy and terror bleeding through from the Black. The man knew the power of objects that had been in close proximity to death. "I'm guessing that ended well for him."

"Better than you could've imagined," said Sanford. "Locke found something else down there, something that could make a demon scream."

Belial had certainly looked like he was pissing in his shorts. Jack left the shelves of bloody-minded objects and turned to Sanford. "All right," he said. "You got my attention."

"Hell wasn't always the place for the Named and their legions," Sanford said. "There were other things, older things. You've seen them."

"I wouldn't call brushing elbows with Nergal seeing," Jack said. "In fact, I'd die happy if I never saw anything like him ever again."

"The demons overthrew their makers, as is the way of all things," Sanford said. "They couldn't kill them, so they locked them away with the old gods. One slipped out here and there, and the demons hunted them and put them back—nothing anyone without a talent would notice as unusual. Wars and nuclear bombs and that sort of thing as cover." He stroked the cover of the red book. "But your little stunt with Nergal cracked the door open, and now they're out. They're all out. Elvis has left the building." He tapped the page. "Basil Locke was the one who first spoke to them, who realized that things other than demons could be called up from Hell."

Jack looked at the scribbling and the diagrams contained in the loose pages of the red book, all of it with the distinct, manic edge of the deranged. He'd seen enough psychotic scribbling, both from his mother while she was on pills and from various mages who'd dipped a bit too deep into the pool of hallucinations and trance magic, to recognize crazy when he read it.

"How do I know this isn't complete shit?" he asked Sanford. "And furthermore, what's it got to do with me and Belial?"

"Belial thinks he can lock a lock that's already been broken," said Sanford. "He thinks if he's the one to put this right by making you his hunting dog, he'll move up the ladder in Hell. But he's afraid of them, too, and we can use that." He touched the sigil. "If we can get them on our side, Belial will never bother you or your wife again."

"She's not my wife," Jack said reflexively. Sanford had to be munching on insanity for breakfast and shitting it out to think he could toe up to Belial using some nebulous spell to control the demon's boogeyman.

"My mistake," Sanford said. "But think of your child, at least. You really think Belial, or any other demon with ambitions, is going to let the child of the crow-mage grow up in peace?"

Jack shook his head. "I've already got that covered," he said. Sanford was tanned and trustworthy, his graying hair and straight white grin making him appear as your kind uncle, to whom you could tell anything. Worse than a demon, because he was only a man, and still trying to cut a deal with things ten times worse than the population of the Pit. "My deal's with Belial, mate," he said. "Not with you."

"Come on," Sanford said. "I'm giving you the chance to slip this yoke once and for all. To never worry again about a demon troubling you and yours."

"I get that, yeah, and it'd be grand," Jack said. "But somehow, I think I'm missing your part of this. I don't believe in altruism. Especially not from slimy gits like you."

"Well, of course not," Sanford said. "This isn't the town of money for nothing, Jack. I'll get what I want out of this, in addition to a warm fuzzy feeling."

"And that would be?" Jack said. Sanford shut the book and drummed his fingers on the table.

"Belial," he said. "Look, I've got every kind of damn thing in here—I have John Wayne Gacy's paintings, I have Elizabeth Short's hair, I have a guitar that belonged to Charlie Manson, and I have the dress Sharon Tate was wearing when his freaks cut her open. I've got objects of power, I've got mage's grimoires, I've got a skull from a sorcerer who was killed by Vlad the Impaler. I have an original edition of *Dracula,* with blood spells written in the margins. But they're things, Jack. And as I get older, things get less and less interesting to me." He gestured at the blank back wall of the cellar. "I want a demon, a living demon, in chains. I want Belial. And if we find what Belial lost, what he fears, I'll get him and you'll get your peace."

"You're fucking nuts," Jack said, before he could stop himself. "You think you can tie Belial down like some kind of pet?"

"I don't plan to pet him," Sanford said, lacing his fingers behind his head. "I plan to study him."

"No," Jack said. "No fucking way. I've seen what happens when men try and put one over on a demon, and I think I'll just back away slowly and leave you to your little catacombs."

"You could do that," Sanford said. "Or you could watch while I let Gator and Parker murder your wife and unborn child, and guarantee that when they're done, what Belial's boogeyman did to those families will look like a flower arrangement." He gave Jack the same slick smile, the let's-make-a-deal smile. "Gator has certain . . . proclivities. Your wife is just his type."

Jack didn't realize he'd moved until he was there, hand around Sanford's neck, slamming the man's skull into the rock. He hadn't had a blackout rage in a long while—heroin didn't lend itself to much except nodding and jittering around looking for your next score. But here he was, slamming Sanford's head into the rough wall until a smear of blood appeared, and he felt fucking fantastic about it.

"She's not my wife," he told the man. "And you leave her the hell out of this."

A fist pounded against the other side of the door. "Sir!" Gator hollered. "You all right in there?"

Sanford laughed at him, as much as he could with Jack's fist digging into his windpipe. "Security camera," he said. "State of the art."

"Sir!" Gator shouted. "We're comin' in."

"You didn't want her involved, you should have been there when Belial was whispering in her ear," Sanford hissed. "But you weren't. You let yourself get beat by something that crawls through the filth at the bottom of Hell and you left her alone. Now what are you going to do about it?"

The door groaned as it started to open, bolts and hinges protesting. Jack let Sanford go, feeling his heart throbbing and bile working its way up his throat. He hadn't properly beaten the shit out of somebody in ages, and the wobbly, lightheaded rush had him flying.

Gator burst in, followed by Parker, and grabbed Jack by the arms, slamming him face first into the desk and scattering Sanford's papers and Locke's book like a flight of startled doves. "You piece of shit," Gator snarled. "I knew I'd have trouble with you."

Parker knotted his fingers in Jack's hair and slammed his forehead against the edge of the desk, short and sharp. Jack saw the flashbulb, and felt the hot, spicy sting of blood in his eyes.

"That's enough," Sanford rasped. He rubbed his neck and fixed his collar. "Just a misunderstanding. Mr. Winter and I have it all worked out now." He fixed Jack with his pale eyes. "Don't we?"

Jack blinked the blood from his eyes. It'd stop, eventually, and leave him looking like he'd been doing battle in the arena. Sanford knew all about him and Pete, and could find him any time he pleased, that was clear. This whole summoning to his broken-down movie-star manse had been a display of might. *We know where you live.* He could accept Sanford's insane plan and play along or he could run again, and know that Pete and the kid would never be safe. Crazy or not, Sanford was right—Belial might honor their deal, he might not, but somebody or something would always be just out of the light, waiting to step out and take their stab at the crow-mage and his offspring. It was why mages didn't get married, didn't reproduce if they could help it. Nobody would willingly dive into the Black, and nobody would put their kid in the way of demons and monsters.

But he had. Jack fucking Winter, father-to-be of the fucking year.

"Yeah, fine," he told Sanford. "It's sorted. You've got yourself a pet mage."

Sanford grinned down at him. "My favorite kind. Get yourself cleaned up and get your baby mama on board. We've got work to do."

CHAPTER 13

Sanford's mansion was high on Sunset Boulevard, beyond even the homes of the movie stars and the techno-billionaires, in the oldest part of Los Angeles, where the old money and the old blood lived. Parker and Gator—Christ, he hadn't been far off, after all—wrestled him back into the SUV, but Gator didn't attempt to put a sack over his head again.

"Sorry I had to rough ya up," Gator said when they were back in Hollywood, dirty palm trees drooping in the sun. "Mr. Sanford pays us to be on top of things. You understand."

"Oh, yeah," Jack said. Gator opened the door and ushered him out onto the sidewalk near a sex shop, a video rental kiosk, and a pay phone covered in obscene graffiti. "Hey, mate," Jack called as Gator took a seat up front next to the silent Parker. "I ever see you again, I'm going to kick your teeth so far down your throat, you'll shit molars for a month."

"You take care now," Gator said, giving Jack another rotted-out grin. With his rough-carved face and bushy sideburns, it had the same effect as a grizzly bear in a wig and Elvis Presley sunglasses grinning at you.

The SUV squealed away from the curb, and Jack sighed. He magicked the pay phone into calling Pete's mobile, and waited on the corner of Sunset and Vine until the Fury hove into sight. The clerk in the porn shop looked at him, looked at the NO LOITERING sign pasted on the window, examined Jack's bloody face, and thought better of it, going back to his copy of *Variety*.

"Oh, good fucking night," Pete said when she saw him. Jack smiled, and felt dried blood crackle on his face.

"You should see the other bloke. Not that I got any shots in, but trust me, he's worse off—face could stop a fucking clock. Looks like zombie Elvis with a bit of Burt Reynolds after an eight-day coke bender thrown in."

"Who in the hell were they?" Pete said. "You leap out of a moving car and when I look back you're being muscled by two villains straight out of a cheap novel."

Jack twisted his spine to and fro, the last kinks from Gator and Parker's ministrations popping free. "I think that was this city's version of taking a friendly meeting." He got down on his hands and knees and examined under the Fury's bumper. Nothing appeared to be amiss, not that he'd know if it was. Cars made about as much sense as the Starship *Enterprise*.

"You lose your spare change?" Pete said.

Jack brushed the road grit from his hands and popped the Fury's trunk, getting the gear for changing a tire and thrusting it at Pete. "Lift this beast up. I need to look at the undercarriage."

Pete rolled her eyes but she obliged, and Jack shimmied through the broken glass and trash in the gutter to stare at the Fury's innards. He breathed on his fingertips to give himself a little light, and the blue fire of his ambient talent gathered around his fist.

In the stark witchfire light, the Fury's undercarriage looked like the intestines of an iron animal, twisted, rusting, and leaking viscous oil. For all the beauty of its skin, it was a twisted mess on the inside.

The hex was hidden on the short side of the muffler, carved sharp and straight, silver metal clean against the grime surrounding it. It was a simple enough trick—just a source to bounce a spell off of, an echolocation widget within the Black. As long as the person on the other end was casting, they'd know exactly where the Fury was at any given time.

Jack slid out from under the Fury and got his kit bag. Pete had a paper mug of tea balanced on the dashboard, and he gestured at it.

"You mind?"

"No," Pete said. "Tasted like shit, anyway."

He used the tail of his shirt to grind the chalk

fine on the hood of the car, and swept it into the cup. "Got a knife?" he asked Pete. One of her eyebrows went up, just a hair's breadth.

"Depends. What are you planning on stabbing?"

"Myself," Jack said. Using blood in spells wasn't exactly the first resort of most mages. Blood tended to complicate things, to attract those that populated the fringe regions of the Black, and to bugger your spell up one side and down the other, until it either summoned a demon or made your liver explode. For quick and dirty hex work, though, blood got the job done.

Pete handed over a small pocket knife, and Jack sliced himself in the familiar path across his palm. You couldn't cut too deep or too often, or scar tissue would make it impossible to get a good amount when you really needed it. He squeezed the runnels into the cup, and then ripped up the end of his shirt and wrapped it tight around his hand.

The clerk in the video shop now had a cordless phone in his hand, and was staring at Jack with something close to alarm. "Please," Jack told him. "I hardly think this is the strangest shit you've seen working in this piss-hole."

Jack mixed the chalk and blood with his finger, and shimmied back under the Fury. He didn't have time to look up any specific, proper symbols to block a tracking spell, but half of magic was the willingness to fly by the hair of your arse, and hope that you landed on something soft. If you didn't have the balls to work spells on the fly, you had no business setting foot in the Black.

He whispered a few persuasive words to the chalk mixture, and then smeared it liberally over the spell, filling the divots the carvings had left with his own blood. The metal hissed on contact, and a little smoke curled that smelled like the inside of a creamatory furnace filled with hair. The hex wouldn't hold for long—once whoever was running the spell tried to find them and smacked a brick wall of Jack's blood magic instead, his trick would cease to be clever. But it bought them a little time, and he hoped it was enough.

"Right," he told Pete, standing up. His knees and his skull let him know that a) he was an old man and b) he was an old man who'd just gotten the shit kicked out of him by two large, efficient goons who had a passion for their work. He could deal with that later.

"Where to?" she said, when Jack slumped into the passenger side of the Fury.

"Venice," he said. "Going to see a bloke about a cat."

CHAPTER 14

Shocking Jack not one iota, Sal's garage was locked up tight, doors pulled and padlocked, and lights dark.

"He better not have done a fucking runner," Jack told Pete. "If I have to chase him all over California, my mood's not going to improve one bit."

"Try not to be a complete cunt," Pete said. "Maybe he didn't know."

"For a man who gets that much of a hard-on over a piece of metal and a combustion engine," Jack said, "he knew. Probably etched that spell on himself. Unlike Mayhew, he doesn't seem like a bloody idiot."

"Just don't burst in there and start causing mayhem and disaster," Pete told him.

"When have I ever, personally and deliberately, caused mayhem and/or disaster?" Jack spread his

128   *Caitlin Kittredge*

hands. He felt justified—the mayhem usually wasn't his fault, and disaster was inadvertent at best.

"Oh, do you really want me to answer that?" Pete said with wide-eyed false innocence. "Because we'll be here for a bit."

"Shut it," Jack told her. He banged on the metal door with the flat of his fist. Seconds went by, then minutes. Sal didn't materialize.

"There's a back door," Pete shouted. Jack picked his way through the rusted field of auto parts that surrounded the garage and tried the lock. Pete rubbed a hole in the grime and peered inside. "Don't see anything."

"He's there," Jack said. "Hiding, probably." He would, if he were in the business of screwing over mages. Jack put his hand over the lock and it popped open. The back of the shop was dark and smelled of stale coffee and motor oil.

"Wait here," he told Pete. "Keep an eye open."

A door marked OFFICE hung open, and Jack heard muted music from behind it. Sal sat behind his desk, a revolver in one hand and a mostly empty bottle at his elbow. "Oh," he said. "It's you."

"Yeah, me," Jack said. "You think I'd be good and gone by now?"

Sal shrugged. The revolver clunked against the desk. "It's a .357 Magnum," he said. "The most powerful handgun in the world. It's a replica of the one they used in the Dirty Harry movies."

Jack ignored his yammering. It seemed nobody in LA could tell reality if it bit them on ass.

"Who told you to put that spell on the car?"

Jack said. "And I'm not going to believe it just happened to be there, on the special car you decided to give especially to me and Pete."

Sal laughed and took a pull off the bottle. "You think I'm scared of you?"

"I think you're pissing your shorts over something, yeah," Jack said. "If not me, then I'd really like to know what."

Sal raised the revolver. "Get out."

Jack shook his head. "You don't want to do that, mate. Believe it or not, I'm your friend in all this."

"Friends, right," Sal mumbled. "Got no fuckin' friends left. Friends are leverage, Jack, you know? Friends can bleed if the sons of bitches can't bleed you."

Sal kept mumbling, but he dropped his eyes down to the bottle, and when the revolver dipped Jack grabbed it and punched Sal just under his left eye. Not hard enough to break his hand, or Sal's cheekbone, but enough to get his attention.

Sal grunted, chair rolling backward, and his bottle teetered and smashed on the floor. A brown puddle bled slowly into the cracks in the concrete floor. "Well, shit," Sal said. "Now look what you did."

"You want your skull to keep its shape, you're going to tell me whatever your scummy little part is in all this," Jack said. He cracked the chambers of the revolver and emptied the bullets out before dropping it on the desk.

Sal grunted, and fished in his drawers for a pill

bottle. He popped the cap and dry-swallowed a handful of small white caplets. "Said I'm not scared of you. What can you do?"

"It's either Mayhew, Belial, or Sanford doing it," Jack said. "So which curtain, Sal? Who wants me kept track of, and why?" He leaned across the desk and grabbed the greasy front of Sal's uniform, lifting him halfway out of his chair. "As for what I can do . . . do you really want to find that out firsthand?"

Sal drove his fist into Jack's gut, and his air went out of him, along with his balance. He went down, bouncing his chin off the edge of Sal's desk and bloodying himself all over again. Sal grabbed the revolver, thick bourbon-numbed fingers fumbling with the bullets, sending copper slugs rolling in all directions.

A decade ago, Jack could've gotten his wind back, smashed Sal's kneecap with his boot, and gotten on with the hard questions. One less trip to Hell, and he could've swallowed down the blood coating his tongue and stood up to trade lumps. But it wasn't, and he hadn't, so he struggled up as far as one elbow, sucking in air that felt like razor blades embedded in his lungs, before Sal aimed the gun at him.

"Adios, you fucking Limey cocksucker," Sal said.

The office door creaked, and Jack expected Pete, and tried to yell. He had a vision of the slug in her chest, the red blossom growing on her skin, the exit wound spraying crimson mist over the hallway behind her.

"Salvatore," a voice said. A man, not Pete. "You know better than that."

Jack let himself fall back to the floor. The concrete was cool, and a flourescent tube buzzed above his head, throwing spider-legged shadows into every corner.

Sal's face was wan, the boozy colors fled and a rime of blue in their place. His eyes were wide and black with panic, and the gun hung limp in his fist before slipping to the floor. "No," he said. "No, I did what you asked."

"Shooting Winter in the face isn't part of the deal, friend," said the man.

"He's working for that demon!" Sal shouted. "The one who's got his teeth in your ass. I was doing you a favor."

"Belial can nip at my heels all he wants," the man purred. "But he's never going to bite down. He's a spineless maggot like the rest. You know what I do with maggots, Sally? I squash 'em."

Sal raised his hands, backed behind the desk, and sat down. "Whatever you say."

The man extended a hand to Jack but kept his eyes on the mechanic. "It is whatever I say, Sally. Don't forget that again."

Jack didn't take up the man's offer. He was pleasant enough looking, what old ladies would describe as a nice young man. His slightly flat features were familiar, too, but Jack didn't bother playing twenty questions with himself on where he knew the face from. He got up, knee and then foot. His head was swimming and his guts still roiled.

"You're a tough guy, huh?" said the man.

"Don't take this the wrong way," Jack said. "But who the fuck are you?"

The man spread his arms. "You don't remember? That's hurtful. I'm the man with the plan, Jack."

Jack lifted one eyebrow. "Lots of stupid cunts have plans."

The man laughed, displaying perfect movie star teeth. "Fair enough. I'm Don." He held out his hand again. A small star sapphire ring glittered on his pinky finger, like an eye protruding from his flesh.

Jack found a whisper of familiarity in the voice as well, but couldn't place it. It bothered him, but not as much as the rest of the mess.

Don retracted his hand when Jack didn't take it. "Careful sort, huh?" He grinned wider, face almost in rigor mortis. "Don't blame you, seeing as I'm the one you've been looking for."

CHAPTER 15

Jack took a step back. A human reaction, to get as far away as you fucking could from predators and the unnatural. A reaction that made him look like a coward, and when Don laughed, it just felt all the worse.

"Don't worry, Jack. I'm not here to make a steak and kidney pie out of you and the little woman," he said. "Depending on how our conversation goes, we could be great friends."

"I seriously fucking doubt that," Jack said. "What's your game, Don?"

"Survival." Don shrugged. "Same as you, Jack. Same as Belial. Lions and zebras both dislike hyenas. Little motherfuckers will eat you clean and laugh while they're doing it."

"And three guesses, but I'll only need one, you're the hyena?" Jack said. Don shook his head.

"No, Jack," he said. "I'm the fuckin' big bad

wolf." He pulled a nail file out of his jacket and cleaned under each finger with a short motion. "But enough about me. Let's repair to someplace a little more hospitable."

"No, I think I like it here," Jack said. Don shook his head.

"I don't want to gut your lady friend out there from crotch to collar, but that doesn't mean I won't," he said.

"You seem to know so much about me," Jack said. "Then you know that threatening Pete is a royally bad fucking idea."

"But effective," Don said. "You don't have soft spots, Jack, except for her. She's going to get you killed one of these days." He snapped his fingers. "Oh wait, she already has. How was your little vacation in the Pit, Jack? Did the dry air do wonders for you?"

"If you're going to try and kill me, do it," Jack said. "Otherwise, shut the fuck up and let me go about my business."

"We're not done," Don said. He opened the office door, but instead of leading Jack back down the hallway, he went to the auto bay. The door was up and a sleek black car rumbled, headlights cutting cones of yellow on the dingy walls of Sal's garage.

"Take a ride with me," Don said. "I promise after it's over, you'll see things my way."

Jack pointed to the back door. "Let me just tell Pete I'm going."

"No," Don said. "Now, or you can clean her insides off your outsides." The door of the Lincoln swung open, and Don gestured Jack into the back seat. The car was old, upholstered in slick hide that shifted like oil in the low light. "She's a big girl," Don said. "I'm sure she can find something to occupy her time until we're finished."

Jack tightened his jaw, but he got into the car. Don needed him alive for something, at least for now. If he really wanted Belial off his scent, he could've just sliced Jack, or let Sal shoot him. And Pete would be well and truly pissed off that he'd left, but she'd get over it. Or she wouldn't, which would probably make his life easier in the long run. Pete hating him was probably how it should go.

"Good move," Don said when Jack settled back against the seat.

"Fuck off," Jack told him.

The Lincoln didn't have a driver, but it backed out of Sal's garage and purred smoothly to the freeway. Don opened the center console between the seats and drew out a thin black cigar. "Care for?" he said to Jack.

"No, thanks," Jack said. "I try to restrict my vices to things that'll kill me slow."

"You're funny," Don said. A cherry sprang to life on the end of his smoke. "Didn't expect that."

"What exactly did you expect?" Jack asked.

"I know a lot about you," Don said. "Been keeping tabs on you, just like Belial. Enemy of my enemy and all that shit. Knew when my spell went dead that you'd head back to poor Sally back there and threaten to beat the piss out of him. Fortunately, Sal knows what side is the right side. He's a good boy."

"Belial is going to find you one way or the other," Jack said. "Whether I'm helping him or not. He's a vicious cunt, that one."

"Belial is more concerned with keeping his little hardscrabble patch of Hell in his control than he is with me," Don said. "I was away for a long time before he ever cared. Nergal made him look bad, is all. I'm older than him, and I'm meaner, but if he wants a stand-up fight, he'll get one. And his little masters the Princes aren't going to like the upset in Hell one bit when I give it."

Don rolled down the window and let the smoke drift out, trailing behind them. The highways were empty, something Jack knew should never happen at this time of day, and the Lincoln traveled so fast he could feel the vibration of the road. "I've walked around the block, Jack. I know when to sit back and let the dogs and the rats fight it out. Whoever's left, that's who I'll deal with."

"So, what, you kidnapped me because you're lonely and wanted to have a chat?" Jack asked.

"Don't be ridiculous," Don said. "You don't have the whole story, Jack. When you do, you'll be on the right side."

"And by right side, you mean your side," Jack muttered. Don grinned at him.

"Of course."

Jack stayed quiet at that. Don certainly wasn't what he'd expected, in terms of a boogeyman who'd frighten a demon enough to go through the trouble of compelling Jack to hunt said boogeyman down. He wasn't sure of Don's nature just yet, but he didn't ping his senses like a ghost or a demon, and he'd never stopped smiling since Jack had gotten in the car. That, more than Don's purported reputation, worried him. You couldn't trust somebody who was always cheerful. There was usually something wrong with them.

The Lincoln left the freeway and started to climb into the hills. The barren scrub blurred by so fast it was only a welter of green and brown, and the flashes of Los Angeles in the gaps came and went so quickly they could be a single frame of film.

"Let me guess: You're going to tell it to me?" Jack said. That was the thing with demons and their ilk—they always wanted to blather at you, to make you understand how right they were, even as they burned and flayed and ate humans alive. Don wasn't human, was certainly who Belial was searching for, but Jack couldn't read much beyond that. He was a blank spot in the Black, something either so old or so strong that magic flowed around him like a stone in a river, leaving a void that shrieked against Jack's sight.

"Going to try," Don said, as the Lincoln cornered, spraying gravel behind it. "It's not a happy story, but I have high hopes for the ending. I'm not one for a downer, just a slow fadeout before the credits roll. I like a twist. You?"

"I like knowing that my day won't consist of listening to smarmy demons talk about themselves,"

Jack muttered. "But so far it hasn't worked out for me."

Don lunged forward, leaving no space between Jack, himself, and the seat behind. Jack could feel springs pressing into his spine and his bones creaking from the pressure.

"I'm not a demon," Don purred. "I don't like being called what I'm not, Jack. It's narrative falseness. It's not fair to the audience."

"Fine," Jack said. He hated that his heart beat faster, that he could hear blood roaring in his ears almost to the exclusion of Don's soft voice. He shouldn't be afraid of flash gits like this any longer. Not after Hell. Not after everything that had come before it.

Don sat back and grinned. "Good. We're here."

Jack looked through the tinted glass. They were at the crest of a hill, a long gravel road in front of him that swooped down into a canyon. Nestled at the foot of the sunset-colored rock, a few gray buildings and a farmhouse with a distinct tilt to it baked in the California sun.

"I'll bite," Jack said. "Where's here?"

Don snapped his fingers and the Lincoln's doors sprang open, mental raven wings poised for flight. "Home sweet home."

CHAPTER 16

Don's boots crunched on the gravel. The heels and toes were silver and flashed in the sun, the stippled snakeskin in between crackling as he walked. "Close enough to the city that no white-knight types poke around," he said. "Far enough to enjoy the beauty of nature." He flicked the end of his cigar away. "Paradise on earth. Gotta hoof it from here. We take a few precautions, being Belial's most wanted and all."

Jack followed Don, the ripples in the Black growing stronger the closer he got to the farmstead.

"You like that?" Don said. "Farmer killed his wife and his daughter back in forty-eight or so. Killed two sheriff's deputies when they came to see what happened. Found out later he had eight whores buried under the floor of his barn. Guess the wife put her nose where it didn't belong. Sad when that happens."

"Sad, yeah," Jack said. "They charge you extra for the story?"

"Something like." Don smiled. "Real estate around here isn't what it used to be. Used to be, you couldn't spit in Los Angeles without coming across a crime scene or a poor sad little murder-victim ghost."

Jack watched a crow alight on the ridgepole of the barn, cawing once before it took flight again. Don curled his lip. "One of yours? Or your bitch hag checking up on you?"

"Wouldn't know," Jack said. Under his shirt, the markings of the Morrigan crawled over his skin, as if the wind had ruffled his feathers.

"Aw," Don purred. "You and Mommy have a fight?"

"Would it make you feel better about your goatee looking like a stripper's pubic hair if I said yes?" Jack snapped.

Don wagged his finger. "You're not much fun to have at the party, Jack, and if you don't cheer up, I might have to throw your ass out."

A sagging porch wrapped the farmhouse, weighted down with mattress springs and a rusty icebox. The crow on the barn took flight, screeching. In the bowl of the earth, the heat pressed down against Jack's skin, radiated from the dirt and from the near-white sky above. The Black here was seared and screaming, hot as an iron and dry as graveyard dust. There were other places that felt the same, but they were concentration camps and mass graves, the sites of enough pain and terror to leave an indelible echo through the layers of life, death, and magic. Jack had never seen so small a patch of earth so infected.

In the bare dirt yard between the barn and house, a small girl sat crosslegged, pushing two dolls together at the apex of their legs. The dolls' faces were blackened and melted, and their hair had fused into thin spikes. She looked up at Jack with pure black eyes that were lidless and did not blink.

"She's our little one," Don said. "Not used to people yet. Still got the marks on her from where I cut her free."

Jack stared back at the girl until she stuck her tongue out at him. "I see you," she whispered. "You want this body? You want me to suck your cock? I see it. Don't lie."

Jack lifted his eyebrows at Don. "Got a mouth on her, doesn't she?"

Don cradled the girl's head against his thigh. "Is that any way to talk to our friend Jack, darlin'?"

"I saw it," she pouted.

"Sure you did. You stay out here and play," Don said. "Jack and I are going to have a little chat indoors."

The girl stared at Jack for another moment with her insect eyes, then went back to smashing her melted dolls together. Human flesh could contain a lot of things, but he still didn't have a sense of what Don and his creepy little bug child really were, under the skin. He could be patient and see what he could see. Don was playing a long game, trying to make him comfortable, and Jack was content to let him think he was as dumb as the rest of the human race and had nothing to fear from this place. The Black writhed inside his mind like a snake, hard to grasp and cold to the touch. He'd be hard-pressed to call up witchfire, never mind sling a hex if he had to. Effectively, he was stuck here for as long as it amused Don to keep him, but he didn't have to let on that he knew.

Don mounted the steps of the farmhouse, rotted boards cracking under his boots. "Come on in," he told Jack. "Meet the rest of the family."

CHAPTER 17

Inside the farmhouse, all was darkness. Light leached from above, through broken spots in the roof, and hit a floor littered with trash and the skeletons of small animals. The stench was even heavier than the darkness, shoving fingers into Jack's nostrils and down his throat. The house stank of rot, old food and older sweat, decades of filth baking in the heat. Even the offal tanks of the Pit hadn't stunk this badly.

Jack pulled his shirt over his nose. At least his own sweat was familiar.

Don jabbed a push-button switch, and a single bulb flickered overhead, casting bird-wing shadows into all the corners. Stairs with most of the treads missing led up, and a hallway stretched ahead, so stacked with ancient newspapers and fruit crates that Jack could barely maneuver it sideways.

"Levi!" Don shouted. "You in here?"

"Back room," a voice croaked, and Don jerked his head at Jack.

"Levi's my brother. You'll like him."

"Will I?" Jack said. "He as convivial as you?"

"He's a laugh riot." Don slithered down the hall passage with the acumen of a snake. Jack dislodged a stack of ancient, moldy *National Geographics*. A rat hissed and scurried deeper into the holes its compatriots had chewed in the stacks of paper.

"For such a flash chap, you sure do love filth," he told Don.

Don shrugged. "Humans notice dirt. For me, your whole world is dirt."

"Suppose it is," Jack muttered. The back room had been a kitchen, at some point, and pipes jutted from the wall where a stove and icebox had once stood. A deep sink crouched in one corner, with some thick, black, viscous substance dripping down the stained porcelain flanks and puddling on the floor.

A mechanized wheelchair, the kind old ladies drove around shopping centers, sat in front of a TV fizzing with static and occasionally showing flashes of a saggy and low-budget porn film. In the chair sat the largest man Jack had ever seen—he overflowed the bonds of the chair, and white stretch marks cut jagged canyons on the back of his shaved head. He breathed with a deep, wet wheeze, something rotten deep in his chest rattling with every puff of air.

"That him?" Levi gave a wet sniff. "He doesn't smell so sweet."

Jack decided that pointing out that the waves of stench rolling off Levi could fell a werewolf wasn't his most prudent course of action. "Your reception is shit," he said, pointing to the telly. Levi grunted, jabbing at a remote with fingers strained with bloat.

"Everything here is shit. Your world is a crapper waiting for somebody to flush the floating turds."

"Come on, now," Don said. "Can you really say that after where you were when I found you?"

Levi coughed, and the floor shook under his weight. He didn't have a shirt on—Jack doubted any shirt in existence would actually keep the rolling hills of his stomach under wraps—and the hair on his chest was sparse and black, matted with sweat. Blemishes dotted his shoulders like a range of volcanoes. "You bring me what I want?" he croaked at Don.

Don fished a grease-spotted paper bag from his jacket and passed it into Levi's waiting hands. The giant ripped it open and tore the wrapper from an In-N-Out Burger with his teeth. Two gulps, and it disappeared down his gullet. He unrolled the magazine also in the sack with greasy fingers, leaving thumbprints on the expanses of naked women in the glossy pages. What Pete called sad porn—junkie girls with empty eyes, tied and splayed, cut and displayed in ways that Jack supposed a bloke like Levi would find right up his alley.

"Got a funny look buying that," Don told him. "You'd think those cunts who work in porn shops have something against the customer. As if I'd want to put it in her. Disease crawling all over the pussy in LA." He turned to Jack. "You hear me? You getting any LA pussy, you wrap up. Fucking city's a plague pit."

"All right," Jack said. The smell wasn't making his stomach any easier to deal with, and he had a sneaking suspicion that if he vomited anywhere near Levi, the bloke would mistake it for dessert. "It's been fun, gents, but if all you did was bring me out here to see the sewage main you live in, then I'm going to say thanks for the memories and make me way home."

"Oh no," Don said. "We're getting down to business. I gotta take care of my brother, though. You understand." He tilted his head. "Or maybe you don't. Most people get close enough to spit on you tend to end up dead, don't they, Jack?"

"You going to tell me something I don't know?" Jack said. "Or is stating the obvious your particular gift?" He got Don's play—he wanted Jack to know that he'd watched him, knew about him, saw all his dirty secrets and got off on them. He could revel in it all he wanted—Jack had enough dirty secrets to keep a team of Dons occupied for a year or two.

"Mouthy fuck, ain't he?" Levi said. He shoved his hand down into the seat of the wheelchair, moving his fat aside, and came out with a packet of biscuits—or cookies, Jack supposed he called them. If he called them anything before he shoved them into his gullet. Levi burped, then tossed the empty packet aside and unfastened the top of his stained khakis. "Good job on the mag, brother. Choice snatch in there."

"No fucking way in hell," Jack said. Dealing with a demon who wanked off to holding a threat over his head was one thing, but watching his morbidly obese brother actually wank off was beyond the pale.

"That's just Levi," Don said. "We're all slaves to our urges, in one way or another." He gestured Jack ahead of him down another narrow hall, lined with doors. "My urge just happens to be a little bit less . . . obvious than Levi's. And yours—well, you've got enough for both of us, don't you, Jack?"

Don shouldered a door open. "I told you I'd explain what we are, and why we won't go back. Why Belial can't cage us." A dirty pair of curtains, which Jack saw had once been littered with pink flowers and happy kittens, closed off the room at the end of the hall. Don gripped them and ripped them open. "A fucking visual is worth a thousand words, isn't that right?"

After Levi and the girl in the yard, Jack figured that whatever else Don had to show him would be more shock and awe. He still stared though, still felt the sink in his stomach and the familiar sensation of his head being too full as his sight attempted to cope with the onslaught of psychic agony wrapped around the figure before him.

"This here is Teddy," said Don. "Teddy as in teddy bear, as in won't you be my. But he won't. Teddy can't be one of us, Jack."

Jack heard Don absently, while the rest of him stared at the thing on the other side of the room. A child's room—walls pale pink, painted with daisies in every color of the rainbow. A name—*Claire, 1961*—was carved above the shape of a headboard faded into the paint.

Against the wall, Teddy dangled, strapped into an upright harness like the type they used on movie mental patients. Hooks hammered into the ceiling held at least a dozen IV bags, the liquid inside green and black. Clusters of flies buzzed around Teddy's face—at least, where his face would be if he'd had one.

Teddy's neck formed a column of pale skin, and at the top a blank, bulbous protrusion twitched this way and that, as if trying to catch Jack's scent. His body was a flat, flabby mass and out of it grew a multitude of limbs, some the size of a child's arm and hand, some little more than angry, infected skin tags. In the center of Teddy's mass, a round mouth rimmed with teeth twitched and sighed as the thing breathed.

Don stepped forward, checked the levels of the IV bags. "Shit," he said. "I'll be right back. Fucking Levi." He kicked the door open, bellowing, "I fuckin' told you to call me if he got low on anything! You think I can find this shit at the fuckin' 7-11?"

Jack was surprised at the stillness after the door shut. Wind rattled the walls, throwing dust against the side of the farmhouse, but aside from the wheeze of air passing in and out of the thing's mouth, it was absolutely silent.

"Holy shit," Jack told Teddy. "I thought I'd seen ugly, but you, mate—you're the clear winner."

You're not much to look at yourself.

The voice didn't so much split his skull as jam a steel rod straight through his sight. Ghosts could talk along the psychic aether, and demons could worm their way into your dreams if you were vulnerable, but actual telepathy was rare, and mostly confined to Fae, a type of creature Jack stayed as far away from as he would a Phil Collins tribute concert in an old folk's home.

"I don't have vagina dentata growing out of me fucking stomach, so I think I'm a leg up on you," Jack said. "Sorry, mate."

You're him, Teddy hissed. *Winter. The man with the plan.*

"If I'd made a plan, do you think I'd be standing here talking to you?" Jack asked. A shiver ran through Teddy's flesh, causing his IV bags to dance and slosh.

I don't know, Winter. Was your plan to take it up the ass from a demon, or was your plan to be smarter than Don?

"Belial and I have an understanding," Jack said. "Can't say the same for your man out there. He's given me no fucking reason to trust him, or that great skin-sack of crap he calls a brother, or you. Never mind Miss Future Spree Killer out in the yard."

Demons lie, Winter. Teddy's mouth gaped and flexed, and a pair of twin tongues flicked in and out. *You know it. Don doesn't lie. Don is older than lies. Better. Don does the things we need done.*

"Don know you're jawing away to me spilling his secrets?" Jack said. If Teddy was talkative, Jack wasn't going to stop him. He was just as inclined to trust a flesh-bag as he was Don, if not more. He couldn't shake the feeling that he'd indeed seen Don before, and that the bloke was just taking the piss with all of the pomp and secrecy.

Don knows what he knows and I know what I know, and what I know could fill oceans and burn forests, Teddy said. *But I'm not really here and neither are you. We're on a road to nowhere, and a highway to hell, and I can't drive fifty-five.*

Jack massaged his forehead. "Well, this has deteriorated quickly."

Don came back into the room, holding a fresh IV bag of green liquid. It looked like pond scum, but Teddy gave a relieved sigh when Don changed out the IV. "You boys getting on?" Don asked, brushing his hands against his coat.

"That thing isn't any more a boy than I am a unicorn," Jack said. "But yeah, we're having a grand old time."

Don pulled up a chair, white and upholstered with a cushion that had once been the same color as the walls. "Sit with me, Jack. Listen to what I have to tell you. After that, if you're still with Belial, well . . . we can discuss it. I don't coerce people, even humans. I believe in that free will you all love so much."

Jack could spot a soft-soap, even one delivered in the skilled, sensitive tone Don employed, but he shrugged. "Talk." Teddy cackled low in his brain.

Talking's what Donny is good at. Talking himself into things, talking us out of our skins and into new toys. Talk talk talk. Open the door, it's just the meter man.

"Hell is ancient," Don said. "Hell is older than Death. Hell was the first piece carved from the Black, before even Death. When the Hag was still hatching from her egg and this world was just a speck of dust floating between stars, there was Hell."

"And then the man upstairs said let there be light, booze, and porn?" Jack said. Don's mouth twitched, and Jack sighed. Fanatics were never any fun, and fanatics who took themselves too seriously were akin to shoving razor blades under your eyeballs and blinking. Whatever stripe their faith, Jack found them tiresome.

"God's a fairy tale for children and the childlike," Don said. "The same as Satan. You know that, Jack. But before the demons everyone is so afraid of, there were other things."

He gestured at Teddy. "Me and mine saw Hell as our own, a place where there was nothing except existence. Hunt, food, mate, sleep, eat. It was a good place. The fires warmed us and the rivers flowed with blood and the meat was slow and fat. But shit happens, as you people are so fond of saying."

"Demons get fed up with you boys taking all the good bits for yourselves?" Jack guessed.

"The *demons*? Strike at *us*?" Don laughed. "Jack, we *made* the demons. We made some from mud, and some from flesh, but one among us lay with somebody—some*thing*—that was an abomination, and she birthed four sons."

Jack narrowed his eyes. As far as creation stories went, this was one where he was sure he could guess the ending. "The Princes."

"They created the six hundred and sixty-six Names," Don said. "Made them in *their* image, not ours. Together, stronger than us. Legion. They murdered who they could, and the strongest of us, the four counterparts of the Princes, they locked away. Four of us plus one, the death-bringer who would just as soon devour Hell as he would their enemies."

"Nergal," Jack murmured. He could still feel the black presence in his mind, the endless, unfathomable hunger for the life of the Black, of Hell and everywhere in between.

"Nergal is a fucking dickhead, by the way," Don said. "Whiny little bitch, all down the days we spent together in that place." He grinned. "Can you guess what the twist is now, Jack?"

"Naughton broke Nergal out," Jack said. "You slipped the gap, and here you are."

"Oh, no," Don said. "I got out long before those necrophiliac morons got their bright idea to spring the asshole. But my kin, yes. They came from the break. Reality is a pretty fragile thing, Jack. Bend it just a little and stress fractures appear. The Princes have kept us under lock and key for millennia— their *masters*, locked away, tortured, and violated like we were nothing. Well, we're free now, like the old times. And we're not going back."

"Look, mate," Jack said. "I got no issues with you doing . . . whatever it is you're doing out here, personally, but I think you're underestimating exactly how far up Belial's arse you've gotten with this little escape routine. He doesn't do well with losing."

"The demons lost a long time ago," Don said. "This business with the Morrigan and Nergal is just the knell sounding the end. Hell is fracturing, politics are king, and things like Belial are scrabbling for power. Time was, they feared our names. So did your kind—every pack of superstitious children has a name for us. They called us Shiva, or said we were a wolf that devoured the world. Four horsemen who ride forth on the last day." Don grinned. "I always liked that one. Got great imagery. Probably why they stick it in so many movies. Point is, it's our time again, and we're riding hard."

"I still don't know what you expect me to do about all this," Jack said. "I don't have Belial's ear. We're not mates who go down to the pub. I can't get him off your trail and stop Hell from throwing you back in the clink any more than I can make Belial do a Riverdance."

"We want you, Jack," Don said. "Because without you, none of this would've happened. My kind would still be cast into darkness. If you hadn't been a good solider and helped the Morrigan wake up Nergal, we never could have found those fractures." He leaned in. "And if you hadn't visited us in Hell, we couldn't have found you now. I want you to be with us, Jack. I want you to be *my* soldier, because together we can turn Belial into a smear on the pavement."

Of course. The dreams—memories—that had woken up the moment he landed in LA. He'd seen the demon's vast prison. And now the inmates had him over a barrel. Perfect.

Jack resisted telling Don that for a supposedly ancient creature, he was a bit of a fuckwit. Nothing could kill a demon. You could exorcise them, send them back to the Pit, but to actually destroy the essence of a demon was something he'd only seen once, and he didn't care to repeat it. "And if I decide that I'd rather not play with your fucked-up little family?"

Don shrugged. "We can't force you, Jack. Like I said, we owe you one. You joined the Morrigan, and you let Nergal free, and you made it possible for everything that came after."

"I didn't let Nergal do anything," Jack snapped. He'd known, hadn't he, that when the Morrigan offered to get him out of the Pit it was too good to be true? He'd taken the deal anyway, because anything was better than Hell. He let her wipe his mind and body clean, and then she'd simply vanished. Not for good—she never left him for good. But she'd left him not knowing what she'd done to him, and without any memory of Hell until now. How much worse could Don's offer be than that?

"You're a nexus for these things, Jack," Don said. "Things that shake the foundations of the world. There've been other men like you, but none that I could get a face to face with." His smile dropped.

"You know, me being imprisoned in the dark by the ants who call Hell their own."

"Suppose I was to do this," Jack hedged. "What's in it for me?"

"No more demons, of course," Don said. "No more Hag dogging your steps. You'd be a free man, and all you'd have to do is help us be reborn."

"You seem all right to me," Jack said. Teddy groaned, and he felt his stomach flip again. "I mean, aside from Jabba over there."

"We burn flesh fast," Don said. "Teddy was supposed to be walking around like the rest of us, but like the song says, you can't always get what you want. Teddy needs a second chance at a meatsuit, and Levi needs a permanent one. In case you hadn't noticed, the rest of them can't exactly cruise up and down Sunset looking for skins. You'd be our agent, in a way. Finding the correct sort of flesh."

"Yeah, that's where it falls down for me," Jack said. "I don't generally hold with rounding up humans for slaughter and possession."

"Possession is a demon word," Don said. "A word for the weak who can't mold the flesh. We used to have bodies—strong, terrible, beautiful to behold. Now, we have to look like everyone else. We have to blend in. You people are like a virus, and we have to mimic you if we don't want the pitchfork brigade at our door."

Jack braced himself for Don's convivality to die a sudden death. "And if I say no?"

"Then we wouldn't be friends anymore," Don said. "And that'd be a real disappointment."

"I do hate to disappoint anyone," Jack said, "but yeah—I don't think I'm the man with the plan, Don. I'm not in it for you or for Belial—I'm in this life for myself. And I don't respond well when things that crawled up out of Hell threaten it."

He drew in a breath, held it. Waited for the surge of black magic that would signal that Don had well and truly ended their powwow.

"I'm disappointed, Jack," Don said. "Very, very disappointed."

Bad luck, pilgrim, Teddy hissed in his head. *You were nice to talk to.*

The blow Jack expected didn't come. The Black didn't surge and the screaming in his sight abruptly faded. His vision went white, and when he came to a wave of vertigo slammed into him and took him to one knee. "Fuck," he hissed, feeling as if he'd been full-body slammed into a brick wall. A trickle of fresh blood worked its way out of his nose, and the cuts on his head smeared more blood across his forehead.

He swiped blood away from his eyes. He was in a men's loo, a single bulb swinging in the draft from his passage. A warped metal mirror reflected his hollow-cheeked reflection, his hair streaked pink from the blood. Jack spun the rusty tap and splashed water on his face, cuts stinging.

"You look like shit."

He turned sharply, but wasn't entirely surprised to see Belial leaning against the cinder block wall, head haloed by Spanish gang tags. "Feel like it, too," he said. "Why, you want to give me a makeover?"

"Sorry about the smash and grab," Belial said. He pushed himself away from the wall and came to Jack, taking his chin in his hands and turning his head from side to side. Jack tried to pull away, but the demon's pointed nails dug into his flesh, and Belial dipped his head and pressed his face into the crook of Jack's neck, inhaling sharply. "Right," he said. "Just had to check on you. Those blokes have a habit of crawling under your skin." He stuck his fingers in his mouth and lapped Jack's blood from under his nails.

Jack swiped at the spots where the demon had touched him. Being close to a citizen of the Pit was like plunging your hand into raw meat—slimy, cold, and unpleasant. "If you fancied me, you should've just said something," he told Belial.

"You'll have to tell me how old Abaddon is looking these days," Belial said. "Fuck-ugly, I'll wager."

Don. What was it with these cunts and their precious nicknames? Gator had been bad enough. "Healthy, actually," he said. "Wears flash suit and talks like a cowboy."

"He always was a pretentious fuck," Belial muttered. "He give you that speech about destiny and how he and his little band of cunt-faced circus children are the true rulers of Hell?"

"Something like that," Jack said. "With more big words and dramatic gestures." He kept an arm's distance between himself and Belial. The demon was being downright chatty, and Jack didn't trust that any more than he'd follow a rent boy down a dark alley in Tower Hamlets.

"It's crap," Belial announced. "They might've been there first, but we outnumbered them. Demons are the true citizens of Hell, and we always will be. Abbadon got loose, but a scrap of memory is all he's ever going to be in the Black. Sooner or later, things will be back as they should be."

Belial closed the distance between them faster than blinking, and Jack wondered why he'd even bothered to try and keep them apart. In a contest between mage and demon, the demon would always win. It was simple physics.

Belial slammed Jack into the mirror, and he felt the sink crack under his lower back, along with the associated column of fire blooming up his spine. His skull dented the reflective metal, and his vision doubled. The demon squeezed his throat, and Jack felt the last of his air flutter and die in his lungs.

"Let's get one thing very fucking clear," Belial hissed. His lips were so close to Jack's ear that his breath sounded like the hot wind that never ceased howling across the Pit. "You try to fuck me, Winter, and I won't care what kind of favored son of the Hag you are. I won't care what kind of magic you and your little Weir can sling. I won't care if Jesus Christ himself shows up riding a unicorn, backed up by Sergeant Pepper's Lonely Hearts Club Band. I will end your fucking existence and that of everyone you care about, and your soul will spend the eternity until the Black and Hell both fall into the singularity under my tender loving care." He let Jack down, and Jack's knees decided it was a good plan to give out and send him tumbling to the floor amid the shards of the sink. Brown water from the ruptured pipes dribbled around him.

"Do we understand each other, crow-mage?" Belial hissed. "Abbadon has been in the dark for more years than even I can count. Yes, he escaped and managed to break the others out, but he's not going to win. And you're mostly certainly going to lose very fucking large if you try and fuck with me on this point."

Jack laughed, which caused him to cough a little blood. He spat it at Belial's shoe and missed. "He's got you good and scared, doesn't he? Never seen you with so much as a hair out of place, and look at you now."

Belial's black eyes were wide, and twin blood flowers had blossomed in his pale, waxy cheeks. Even his pristine suit was wrinkled and looked more like it had spent the night on a street corner than one of Hell's posh palaces. "You watch your mouth, crow-mage. I doubt you'd be laughing at me if the Hag hadn't scrubbed your memory all shiny-clean."

Jack pulled himself to his feet. Belial didn't know his memory was knitting itself back together, and he intended to keep it that way as long as possible. "For the record, I told Abbadon to go fuck himself, and I'm telling you the same thing. I've seen him and those things he hangs about with, and I'm not accustomed to admitting it, but they're beyond me. You knew there was no way I could put those cunts back underground by myself. You're just setting Pete up to fail. You probably think this is funny."

"Trust me," Belial snarled. "This is not my happy face."

Jack kicked open the door, into the face of a very surprised bartender with a goatee. "Hey!" he said. "One guy in the john at a time. You two take it somewhere else."

Belial twitched his cuffs and straightened his tie. "Gladly," he said. "And might I remind you, Winter, you're still on the hook, regardless of what you think. I wouldn't be using you if I had a choice, believe me. Abbadon and his friends belong back in the darkness where we sent them, and you're the man for the job, whether you know it or not. Get it done."

"Fuck off," Jack muttered, but Belial did his peculiar trick where you blinked and he'd simply gone.

"Listen, buddy," the bloke said. "Either order a drink or get the fuck out, okay? I don't need the George Michael action in the fucking bathrooms."

"You've got pubic hair on your face," Jack told him. "Might want to wash."

The kid opened his mouth, but Jack shoved by him. He was in a dank bar, neon beer signs casting the only light. He reached behind the bar, grabbed the first bottle of strong whiskey he saw, and kicked open the swinging door to the street. He was back on Hollywood Boulevard—exactly where he'd started.

Jack sat down on the curb and opened the bottle, taking a long pull. Everything hurt. It was an unfortunate side effect of slagging off things that were higher in the food chain than you, and he'd accepted it.

The whiskey was shit, and it burned all the way down, lighting his already upset stomach aflame. Jack scanned up and down the pavement, until he caught a kid in a tracksuit and a do-rag nodding against the front of the hipster bar. He might be white, and old, and straightened out, but he still knew a dealer by scent.

"Oi," he said to the kid. "Need to borrow your mobile."

"Fuck you," the kid said promptly. "Go suck cock and buy your own, old man."

Jack set the bottle down—it was shit booze, but it was all he had. He wrapped one hand around the green-tinged gold necklaces at the kid's throat, and the other around his balls. He'd had to do this entirely too often lately, he thought. "I'm just going to borrow it," he said, adding a squeeze for emphasis.

"*Fuck*," the kid hissed. "You crazy, fool? You know whose corner this is?"

"I'm sure he's a terrifying gent, and that I'm well and truly fucked, but right now I need to make a fucking phone call and you're standing in my way," Jack said. "So you can either be a helpful lad or a soprano. I really don't care at this point. Not having the best of days."

The kid considered for a moment, and then shook his head, pulling a gleaming smart phone from his tracksuit. "You're a fuckin' crazy white dude, aren't you?" he said.

"Been accused of it, yes," Jack said, and dialed Pete.

"Oh, for fuck's sake," she said. "I thought you were dead. I've been driving circles around Los Angeles looking for your corpse."

"I'm fine," Jack said. "Need a lift, though, if you can manage it."

"Is the car safe to drive now?" Pete asked. "I don't fancy another go-round like at the garage. Where did you *go*, anyway? One moment you're talking to that git Sal and the next he's falling all over me, blubbering about 'them' taking you away." She sighed. "Where are you?"

"Hollywood and Van Nuys," Jack said. "Thanks, luv."

"Fuck you," Pete told him. "Only doing this so I don't have to claim your body at the morgue. Damned inconvenient."

Jack polished off more of the whiskey while he waited, undisturbed by the dealer once he handed the mobile back. How he was going to explain this royal mess to Pete, he didn't know. Maybe he could drink enough to forgo explaining anything, but that would take a lot more than one bottle of paint thinner disguised as booze.

He wasn't about to blame Pete for all this, even though it was tempting—she'd done what she'd thought necessary in the moment. When things like Nergal loomed on the horizon, people got scared and stupid, made decisions they didn't think they'd ever live to regret, because they wouldn't be living at all.

Abbadon had said that Jack had made it all possible. He'd made his own decision, when he was in hell and the Morrigan had come to him. He had certainly never thought he'd live to regret that one. And now the regret was all over him, under his skin.

Jack looked at his own hand gripping the whiskey bottle, at the black curlicues that terminated just short of his knuckles. It wasn't ink—it was part of him, or part of the Morrigan that was in him. The thing that had only manifested as sight and Death dogging his steps tenaciously before now was visible, telling anyone who cared that Jack Winter was inexorably bound to the mistress of death and destruction.

He was pissed enough for there to be a warm buzz in his skull when the Fury rumbled to the curb, but at least it shut up the persistent circle-jerk of whispers inside his skull. *All your fault. She's not done with you. None of this is over.*

"Jesus, Jack," Pete said, jumping out of the car and crouching beside him.

"Not him," Jack said. "Wager I could take on that bloke. Pacifistic and shit, wasn't he?"

Pete took his arm and Jack let himself be pulled along and installed in the back seat. Between the thumping he'd taken and the whiskey, he was ready to fall asleep for a decade or two and wake up when everyone had a jetpack and nobody gave a fuck about Jack Winter.

"I'm not going to ask where you got off to or what happened," Pete said as she put the car in gear. "But if you don't want another bruise or two in the collection, you're going to tell me once you stop stinking like a transient who sleeps outside a distillery."

"Fair enough," Jack mumbled. He tried not to drift off, tried to stall the dream that had to be coming by counting the turns the Fury made. "We can't go back to Venice," he said. "They know Mayhew."

"I made arrangements," Pete said. "You concentrate on not bleeding on the seats."

"Figure this heap is ours now," Jack said. "Seeing as Sal's not on the side of angels." This wasn't his sight or a spell—this was just tired, a fatigue he never would have felt even five years ago.

"Thought there were no angels," Pete said. Jack's eyes fluttered closed, and he couldn't prop them up any longer. He was going under, and he'd just have to hold his breath.

"Not in this world, luv," he mumbled, before the hot, dry wind filled his lungs, and he was back in Hell.

CHAPTER 18

Belial kept a hand on his shoulder, almost constantly. He never spoke above a whisper, but Jack heard every word. Belial knew he would—his sight echoed, and his skull split and re-formed again and again as the demon hissed into his ear. They walked every inch of Hell, Jack's bare feet blistering and rotting as cinder and offal worked their way in.

"I want you to see," Belial whispered. "I want you to see what Hell is, Jack. The vast majesty of it. See it and know that from now until we all fall into a star, this is your home."

He ran his sharp nails along the back of Jack's neck. "This is your fate."

The demon's lips brushed his earlobe. "This is where you belong."

Pete nudged him, and Jack saw an alley, brick buildings reaching to block out the bleached sky. Cars and people sounds moved past the mouth, but it was silent and shaded, much like the alley next to his flat at home.

Was it his home? It wouldn't be the first time he'd been unceremoniously chucked out of a city he'd once considered friendly. But London was different. London was the only spot where he could sleep, without dreams. The only spot he'd allowed roots to reach below the surface. He knew the Black there. Everywhere else was the Wild West.

"Come on," Pete said. "Your creepy friend from the bar said we could lay low for a few days."

"Sliver?" Jack got out of the Fury and tried lifting his arms. A dozen knives, from his skull to his knees, stabbed him for his trouble. He twisted the kinks from his back, trying not to gasp as his tender ribs vibrated.

"Yeah, him." Pete grabbed her bag, his kit, and a disintegrating cardboard box from the trunk. "What's wrong with his face?"

"For a wraith, nothing," Jack said. "He's an all right sort."

Pete shouldered open a metal door marked FIRE EXIT ONLY. Considering that it was propped open with a cinder block, Jack figured the building either had a lot of fires, or had stopped worrying about the eventuality.

"We never have any normal friends," she said.

"Normal's overrated," Jack said. The door swung shut and only a single bar of light illuminated the metal staircase, leading up and up. He smelled piss and stale air, and pulled Pete behind him. "Let me," he said. The Black here was like smoke curls from a candle just snuffed—thin and ethereal, the boundaries of the daylight world worn to practically nothing.

On the one hand, Abbadon and his merry band of freaks would have a hard time finding them in the swirling hotspot of magic. On the other hand, anything could be lurking in the dark and his sight would only hear the static of the nexus.

"Fine," Pete muttered, shoving the box at him. "Take this, then."

Jack accepted the burden, and saw in the slice of sunlight that Pete was pale, with sweat beading on her forehead. "You all right, luv?"

"Fan-fucking-tastic," she said. "Only been vomiting more than that bloody child from *The Exorcist*. Had it with this fucking pregnancy, I'll tell you that much. I want to climb in the TARDIS and fast-forward to when the kid is about eleven." She set her jaw and followed Jack up the stairs. He tried not to listen to her sawing breath. Pregnant birds threw up. His mum had certainly never let him hear the end of it. *Morning sickness out the arse, and what do I get? Ten fuckin' hours of labor to pop out the world's most ungrateful little cunt.*

It didn't mean anything, and fussing over Pete would just make her chuck something at his head. Maybe if he repeated it enough times in his own head he'd believe it. Pete would be all right. The kid would be all right. He just had to play the game a bit longer, and he'd no longer be in any danger of fucking either of them up.

And that was the way it should be. The way it

had to be, unless he wanted to raise another Winter to get nicked by the cops, slam handfuls of smack, and drift through the Black as useless flotsam.

"Here," Pete said. "Sixth floor. Said the key would be on the jamb."

The hallway of the flat wasn't much better—someone had made an attempt to cover the stained diamond-shaped tiles with green lino, but most of it had been ripped back up, leaving jagged continents. The wood paneling and sooty lamps had probably once been grand, but that had been decades, if not centuries, ago. The high ceiling merely served to create a smog layer inside, a miniature of the outdoors, made of cigarette smoke and stale stench from cooking oil.

A pair of junkies crouched by the elevator, a gated type with a hand-scribbled sign reading OUT OF ORDER. The pasteboard was yellowed and a variety of creative and obscene graffiti covered the black letters.

The girl, one half of her head shaved and one covered in blue dreadlocks, stretched out her hand. "Got any change, brother?"

"None you could spend in this country, sorry," Jack told her.

"Oh, you're British," she said, and gave him a dreamy smile. "That's cool."

The boy nodded, skinny arms quivering as they wrapped around his knees. The bare flesh poking through his pants was scraped raw, concentric lines making hash marks in the skin. His arms were in the same condition. Ice could make you scratch that way, think there were insects and demons crawling in and out of your flesh.

"Down here." Pete fitted a key into the last flat in the hall and stepped inside.

Jack paused on the threshold, but there were no hexes on the flat, just the swirling ankle-deep tide of the Black. He'd need to fix that.

The flat smelled of ammonia and stale fag smoke. A roach scuttled along the back of the kitchen sink, and the walls were the yellow of stained teeth. A broken shade let in a little light, but otherwise, except for a stained mattress, the single room was empty.

"Home sweet fucking home," Jack muttered. Pete sat down on the mattress and put her head between her knees. Jack dropped the box and sat next to her.

"All right, luv?" he said. He weighed his risk, and then put a hand on the center of her back. Touching Pete was usually like putting your hand in something warm and sweet, a blissful hit of the best narcotic his brain could imagine. Now it was like grabbing a high-voltage wire with his bare hand. A rush of her talent fed into his and tried to convince him to expel the cloud of power as a hex or a spell that could blow a hole through the flat's wall.

He hadn't really touched her since the pregnancy— he'd brushed her hands, sure, or put his arm around her while they watched telly if she was in a good mood, but there hadn't been any close contact, and he certainly hadn't tried to fuck her. That would be a fast ticket to the A&E, considering Pete's usual mood. He hadn't expected to feel the touch of the Weir so strongly—stronger than it had ever been.

Stronger than before the Morrigan touched you, *you mean,* his treacherous inner voice whispered. Jack fucking hated the voice. It always told him the truth.

Pete surprised him by leaning her weight on his chest, nestling her head in the crook of his shoulder. "We ever going to make it back?" she said.

"Don't know." Jack didn't have the heart to lie to her. She would've known, anyway. "Doesn't look good," he said.

"You going to tell me what happened now?" Pete said.

He should move his hand. Move it before Pete's talent overwhelmed him, made him drunk on the rush of the Black through his brain, and he did something stupid. But she was warm, and small under his hand, and he could feel her ribs move when she breathed.

Jack kept his hand on Pete while he gave her the short version of meeting Abbadon. "Fucking nutter," he finished. "Thinks he can take on Belial and the rest of Hell. Probably wants to grab his He-Man sword and go toe to toe with the Princes, stupid git."

"Why is that so stupid?" Pete got up and ran water into her hand from the rusted tap. She swiped the sweat from her face and drank another fistful.

"Because he's talking about destroying Hell?"

Jack spread his hands. "Nobody can go up against demons, Pete. A demon, maybe. But not all of them. Besides the six hundred and sixty-six, there's their legions. Berserkers, Phantoms, Fenris. Millions of them, Pete. It's like a hobo shouting at taxis—funny to watch, but completely ineffective."

"I don't think you'd need to take on millions," Pete shrugged. "Just the ones who control the millons. Even the Named would fall into line. They're demons, Jack. You told me they follow the leader. They value the rank and file. If someone were to knock down the Princes, I bet all but a few would fall in."

Jack massaged his forehead. If he was honest, he'd had the same thought. "Abbadon's too crazy to be organized," he said. "Too much time in solitary. His mind is porridge."

"He was the first thing in Hell, Jack," Pete said. "To be only one of four survivors, over countless millennia—he might be crazy, but he's a hard man. If he was a human, he'd be the worst kind of bastard. Seen them time and again in the prisons when I was on the Met."

"Even so," Jack said. " 'M not being his errand boy. I got enough of that with Belial."

Pete sat back beside him, mattress bowing under her weight. Her shirt was loose—one of his; he recognized the faded SUSPECT DEVICE lettering across the front—and if he hadn't known, he wouldn't have been able to detect the slight swell of her stomach. It was there, though, and she let out a small sound as she sat back down.

"Can't wait to swell up and have to visit the loo every ten seconds," she said. "My mum was all, 'childbirth is a miracle and a beautiful gift from the unicorn faeries,' but all my sister could talk about was how big Mum's feet got when she was ready to pop with me."

"Your feet look fine to me," Jack said. "You're not your mum."

"Thank fuck for small favors," Pete muttered. She flipped open the top of the cardboard box. "So, Abbadon. You manage to figure out why he's after these families?"

Jack had been actively trying not to think about that, but after seeing things like Teddy, he couldn't very well ignore what his eyes and his logical mind were both shouting at him. "Got an idea, yeah."

Pete pulled out the stack of files Jack had first seen on Mayhew's desk. "Good, because I've gone over these fucking police reports ten times apiece and I still can't see any reason behind the murders."

"I think Abbadon and his pals are trying to grow themselves new bodies," Jack said. "Saw one out at his little ranch of horrors that had gone wrong. Horribly wrong."

"But they're corporeal creatures," Pete said. "Don't they have flesh of their own?"

"I think they can't pass out of Hell," Jack said. "When they were born, there was no here. There was just Hell, and a void. At least if I understand his ramblings correctly."

Abbadon's flesh was working all right, but the others were falling apart. Teddy was the worst, but there was nothing normal about the way Levi's and the girl's flesh had reacted to the intrusion of something ancient and malicious beyond measure.

"The kids," Pete said. Jack nodded.

"I don't think either the Case baby or this recent one are dead," he said. "I think they're being used as vessels."

Pete's face went pale, and she swallowed hard. "Christ."

"Yeah," Jack said. "Not exactly an acceptable hobby."

"To have something like that, randomly deciding to slaughter you to get at your kid . . ." Pete trailed off, and paged through the pictures again.

Jack patted himself down for fags and found his pack partially crushed in his pocket. He lit one, dragged. He didn't want to tell Pete that he had a feeling the Cases' and the Herreras' slaughter wasn't all that random. Ancient creatures of Hell didn't simply latch on to you because they liked the cut of your jib.

Abbadon had escaped the great iron prison Jack had found while in Hell. Had escaped a full ten years before Nicholas Naughton had tried to awaken Nergal and sent the rest of the domino tiles flying.

Abbadon had had help. Nobody escaped Hell without it. Jack sure as fuck hadn't.

"I need to see Mrs. Herrera's body," he said. "It'd still be on ice, yeah?"

"They keep unsolveds for as long as there's room and they don't go ripe, 'least they do back home,"

Pete said. "I imagine she'd still be about. File said they had no family to claim the remains anyway."

"Right," Jack said. "Let me put up some hexes on this shithole, and then we're going to go find out exactly what the fuck Belial has gotten me into."

He dug through his kit bag and found chalk and a few of his dried baggies of herbs. He didn't put much stock in kitchen witchery—that was the provenance of white magic, the sort of person who believed nailing a few twigs and a twist of colored thread above the doorjamb would keep out anything that meant you harm.

Only the Black could do that, and bending the Black to your will wasn't something a white witch would ever truck with.

He chalked the barrier marks around the doorjamb and across the threshold, something to focus the hex. Protection hexes, good ones, took time, but Jack could pull a quick and dirty barrier together in a few heartbeats. That was important—if something was clawing at the other side of your door, speed trumped elegance every time.

He laid a line of salt from his ancient tin and followed it up with a line of herbs. He reached out, touched the electric swirl of the Black just beyond sight, and pulled it into the chalk, into the salt, tugging and weaving it into a crackling barrier across all the thresholds of the flat. A twinge in the front of his skull, and it was done. Anyone trying to come at him would get enough of a jolt to reconsider their life choices.

"Let's get this done," he told Pete. "I'm ready to be out of this miserable city."

Pete collected her mobile and her bag, but before Jack could stow his kit, fists pounded on the door. Pete rolled her eyes. "Probably just some crackhead."

Jack touched the door with splayed fingers, but nothing spiked his sight. "Yeah? What?"

"Hey, dude." The female junkie's voice was thin and papery through the water-stained door. "You got a place we could maybe piss? The gas station is like half a mile away."

"Fuck off," Pete said. "This isn't a hotel."

Jack sighed. "What's the harm?" A girl couldn't just find a convenient alley, like he had when he was a junkie. He could practically feel the grimy film that built up on your skin when you were concerned with showering maybe once or twice in a month. The stale taste in your mouth of fags and the bite of bile, because you hadn't eaten in recent memory and didn't want to. Your veins burned you from the inside out, burned out hunger and everything except the need to chase the fire, reignite it when it got low.

Pete threw up her hands. "Whatever. Just be quick."

Jack undid the deadbolt and opened the door a crack. Saw the girl's bloodshot eyes and rigid face, and tried to slam it again, but she thrust her steel-toed boot into the gap and then threw the door off its hinges with a boom.

He went down hard, the door landing on top of

him. If it hadn't been half-disintegrated with dry rot, it would've crushed his ribs, but instead the junkie girl landing on top of him finished that job. She crouched atop Jack and leaned down, nostrils flaring wide. She wore a piercing, a ring with a jewel bead that shimmered in the low light as she inhaled his scent.

Jack thrust against her with his whole weight, but she wrapped a hand around his neck. "You really think you can just run from me? You think Belial can protect you?" The voice was low and masculine, and as it twisted out of her narrow throat it sounded like a creature trapped far below ground.

Out of the corner of his vision, he saw Pete moving—she held a thin metal tube he recognized as her collapsible baton that she'd carried as a detective, and still kept in her bag for rough spots.

Jack looked back at the girl. Blood vessels had erupted across the surface of her eyes from the strain of Abbadon's magic, and her breathing was sawing in and out of her throat. "What part of no don't you understand, Donny boy?" he said. "I'm not interested in your jailbreak. I have to live in this world same as everyone else. Don't particularly want to destroy it."

"Then you'll burn like the rest," the girl hissed. "Like all the other sons of bitches who stood up to be counted against me."

Pete raised her baton, but on the downswing the shape of the male junkie slammed into her, knocking Pete into the wall hard enough to leave indents in the stained plaster.

"Shit . . ." she gasped, as the boy straddled her, wrapping his fingers in her hair. He had a knife, a rusty little Swiss Army number like a boy playing at wilderness adventures would carry, but he jammed it into the fold of Pete's jaw.

"Stay down, whore," he rumbled. Levi. Jack would know the wet, smothered gasp of the voice anywhere.

"I'd hoped you'd be one of us," Abbadon snarled, "but now you're useless to me. Loose ends get cut, Winter. Your little demon boyfriend can't protect you now."

Jack felt the cool metal of Pete's baton brush against his fingers, and he struggled under the door and the weight of the girl, batting it back toward Pete. Her fingers closed around it and she whipped it up and across the boy's face. A welt of bruise blossomed up one cheek and Jack saw a tooth fly, borne on a spray of blood.

The girl turned her head for a split second, and Jack braced his hands against the blistered paint of the door and shoved. She tumbled off him, and Jack scrambled onto her back, grabbing her by the hair and slamming her head once into the floor, short and sharp.

The girl went still, but the boy was less tractable. Pete was up now, and hit him again with her baton, and again, until he fell, twitching and bleeding. Jack scrambled for his kit bag. Exorcisms, unlike barrier hexes, were not something he could perform on the fly, but it wasn't like a demon had actually crawled inside the junkie. Levi was just riding him, using him like a puppet.

He flipped the top off his salt tin and dumped the full contents over the junkie's body, watching the flakes turn pink as they stuck in the runnels of blood across the boy's face. "Get the fuck out," Jack snarled, and pushed, with his talent, as hard as he could. He contacted the expanse of Levi's power—sticky, dark, endlessly hungry. A vast maw, a thing that could devour the world and never be sated.

Jack shoved, using the salt as his vessel, and thin green flames rose from the junkie's body as the Black clashed with Levi's talent. The junkie spasmed, then rolled on his side and vomited a thin stream of sticky bile laced with blood.

Jack grabbed Pete by the hand, slinging his kit bag with the other. Abbadon knew where they were, and his hexes had done precisely shit. Keep moving—that was the only way to defeat a predator. Run until your feet are bloody and then run some more.

"You all right?" he said. Pete was pale, the only spots of color high in her cheeks.

"I'm fine," she said tightly. "Fucking go."

They made the reverse journey down the stairs and into the Fury. Pete let out a small sound as she lowered herself into the seat, and Jack tossed his kit to the floor, taking her chin between his fingers. He knew that sound, had made it himself when he thought everyone, his mum and Kevin and the rest, had stopped listening. The sound came after beatings, after falls, after you'd swallowed the blood and the bruises had flowered fully on your skin.

"What's wrong?" he said.

"Nothing," Pete snapped. "Just took a hit from that fucking junkie, is all. I told you not to let them in." She sucked in a breath, and passed a hand across her abdomen before shoving the key into the Fury's ignition. "Stupid," she told Jack. "So stupid."

Jack couldn't disagree with her as they drove away, but he at least had the comfort of knowing he was going to make Abbadon answer for this, and for everything else. Belial couldn't threaten him and Abbadon couldn't scare him, but now he'd fucked himself. Jack could take a beating, take a knife in his own back, but Pete was a different thing. Abbadon didn't know that yet, but he would.

CHAPTER 19

By the time they pulled off the freeway at North Mission Road and took the turns that brought them to a complex of brick buildings that looked more like an old-fashioned movie studio than a mortuary, Pete had gotten some of her color back and she'd stopped wincing every time she took a breath Jack felt his own chest unknot.

Pete parked in the visitor's area and turned to him. "It'd take more than that to hurt me and the kid," she said to Jack. "Don't worry, all right?"

"Can't make any promises," Jack said. "I'm never going to not care if you're getting hurt, Petunia. You know that."

She winced at her full name. "You leave off calling me that. Know how much I bloody hate it." She shoved the door open and perched a pair of sunglasses on her nose. "Tell you one thing, I'm not saddling this child with a name that'll follow them through life, giving them endless shite. Been wondering even more lately what the hell my mum was thinking."

"You given it any thought? A name, I mean, not your mum," Jack said. The mortuary started at one of the brick buildings, with a peaked roof covered in red clay tiles, and continued in a modern gray box that told Jack in no uncertain terms via several signs that visitors were not allowed.

Pete shrugged. "I'm not much good at names. Figure I should stick my Da's given name in there somewhere if it's a boy. What about you? Your mum? Lawrence?"

"Lawrence, maybe," Jack said. "My mum . . . are you mad? I'd never do that to a kid. Fucking bitch is dead and she's going to stay that way, not live on forever saddling some poor offspring of mine with her name."

"Well, excuse me very fucking much," Pete muttered. "Just thought I'd ask."

Jack was saved from having to think about what his mother's reaction would be to him naming a living being after her by Detective Shavers, who came from the low gray building. "Let's get one thing straight," he told Jack. "I'm not happy about this."

"You don't have to be happy," Jack said. "I'm not thrilled to see you either, mate."

Pete jabbed him sharply in the ribs. "Thanks very much for setting this up," she said.

"It's not for you," Shavers snapped. "I've had Ben calling me eight times a day, drunk off his ass, crying about the dead families. I can't deal with this shit, Ms. Caldecott. Whatever you've stirred up in his head, look at the body, say what you have to say, and calm it back down."

"I don't think I can do much about Mayhew," Pete said. "In case you hadn't noticed, he's not exactly a stable individual."

"If you don't fix this, I'm going to arrest you and throw you in county myself," Shavers said. "And I will personally ensure that your boyfriend's in there with you, in a cell with a roommate who has a thing for blonds. That clear enough for you?"

Jack thought that Shavers could do with a good pop in the mouth. Knock out a few of those film-star teeth, and see how he'd act then. Coppers were, at the root, mostly the same. There were a few, like Pete, who thought they were genuinely on the side of justice, if not always the side of Good, but most were like Shavers—little men, with a little bit of power, using it to the hilt to fuck up everyone else's day.

Shavers led them into the morgue proper and got them visitor's badges, the kind given to families identifying the corpses of their loved ones. The only other person with the same colored badge as Jack was a sobbing Mexican woman with gray hair wrapped in an orange scarf. A morgue worker stood by her, not close enough to get grabbed, but close enough to look uncomfortable.

Shavers showed them the way to the cold room, then pulled out his mobile and left.

Pete opened the refrigerator door, as small and

square as the reliquary for a person's ashes. Mrs. Herrera was naked, covered in a plastic sheet. Blue around the edges, her eyes were shut, but nobody would ever mistake her for being asleep.

Jack got out a pair of rubber gloves. Who knew what kind of shit the morgue workers did with the unclaimed bodies? Nothing he wanted all over his skin. He took the sheet off and looked Mrs. Herrera over. She'd been in good shape when she was alive. The gaping cavity in her abdomen had been sewn up with rough stiches, and she could have been a trophy wife recovering from a tummy tuck. Her breasts were natural, flat brown nipples and not much volume, as far as tits in Los Angeles went.

Jack checked her arms, the inside of her thighs. No track marks and no tattoos. In the parlance of the Black, that made her practically a nun. Ink and smack were the two most common things to go under the skin if you had a talent.

He gestured to Pete. "Help me roll her."

Pete didn't flinch—she had ten times the experience with stiffs that he did. "You looking for anything special?"

"Don't know," Jack muttered, running his fingers lightly down Mrs. Herrera's spine. It could have been random. Abbadon could have seen a pregnant woman at the market, at the cinema, anywhere at all. He moved among humans like a shark, and he could have happened on her by chance.

He couldn't believe that, though. Not really. Abbadon was smart, and people weren't all the same. One could be possessed as easily as breathing, while the next would fight to their dying heartbeat against psychic invasion, killing themselves and wearing Abbadon down to a nub. A fugitive from Hell couldn't afford to take a chance like that. He'd chosen the children for a reason.

Jack found what he was looking for under the fold of Mrs. Herrera's buttock. She had an arse toned in life by the sort of workout that came with private gyms and trainers named Sven, but the small shadow was a flaw, the sort of flaw a woman like her wouldn't allow.

Pete got a pen light from a tray of instruments and shone it on the mark. "What the hell is that?"

Jack used his thumb and forefinger to spread the skin tight, touching the raised ridges with his other hand. The slightest bit of power was still there, mostly faded by death. No blood, no life.

"A brand," he said. Seeing the simple lines, in the shape of a twinned cross surrounded by a broken triangle, stirred a memory that he'd just as soon forget. Another pretty girl, skinnier and paler, but beautiful nonetheless. Hollow, lifeless eyes. Skinny fingers that wrapped around his wrist and left marks when he yanked himself free.

Her name had been Fiona Hannigan, and she was dead now, but she'd been into the same shit as Mrs. Herrera.

"I can see it's a brand," Pete said. "You look as if you've swallowed a mouthful of embalming fluid. What's it mean?"

"It means she was part of a sect," Jack said.

"Not a sect, really—like a club. It's a calling card for sex magic. She was one of the cattle. One of the conduits they used for ritual." He threw the sheet back on Mrs. Herrera. He didn't need to look at the brand any longer.

A baby conceived during a ritual, already tainted by black magic, would be the perfect flesh for something like Abbadon. Jack honestly wondered why he hadn't thought of it before.

Pete was chewing on her lip, a gesture that she reverted to when she was nervous or going over some particularly nasty truth. "You said one of them went wrong," she said. "One of the things riding with Abbadon."

"Yeah," Jack said. "Fucking disgusting. Looks like a twat with teeth. Think it was the Herrera baby, poor soul. Abbadon took the Case child for his own flesh, and fuck knows where he found bodies for the other two. They're not working out much better, I can tell you that."

"And I can tell you they're not finished," Pete said. "You can't go against the Princes a man down."

She was right. Pete was usually right. That was the maddening thing about her. Jack shoved a hand through his hair. It was still stiff with blood. He needed to wash, needed a drink. Needed to get out of this city, where there was nothing but a black hole of pain and misery to fall into, until you smacked the bottom and came apart like a doll.

"There can't be too many cabals of fuck-mages, even in a city like this," he said.

"We can't let that thing get its hands on another kid," Pete said. "Nor slice up another family like they're a fucking fruit cocktail." She stripped off her gloves and threw them in the biohazard bin.

"Don't worry," Jack told her. "I know somebody who'll know exactly where we can find ourselves a pregnant sorcerer."

CHAPTER 20

Sanford practically bounded down the drive when Jack rang at his gate, Gator and Parker in tow. "Jack! You have some good news for me?"

"Not even a droplet of piss for you," Jack told him. Parker grunted, and Sanford blinked.

"Then, pardon me, but what the fuck are you doing here?"

"Got a proposition for you," Jack said. This had to go just right. If he slagged Sanford off, that great cunt Parker looked like he'd be all too happy to leave him stone dead in a canyon somewhere, food for the coyotes that Jack could hear yipping even now in the hills behind Sanford's house.

"For me." Sanford cracked his knuckles. "This should be good, considering how I believe I told you exactly what I needed from you, and the consequences if that didn't happen."

"Yeah, well," Jack said. "You really know so

much about me, you'll know that following orders from gits in slick suits isn't exactly my forte."

Sanford rubbed a thumb across his forehead. "Shall we take this somewhere more conducive to negotiation?" he said. "You look like a man who could use a drink. Possibly a flea bath."

This time, there were no pleasantries by the pool. Sanford took Jack to a study, full of film tear sheets from pictures Jack had never heard of, a set of fake fencing swords and the rubber head of a swamp monster hanging on the walls. "Basil was quite a collector," Sanford said. "Somewhat notorious for stealing from his sets, actually. Have you seen any of his films?"

"Can't say I'm a movie buff," Jack said.

"Right, you were in that band," Sanford said. "Probably thought you were too cool for cheesy old B pictures. Anyway, I recommend *My Soul Condemned*. Nasty little noir picture, better than most of the crap Basil was featured in."

He poured scotch from a decanter into a crystal tumbler and Jack drank, but it was cheap stuff that lit a fire all the way down. The *fuck you* scotch, reserved for guests you really wanted to shove into the pool and hold there until they stopped twitching.

"Now," Sanford said, lighting a cigar from an inlaid box on his massive desk. "Why don't you tell me what's got you in such a lather?"

Jack told Sanford about Abbadon. Watched his face for any sign of a twitch of guilt, but Sanford was better at the game than that. He smoked, he drank, he smiled and made conciliatory faces in all the right spots.

"Well, that's certainly an exciting story," he told Jack when Jack finished. "But I don't see what it has to do with me."

"You want Abbadon on your side," Jack said. "So you can poke and prod Belial for the rest of his miserable existence. You can't hope to hold him on your own, but with some of Abbadon's magic, you'll have the pet demon you've always wanted." He steepled his fingers. "You tell me where the local sorcerers meet to fuck each other's brains out, I guarantee I can deliver you Abbadon."

He didn't make a habit of hooking men like Sanford together with creatures like Abbadon, but Sanford didn't know that. He thought threatening Pete and the kid would keep Jack in line, and Jack was content to let him go right on thinking it. Besides, he needed Sanford, at least for a little bit longer. Then it might be amusing to watch Abbadon chew the prick up and shit him out.

"Interesting," Sanford said. "And what's the upshot for you?"

"You leave Pete alone," Jack said. "Call off your pet sociopaths and let her go about her life."

Sanford rolled his eyes. "What a predictable twist," he said. "I'd never sell a picture with a line like that."

Jack held Sanford's eyes. "Good thing this is real life, then." He leaned forward and set the empty tumbler on the edge of Sanford's desk. Sanford didn't flinch, but he wasn't acting like Jack had brought him the wrong sort of coffee any longer, either. The temptation to get what he wanted was going to rule him. Jack leaned back in his chair. "So? You know any place like what I'm talking about?"

Sanford exhaled a cloud of smoke. "You fuck me in the ass over this, Jack . . ." He leaned forward and stubbed out his cigar, one vicious movement that rattled the ashtray. "I'm not going to need to hurt Pete and your kid. You'll wish you were dead either way."

"Story of my fuckin' life," Jack said. "Let's get on with it, shall we?"

CHAPTER 21

Sanford and Jack rode in an old Lincoln limousine, a great rolling coffin of iron and chrome. Parker drove and Gator stayed behind, a development that clearly infuriated him, veins bulging out of his bull neck. "I don't trust that Limey fuck, sir," he told Sanford.

"That's all right," Sanford said, giving Jack a mild smile. "Neither do I."

Parker stayed quiet, guiding them down from the heights of Sunset Boulevard and back into the maze of downtown.

"It's a real shame what's happening down here," Sanford said. "Used to be a high-class neighborhood back before the crash. Now it's full of spics and crackheads, and all of these old buildings are crumbling." He gestured at an Art Deco cinema, marquee lit up to advertise a live performance of *The Rocky Horror Picture Show*. "The Million Dollar

Theater. Back in old Basil's day, all the premieres were there. Swank spot." He pointed to a brick building across the street, a nondescript four-story box surrounded by tourists with cameras. "They filmed *Blade Runner* in there, the Bradbury Building. Crazy ironwork. I'd've loved to get a shooting permit for a feature I did a few years ago, but it's all rented by the LAPD now and they're real assholes unless you have a buddy on the force."

The limo pulled to the curb, putting an end to Sanford's rambling before Jack had to choke him with his own shoelaces. The man loved the sound of his chatter like few Jack had ever met before. That was fine—the more Sanford talked, the less he had to.

Parker opened the door, but let it swing back at soon as Sanford was out. It clipped Jack in the knee, and he cursed. Parker's lips twitched with the thinnest ghost of a smile before Sanford went to a metal door sandwiched between a convenience mart and a shop selling *quincenera* dresses and hit the buzzer.

"Let me do the talking in here," Sanford said. "I have a relationship with these people. You're an outsider, and they don't like that. Me bringing you at all is putting my whole reputation at risk."

"I'll do me best not to use the wrong fork or spit on the carpet," Jack said. Worrying about offending sex magicians was like being concerned with hurting a hobo's feelings—you could spare the worry, but why bother? Sex magic spoke to a particular kind of ego, worse than the usual sort of cunt who turned to black magic. None of the sorcerers Jack had run across were much better than pimps with a little bit of talent and just enough charm to lure damaged boys and girls into their games for power. He supposed there might be some who used fucking as a genuine focus, a form of power-raising that was consensual and at least in the gray area between outright black magic and the white stuff that everyday sorts associated with witchcraft, but he hadn't met them. The more depraved the sex, the more pain the subject was in, the less they wanted it, the bigger the entity you could attract. And the sorts of things attracted to blood, sex, and suffering weren't cuddly and inclined to sit down and have a cup of tea.

He couldn't worry about that now. He wasn't on a mission of mercy. He was here to find a pregnant sorcerer, warn her that something was coming to slice her like a Sunday roast, and get the fuck out. Let Sanford and Belial and Abbadon duke it out. He was finished with being batted back and forth like a toy mouse. LA couldn't be in his rear view soon enough.

The buzzer rang, echoing through the rusted speaker, and Parker held the door for Sanford. He began to let it go on Jack again, and Jack stared into his blank dark eyes. "Do it and I'm putting your head through."

"You threatened to kick our teeth in, too," Parker murmured. "Promises, promises."

Jack followed Sanford up a narrow staircase, threadbare Persian carpets muffling his boots. The

walls were stamped tin, painted over with blood
red that pooled and dripped at the floor. A single
bare bulb flickered above Jack's head, giving Sanford an entirely undeserved halo as he crested the
landing in front of Jack.

Sanford knocked at another door and looked at
Parker when a deadbolt clacked. "We'll be out in a
few minutes. Just hang out."

Parker grunted, and glared at Jack with hostility
naked as a spitting electrical wire. Jack patted him
on the shoulder. "Cheer up, mate. You'll have time
to work on your tan."

The door swung open, and a small woman looked
Jack up and down. "You didn't call ahead for a visitor," she told Sanford.

"Come on, Anna," he said. "You know I'm a good
boy."

One of her painted eyebrows went up. "Hmph,"
she said, but stepped aside. She was pudgy, in the
way that short women seemed to grow outward, not
up, and wore a black silk dressing gown and heels.
She didn't have the hollowed-out stare of most sex
sorcerers' fuckmates. A madam, Jack decided, somebody who wasn't to the taste of whatever entity this
sorcerer was feeding in exchange for power.

"We don't have any more recordings for you,"
she told Sanford. "Next ritual is at the new moon.
You're welcome to attend, as always."

"Hold up," Jack said to Sanford. "You use their
rituals for spank material?" He shook his head.
"Got to hand you that one, mate. You're sicker
than I thought."

"Please," Sanford said. "Shut the fuck up. Did I not make myself clear?"

Jack ignored him and looked at Anna. "Where's your loo?"

"Down the hallway, second door," she said. Jack started walking without another word.

Sanford was somebody who liked the wheedling almost as much as the result. They could be here until Christmas while he danced around with Anna and her fellow perverts, trying to couch his question in the most honeyed terms. Tell a sorcerer an ancient entity from the blackest part of the Pit was after one of their flock, and they'd probably welcome it with open arms. Sanford had to avoid that at all costs if he wanted his prize of a living, breathing pet demon than he didn't have to share with anyone.

Jack had no such compunctions. He'd kick down every door in this shitty warren of flats if he had to. He opened the loo door loudly, running water and flushing the toilet, and then slipped out and down the hallway.

He thought it might have been offices at one point, in the past when men wore hats and women all had blood-red lips and low, husky cigarette purrs. The wavy glass door showed shadows, and moans and sobs came from behind a few. Jack tried those first.

A boy who couldn't have been much older than Sliver glared up at him. His bare torso was covered with thin welts, and a black halo of makeup had collected under his eyes. "Get the fuck out," he said, swiping the runnels on his cheeks.

"Sorry," Jack said.

"Don't be sorry, get out!" the kid snapped. "I'm off duty, all right? Find somebody else to fuck with."

"Can I help you?"

Jack turned to tell whoever it was to fuck off, but instead found himself face to face with a pleasant-looking blond girl whose stomach under her Killers T-shirt was swollen round as a sport ball.

"Yeah," he said. "As a matter of fact, I think you can."

"Excuse me," the boy said loudly. "Can you two have your girl talk somewhere other than my room?"

"Calm down, Travis," the girl said. "Nobody wants to be in your room." She ushered Jack out and shut the door. "Sorry about him. He's new."

"He always that cheerful?" Jack asked her.

"Usually he's pretty good about new people," the girl said. "But he had a rough night. The indoctrination can be tough." She gave Jack a serene smile. "The first time I let the power inside me, I puked my guts out. But Anna helped me, and now look." She ran her hands over her stomach.

"A veritable bundle of joy," Jack said. "Anna, she's like your mum?"

"Oh, no." The girl shook her head. "Anna leads the rituals. She's the one who shares the power with us, and who showed me how I can use my body to communicate with it." She gave a small shiver. "Anna's so much more than a mother."

A female sex magician. Well, he'd heard of stranger things. Jack took the girl by the arm. "What's your name?" Her talent was barely a flutter, just enough that she'd feel disconnected from the daylight world, a vague feeling of unease she could never identify. It made her a thick piece of juicy meat to people like Anna.

"Kim," she said. "My ritual name is . . ."

"I don't give a fuck," Jack said. He turned them around and aimed them at the glowing red sign showing the exceptionally stupid where they should go in case there was a fire. "You're the only pregnant one here, yeah?"

"Yes, for now . . ." Kim twisted in his hand. "You're hurting me."

"We're going," Jack said. "Come with me."

"No!" Kim said, jerking free. "I'm not a whore, dude. If you're here for a ritual, then talk to Anna. You can't just drag me off to fuck any time you want."

"Listen, you brainwashed twit," Jack said. "If you don't leave this place right now, then you are going to end up dead and your child is going to be a vessel for something so horrible your tiny mind can't comprehend. Look at my face and see if I'm lying to you."

Kim stared at him, catching her lip between her teeth. "My baby?" she said. "Anna wouldn't hurt my baby. Children are a gift, a product of the most sacred kind of union . . ."

"What utter shit have they been feeding you?" Jack said. She was letting him walk her, at least, and he shoved the door open with his free arm.

A klaxon began whooping, and Jack resisted the urge to ram his head into the wall. "Listen to me,

Kim. Your little circle-jerk here has been targeted by a predator who is much bigger and hungrier than your Anna. She might think she's struck a bargain with him, but she can't stop what he wants to do with your kid and any others who come into the fold. Nothing can. If you care about the kid at all, you'll come with me now."

Kim swallowed hard, lacing her fingers across her stomach. "Who are you?"

At the far end of the hall, Anna and Sanford appeared, Parker in tow. "Stop him!" Anna shrieked. "He's got a girl with him!"

"I'm Jack," Jack told Kim. "Nice to meet you. Now kindly get yourself together and fucking run."

Parker reached under his coat, hand coming up. Anna raised her hands, and Jack saw purple witchfire crackle around her fists. "Fuck," he muttered, throwing a shield hex to bounce Anna's spell back at her. His head throbbed, and Anna's power jittered through the light sockets and across the walls, throwing sparks.

Kim stared at Anna, then back at him. "You're crazy," she whispered.

Jack watched Parker bring up his pistol, work the slide. The hex might hold; it might not. Bullets were iron projectiles, and they were decent at punching through spells even when the mage throwing them wasn't beat to shite and working on half power. "Look," he said to Kim. "You've got no reason to trust me, but I don't want anything from you. I've got a kid of my own, and I know you'd die before you let anything happen to yours. I'm just here to see that you don't have to."

Kim looked back at him and didn't say anything else, just started moving, down the stairs, as fast as she could with her extra weight.

Jack slammed the fire door, twisted the deadbolt, and, for good measure, sent a burning curse into the lock that turned the works to slag. It wouldn't hold a sorcerer like Anna for long, but it'd give them what he hoped was enough of a head start.

"Are you some kind of psycho?" Kim asked as they reached the bottom level. Jack worked his lock-pick charm on the padlock and chain keeping the door to the next building shut, then hustled Kim through.

"There's some debate about that," he said. "But right now, I'm the sanest person you know."

A shadow loomed up in front of him, and Jack didn't have time to move before Parker slammed a fist into his face. "Bad luck, pretty boy," he told Jack, taking Kim by the arm and pulling her behind him. "The bitch doesn't belong to you."

"I doubt she belongs to you either," Jack said. "Unless you're the proud father."

Kim's eyes went wide at the idea. "I don't know this asshole!" she exclaimed.

"Not someone you want to know, either," Jack said. His cheekbone felt flat and numb—Parker hit like a hammer. Trying to hit back would just end with him in an emergency ward pissing into a tube.

He hit with a curse instead, the leg-locker flinging Parker to one side of the tunnel and chipping a dent out of the cinder block wall. Jack grabbed Kim's hand and jerked her along. She couldn't run very well, more of a waddle, but Jack jerked her up the steps and burst into the foyer of the building next door, coming face to face with a surprised Japanese man holding a long-lensed camera.

" 'Scuse me," Jack said. After the claustrophobia of Anna's lair, the light made him squint.

Kim pressed close to him. "What's going on?" she whispered. "Who was that guy?"

"An arsehole," Jack said. "Somebody who doesn't have your kid's best interest in mind."

"Excuse me." A heavyset woman in a blue blazer tapped Jack on the shoulder. "The lower level is strictly off limits to visitors."

"Yeah, sorry," Jack said. Sunlight dappled the red tiled floor, and a spike of pain went through his forehead when he looked up. He was surrounded by cold iron—run under the water of a free-flowing stream—iron rails, iron decoration, iron elevators running up and down on iron chains. The entire building was seamed with iron, a box designed to kill anything magic that crossed its threshold.

"Well," Jack muttered to himself. "Shit."

Kim blanched, putting one hand on her stomach and one on her mouth. "Oh my god. This place sucks."

A tour group, consisting of a pod of tanned twenty-somethings chattering in German, entered the lobby, and Jack pulled Kim into the midst of the crowd. He couldn't throw hexes in here, but nobody could find them from the outside, either. Sanford and Parker could watch the street, but with the steady flow of tourists and bored-looking office workers that Jack guessed were cops, he'd have to spot them first. A little luck, and he could have Kim on a bus back to Bum Fun, Kansas, or wherever the hell she'd come to this city from by nightfall.

"This is the Bradbury Building," intoned the tour guide. "Built in 1934." A translator repeated, and the Germans cooed appreciatively.

Parker burst out of the cellar door, and the security guard started for him. He hit her, one jab straight into the throat, and she collapsed to her knees on the tile, choking.

"Dammit," Jack muttered. There went his plan to slip out unnoticed when the Germans returned to the filth, noise, and vomiting hobos of downtown LA.

Parker made a beeline for them, and Jack did what came naturally, ran like hell, up the stairs and past a cord blocking the unwashed masses from the second floor. He pelted down the landing, and against a normal bloke he and Kim would have had a head start. Parker, however, eschewed the stairs entirely, leaping straight from the lobby to the first balcony, landing on a floor with a crash that cracked tiles. His knobby muscles rippled under his black shirt and he dropped into a crouch, nostrils flaring at Jack as he used his body to make a barrier between him and Kim.

"Holy shit," she squeaked from behind him.

A demon would never be able to form-shift amid

all this iron, which left Jack with several distinctly unpleasant possibilities as to what, exactly, Parker was. Not a werewolf—the enchantment would have been obvious during all the contact they'd had, in the form of Parker kicking the hell out of him.

Something organic, something in the blood. Something that was causing black claws to erupt from Parker's hands and his teeth to overshoot the bounds of his mouth.

He crouched on his haunches and hissed at Jack, the back of his coat splitting to allow two long, leathery wings to erupt, covered in effluvia from his shift from ugly man to fuck-ugly bat-creature.

"Freeze!" One of the cops—anyone anywhere could tell he was one, rumpled suit and cheap shoes and all—aimed his pistol at Parker's back. When Parker let out a screech, the copper fired. Two rounds caught Parker between the shoulder blades. He jerked and turned on the man, closing the space and his teeth around the copper's throat. A spray of arterial blood hit the wall and washed the tiles. Jack shoved Kim.

"Move your arse." There was a second landing, a set of stairs near the rear door of the building. They had to move, before Parker realized he'd lost track of them. Before Sanford showed up. Before the LAPD decided to ventilate his torso just for the fun of it.

Parker gave a great flap of wings, and with a screech leaped over Jack and Kim and landed in front of them. Kim let out a moan. "What the fuck *is* he?"

Parker's ears had elongated, and a patch of ugly, wire-brush fur had grown across his face like the world's most unfortunate set of mutton chops.

"I said the bitch wasn't yours," he hissed. "She's going to whelp, and the kid is Abbadon's. You promised the boss Abbadon. This is the quickest way and fair's fair, Winter."

"Fuck off, bat boy," Jack told him. "Go back to sucking on diseased goats." He moved a step to the right, experimentally, and Parker matched his move. Jack pulled Kim close, so he could feel her swollen stomach against his back. "When I move you run like fuck for those stairs and don't stop until you're in broad daylight. Find a cop in a uniform and stick to them like glue."

Kim shook her head, her eyes going wide. "No . . ."

"Don't give it a thought, luv," Jack told her. "I'll be right behind you."

He let go of her hand and put his attention on Parker. Try to avoid a stand-up fight, and fate saw that you got exactly that. Bitch that she was. "About the teeth-kicking," Jack said to Parker. "Now seems as good a time as any."

Parker grinned at him. "Big words for a little man."

"Words at all coming from your ugly mug," Jack told him. "Amazing, really." He cocked his head, put the weight on the balls of his feet. Prepared himself to take the hit. He was used to that, at least. Sometimes you just had to take it, taste the blood, spit out your ruined teeth, and get on. "Tell me," he said to Parker. "Are you mean because you're ugly? Or are you ugly because your mum sucked the cock of a rabid werewolf and vomited you out afterward?"

Parker launched at him. Kim screamed, but she ran, caroming off the wall, digging her feet in and heading for the stairs.

Jack went over on his back, slamming into the rail with Parker on top of him. The lobby below was in chaos, some tourists screaming, some snapping away with their cameras. The coppers were rushing about, but after what had happened to their mate, none seemed anxious to get close to Jack and Parker.

Parker's breath smelled like a sewer in the height of summer and was as hot as an oven on Jack's face as Parker snapped his black teeth. Jack threw up his arm, and Parker clamped down on his leather, and through it to flesh. The pain took a moment to come, but it did, hot as coals and deep as marrow. The only bright spot was that it wasn't his neck.

Jack jammed his boots into Parker's belly, the steel toes meeting soft flesh, and shoved with all his strength. Something gave out in his back, but Parker went flying over his head, slamming into the cage that blocked the elevator shaft. The car was on the top floor, and he fell, hitting the bottom of the shaft with a scream.

Getting his feet under him was a trial. Jack felt the sting of cold air on his arm, and saw a half-moon of bloody, rent flesh under his shredded leather. He could deal with it later. If there was a later.

The elevator shaft rattled, and Jack went to the edge. Parker was climbing. One wing was twisted and broken, leaking brackish-colored fluid, but his claws still worked, and he scaled the shaft, snarling and screeching with each movement.

Jack shot a glance over his shoulder. Kim was nowhere to be seen. Good. One less thing he had to worry about.

"You son of a bitch," Parker rasped. He wasn't moving fast, but like a high tide, he'd inevitably reach Jack. "You fucked up now. You should've killed me."

Jack looked upward into the lift shaft. The car hung above his head, near the peaked roof of the shaft. It was suspended from the three landings of the building like a cage, and the chains that raised and lowered the car rattled as Parker climbed.

Jack tried a hex, even though the answering echo of emptiness told him that in this place, the Black did not exist.

Parker's claws grabbed at his boot, but they couldn't get through the steel and pin him in place. Jack wrapped his arm through the chain and kicked with his free foot, cracking Parker in his elongated jaw. Parker slipped a little, but kept his hold.

Jack tried the curse again, as reflex more than anything. Magic was his armor, his sword, all he had. He wasn't strong, and wits alone weren't going to take a pissed-off chupacabra off his arse.

The cold started in his fingertips, as if he'd gone outside on a snowy day in Manchester and forgotten his gloves. It spread up his arms, down his back, deep into his chest, and around his heart. His blood roared through his ears like a freight train. Parker stopped struggling, his rheumy yellow animal eyes going wide.

Jack watched the ink of the tattoos, the Morrigan's marks, shift and wriggle under his skin, giving birth to new shapes that moved with a life of their own. Feathers sprouted on his skin, covering every inch of him from scalp to sole.

The word sprang to his lips unbidden, the cold spreading to his mind and killing the panic and the scrabbling fear, everything except the dead-eyed logic that lived in the lizard part of his brain.

"*Aithinne.*"

The cables holding the lift car glowed, and turned to slag, in the space of a breath. Parker jerked his head up, but the iron car fell too fast, and it took him to the bottom of the shaft, pinning him under its crushing iron weight.

Jack fell back on the tiles, slamming his bad arm hard and starting the flow of blood afresh.

The cold retreated, and when he came back to himself he picked his arse up off the floor and ran. The chaos inside the Bradbury Building served him well, and he ducked across 4th Avenue and into the lobby of the Million Dollar Theater as a herd of cop cars screeched to a stop, jamming up traffic and starting a cavalcade of horns.

He caught a flash of blond hair and saw Kim peeking at him from the women's loo. "I didn't know where else to go," she said.

"You're all right, luv," Jack said. Kim pointed at his arm.

"Your jacket is all torn up."

"Arm, too," Jack said. He looked down. Time to assess the damage, see if he'd make it as far as somebody who'd stitch him without asking too many questions.

His arm was smooth and bloodless. A thin line of scars, narrow and square as standing stones, was all that remained to show his arm had once been torn to hamburger.

Kim leaned in to examine his arm, and then shrugged. "Seems all right to me."

"It does, at that," Jack told her. He could think about it later. Figure out how it had happened later. Decide what the fuck had gone on back in the Bradbury Building with Parker. Later. All later.

He guided Kim to the back exit and out onto the street. The safehouse Sliver had given Pete was out of the question—Abbadon had found it and walked through his hexes without a second thought.

"You got a mobile?" he asked Kim. She tilted her head at him, pale brows drawn together. "A mobile phone," Jack snapped. "You got one?"

"Oh, yeah." Kim passed him a bright pink hunk of plastic, the screen displaying a photo of herself and another, equally blond and vacant-eyed girl with their cheeks pressed together. Jack handed it back.

"I can't work something that doesn't have buttons. Dial the number I give you."

Kim did as he said and Jack explained, in as few words as he could and with as little detail as possible, where to find them.

Pete arrived about half an hour later, and Jack put Kim in the back seat of the Fury. Pete looked her over and cocked one eyebrow at him.

"I know," he told her. "Just . . . don't make a big deal of it, all right?"

"Bigger deal is where we're going to hole up," Pete said. "Considering this bastard apparently has a live feed of where you are at all times."

"There's a couple of motels on Sunset," Kim piped up. "My girlfriends and I used to crash there. Nobody pays attention to who's in and out, and if you slip the night clerk a fifty he'll say he hasn't seen you."

"Fine," Pete said. She turned the Fury toward Hollywood, and dealt with the clerk at the Sunrise Motel while Jack took Kim to her room.

"Why're you doing this?" Kim said. "You're just going to piss them off, you know. And then I'll be right back where I started."

"You wouldn't have come with me if you believed that," Jack said. "You know Sanford and those gits back there want to take your kid and you know what would happen when they did. You're not like them, at least not all the way."

Kim sat on the bed, rotating her spine so it popped. "Fuckin' kid weighs a ton," she said. "They don't tell you when you get pregnant it's like having that thing from *Alien* growing inside you. Making everything swell up, making you puke nonstop, kicking you in the ribs all night."

Pete came in and shut the door. "This place is about as lovely as a sewage treatment plant in Aberdeen," she said, "but I don't think anyone human followed us. Most of these people wouldn't know if Jesus Christ himself was riding down Sunset on a pony at the head of a zombie parade."

"Is she your wife?" Kim said.

"No," Jack said, in concert with Pete. Pete shot him a look, then turned her attention to Kim.

"You must be hungry, luv. What can I bring you?"

"I like burgers," Kim said. "Burgers and chili fries."

"I'll be back," Pete said. Jack followed her to the door and caught her hand.

"You sure about this?" he said. Pete gave him a smile.

"I'll be fine. Can't hide in a shitty motel forever, can we? The girl's got to eat, and so do I." She turned her hand in his, and squeezed, before lifting his arm to examine it. "What happened to your jacket?"

"Something thought it was tasty," Jack said. Pete stood on tiptoe and planted a kiss on his cheek.

"Take it off. You look homeless." She left, and Jack locked the door after her and went about chalking a hex. Not that it would do shit against Abbadon, but it was familiar and he needed something to do.

Kim spoke from the bed. "She really loves you."

"Don't know about that," Jack said. "Tolerates, maybe."

Kim folded her hands over her stomach and swung her feet up on the bed. "Put the TV on. I don't want to hear the hooker in the next room faking her way to twenty bucks."

Jack turned the telly to a news program and sat next to Kim. "Got some experience with that?"

She sniffed. "That obvious?"

"People like Anna prey on people on the game, and junkies, and runaways. Lost souls. I doubt it was your fault."

"I had a kid," Kim said quietly. "Before this one. I was seventeen. He was born addicted to meth."

"I'm sorry," Jack said.

"When this happened, I was clean and I was living at Anna's," Kim said. "Getting fucked by her kinky friends wasn't so bad. She fed us and we weren't prisoners. Place to live. It wasn't rape. More than I can say for when I was hooking."

"Did you really think you could raise your kid in that place and everything would turn out fine?" Jack asked.

"I don't fucking know," Kim muttered. "I don't even know who the father is, but I do know the baby's going to be healthy this time and I'll take it from there."

"Until Abbadon takes it from you and uses it as a vessel for one of his pals," Jack said. "He screwed up with the last child. He won't take that chance with you."

Kim sniffed again, and in the light of the TV Jack saw wet lines on her face. "What am I supposed to do?" she demanded. "If it's not that, they'll still take the kid. That guy you came with, Sanford. He told Anna when I got it in me he wanted to adopt it. Legal and everything. I thought it'd be great—he's rich, and he could give the kid stuff I couldn't." Kim started to sob in earnest, her shoulders fluttering like wings. "When I found out . . . what he wanted it for . . . I knew this wouldn't be any different than my other boy. But you don't ask a man like Harlan Sanford questions. You just give him what he wants."

Jack peered through the curtains. Concentric cigarette burns let in the lights of the boulevard, the endless line of cars, and the hard diamond glitter of the Hollywood Hills beyond. "That you do," he murmured.

"Hey, where's your woman?" Kim said. "I'm fucking starving."

"Excellent question," Jack said. A burger shack sat diagonally across the parking lot from the motel, and he peered through the curtains again. Pete's small, thin shadow was nowhere to be found.

"Stay here," he told Kim, stepping onto the landing and shutting the door behind him. "Pete?" he called.

The parking lot was empty, mostly full of rusted-out cars and a few caravans, their windows covered with tattered curtains. "Pete!" he shouted, leaning over the rail to check the breezeway below.

"Hey!" A door banged open, and a shirtless bloke with a gut leaned out, glaring at Jack over piggy cheeks. "Shut the fuck up," he snarled.

Jack pointed a finger at him. "Go back in your room." He felt a wave of the Black batter against him, and knew from the man's expression that his eyes were flaring ghost blue.

The door slammed, and Jack started down the stairs. He'd panicked reflexively, and his heart was thumping fast enough that he could've just taken a snort of speed. "Pete!" he shouted. The motel sign in the window of the reception office glowed blue, telling him there was VACANCY . . . CLEAN ROOMS . . . AIR CONDITIONING. The sign flickered as he passed.

He jogged across the lot to the burger shack. The interior was lit with harsh bulbs that washed out all the color, from the faded food pictures hanging above the counter to the teenager swiping a mop half-heartedly across the gray floors. He looked up when Jack banged the door open. "Fryer's off. We're closing in ten minutes."

"You see a woman in here?" Jack asked. His heartbeat had taken on a rhythm, a drum line of panic. *No, no, no, no* . . . "Black hair, leather jacket, about so big?" He held out his hand to Pete's height.

The boy shrugged. "Nah, man. Nobody like that."

"Maybe I can help." Jack was only half-surprised to see Gator step out of the shadows of the corridor to the loo.

"Where is she?" he said. He pulled the Black to

him, felt his talent flare in his mind. He'd burn Gator where he stood if that was what it took, and he wouldn't feel one iota of regret.

"She's fine," Gator said. "You know, it didn't have to be this way. Y'all made it real difficult for us to do what needs to be done." He shook his head. "Mr. Sanford's real upset with the two of you. He had me put Miss Caldecott up in one of his properties as insurance."

"Insurance for what?" His hands were sweating, and he was numb, but not with the unearthly cold he'd felt when he'd killed Parker. This was fury, and he recognized it. Rage and Jack were old friends, drinking partners, had spent long evenings together when he was younger and more foolish. It gifted him with broken bones and busted teeth and stints in lockup, but rage was a good friend to have when you were looking at someone like Gator who'd just kidnapped your pregnant girlfriend.

"For Mr. Sanford," Gator said. "He has to make sure you won't get crazy and go off on him."

The door creaked again, and Sanford entered. He took a seat in the first booth by the door, and gestured Jack into the bench opposite. "I apologize for the hardball, Jack," he said.

Jack sat. He couldn't think of a better response. Well, he could burn Gator's face off and kick Sanford until even his own mother wouldn't recognize his corpse, but that wouldn't help Pete. He had to stay calm, for Pete. Get Sanford to tell him what he'd done with her. Play the game and not panic, not react like every bit of him was screaming to.

For once, he could keep it together long enough to actually be the one who made things right again.

"Isn't this nice?" Sanford said. He gestured at Gator, who slipped the teenager a few bills.

"Get that fryer goin', boy. Bacon cheeseburgers all around, and make me up a batch of those cheese fries. Extra cheese."

The teenager looked at the three of them in turn, and then shrugged and went behind the counter, hitting switches to turn on the lights and the cookers.

"In Hollywood we call this a sit-down, Jack," Sanford said. "A meeting between opposing parties to find a mutually beneficial outcome."

"Where is she, Sanford?" Jack splayed his palms flat on the table. If he could keep his eyes on them, he could stay calm long enough to figure a way out of this. The ends of his tattoos curled around the base of his thumbs, crept between the webbing of his fingers. The fury of the Morrigan wasn't going to do one fucking bit of good now. Pete depended on him not slagging Sanford off. She depended on him being clever, which didn't come naturally. Smashing someone in the face was much more instinctive.

"She's fine," Sanford said. "You think I'd manhandle a pregnant woman? You really have a low opinion of your fellow man, Jack."

"Things like you aren't men," Jack said. "A man wouldn't take a woman's baby to be used as a piece of fucking Tupperware for something like Abbadon."

"You really think that child would've had any

kind of life with somebody like Kim in a place like Anna's?" Sanford nodded his thanks to the teenager as he set down baskets of burgers and fries. "She was a junkie and a streetwalking whore when Anna found her. That's not a mother, Jack. That's a bitch who drops a litter."

He took a bite of his burger and licked his fingers. "You should try this. They know how to do meat right here."

Gator took a fistful of cheese fries and shoved them into his mouth. "Sure do. Just like home."

"In a way, Jack," Sanford said. "You owe me one. You knocked off Parker without so much as a sorry."

"Yeah, well," Jack said. "You let your pet monster off the chain, Sanford, and I put it down. You want to have a moment of silence? Maybe light a candle? Didn't know the two of you were so close."

Gator grabbed him by the back of his neck, slammed his head into the plastic tabletop, and held it there. Jack could smell the chili powder and grease on his fingertips. "He was my friend, asswipe."

"Gator." Sanford ticked his finger back and forth like a metronome. *One, two, three.* "That's enough."

"You and me ain't finished, boy," Gator whispered in Jack's ear. "Sooner or later, I'm gonna get you alone, and then the pain's going to come."

"Looking forward to it, darling," Jack grunted.

"Let him up," Sanford ordered. "Now."

"Sure, boss," Gator said, and Jack straightened up, rubbing feeling back into his cheek.

"Now's the part where you threaten again to kill

Pete if I don't help you, right?" Jack folded his arms. "Get on with it, then."

"That threat never went away," Sanford said. "But allow me to motivate you, rather than try more useless scare tactics. Abbadon knows you screwed him. He knows you tried to take his vessel away, and he won't stop until he finds you. You think a couple of bespelled junkies are the extent of his reach? They're not. Not by a long shot."

Jack gave voice to the whirlpool that had been brewing in his head since he'd found Kim. "What're you up to, Sanford? You know an awful lot about Abbadon for somebody who's only heard about him this morning. From me. Always a little bread-crumb when I got off the trail. Always a convenient helping hand."

He stood up, shoving his elbow into Gator's gut on purpose. "Fuck you and your game, Sanford. Either you tell me what you're really on about or I'm walking. I'll figure out where Pete is on my own, and you know what'll happen to you when I do."

Gator bared his teeth, gold gleaming almost black under the harsh light. "Maybe, but you know we'll mess her up 'forehand."

Jack turned his eyes on him. "You lay one finger on Pete and it'll be the last thing you live to regret. Make no mistake."

Sanford spread his hands. "This is all completely unnecessary posturing on your part, Jack. Fact is, if you knew the truth, you wouldn't have helped me."

"And now?" Jack said.

Sanford grinned, that maddening grin with vast emptiness behind it. "Now I suppose it doesn't make a difference. You needed persuading, and I persuaded you, and nobody needs to gnash their teeth over it. Do as I ask and Pete will be sound as a pound. That is the expression, correct?"

Jack found that rather debatable, personally, but he just nodded. Information over reaction. Calm over chaos. That was how Pete would do it. Pete would protect herself, and him, and Kim. She'd get to the bottom of it and find out what Sanford and Abbadon were really up to.

"Fine. You got me," Jack said. Sanford clapped his hands together and then wiped them with a wad of paper.

"Excellent. Gator, pay up and go get the whore. We can't have her running around in her condition."

Gator pulled a wad of cash from his pocket and shoved it at the teenager. "You did good, kid. Never saw nothing, right?"

"Y-yes, sir," the kid stammered. "Have a good night, sir."

Sanford escorted Jack to the same black SUV, but this time they both sat in the back seat. Presently, Gator came back, prehistoric brow set in a frown. "Whore's not there."

"Fuck," Sanford muttered, passing a hand over his face. "Abbadon can deal with her, then. Women are a pain in the ass, Jack. Don't let that one you've gotten saddled with tell you any different."

Gator drove, but they didn't go to Sanford's house. They drove far to the east, past the outlying bits of Los Angeles, past Riverside and Thousand Oaks and into the high desert, until Jack could look down the mountains behind him and see Los Angeles spread out like a handful of broken glass under a streetlamp, gleaming and shattered into a thousand fragments.

"Bright lights," Sanford said. "Blinding, really. Hard to see what's staring at you from the dark outside."

"I know what is," Jack said. "So where the fuck are we going?"

"To the truth," Sanford said, as the car slowed and they turned up a long drive, lined with the wispy, dancing forms of cypress trees. "About me, Abbadon, and all of it. What you wanted, isn't it?"

Jack looked up the drive to the dark shadow of the house beyond. The Black was thick here, almost thick enough to touch, springing from the center of the roof and swirling across his senses in a tsunami.

"Not really," he told Sanford, but he got out of the car, gravel crunching under his boots, and walked toward the deep well of the Black anyway.

PART THREE

RESURRECTION

"Kiss my ass."

—Last words of John Wayne Gacy

CHAPTER 22

There was silence when Jack approached the house, except for his boots on the gravel drive and the click of Gator's lighter as he lit one of his brown, wormlike fags. No birds, no coyotes, not even wind disturbed the space around the house.

Places like this were rare, places where the Black exerted such perfect control over the environment of the daylight world. Usually they were concentration camps, mass graves, sites of massacre or cold-blooded murder. Jack had backpacked in Belgium and stood in the perfect stillness of the Ardennes Forest, watched the green- and gray-uniformed spirits flit among the trees, and heard the absolute stillness of the Black, which had absorbed the deaths of thousands on the soft, spongy ground.

Sanford at his shoulder made him jump. He tried to disguise it as working the kinks from his neck, but Sanford's grin told him he hadn't managed it. "Aren't you going to ask me where we are?"

Jack shrugged. "Wouldn't want to rob you of tour-guiding."

"You know," Sanford said, starting for the front steps, broad as three bodies laid end to end, "that whole smartass defense mechanism isn't fooling anyone." He looked back at Jack, his eyes pools in the low light. "Everyone is afraid of something, Jack. Even you."

Gator shoved Jack from behind. "Move it, pecker-wood."

The doors opened at Sanford's approach, and he shoved them wide. "You said you wanted the truth, Jack. So come in."

Jack looked up out of habit. Nothing was carved into the doorframe, and no hexes hung in place, but the psychic void inside would be enough to deter all but the most ignorant of mages. Which placed him squarely there, he supposed. Jack Winter, tilting at windmills and leaping off cliffs.

The foyer was laid out in tiles that rang under his heels. Dead leaves skittered in the corners when the door shut. A fountain dominated the center, a nymph being swallowed by a many-eyed, tentacled sea beast. The nymph had long lines of rust traveling down her breasts and the apex of her thighs, water long gone.

"Nice place," he said. Sanford flipped an old push-button switch and a single bulb in the chandelier above flickered to life.

"It gets the job done," he said. "Built by an orange

farmer in the twenties. Howard Hughes stayed here. And Basil Locke bought it in 1939."

Gator was still in the doorway, shifting from foot to foot, and Sanford snapped his fingers at him. "For fuck's sake, nothing is going to bite you. Get in here."

Jack watched the big man's back stiffen. Maybe Gator wasn't as colossal a moron as he appeared. If Jack had a choice, he wouldn't be here either. While Sanford puttered around, he went over the list. Pete wouldn't be here—he would've felt her, if she was anywhere on the grounds. She wouldn't be at Sanford's house. Too obvious for a man who loved a twist ending. That left a myriad of places Jack hadn't guessed at yet, which meant he had to go along with Sanford a little longer. He just hoped he didn't lose his temper and stave the bastard's face in before he made sure Pete was safe.

"Locke made a couple of films overseas," Sanford said. He walked, turning on lights as he went, until they stood in a vast atrium that overlooked the view of Los Angeles, far in the distance. "Genre stuff, nothing that the international audience was interested in. But he met a nice young man named Heinrich Himmler in Germany, in 1938. What a Russian-born lapsed Jew was doing partying with fledgling Nazis, I couldn't tell you, but he picked up some interesting theories. Did you know that both Himmler and Hitler were deeply involved with the Thule?"

"Everybody knows that," Jack said. "It's not exactly a state secret."

"The Nazis didn't understand the Black," Sanford said. "Didn't understand that to use magic you had to have your frequency tuned in the first place. Have the knack. But Locke did. And when he came back, he bought this mansion. Spent more and more time up here. After 1942, he never made another film. He died here, in obscurity, with massive debts. A couple of studio heads kicked in and bought the place out of pity, used it for a few location shoots, but as you can tell . . ." He gestured around the empty room. A single ratty sofa, the kind of plaid that always seemed to be stained with beer and cum no matter how clean it was, sat in one corner, its arms chewed by rats.

"Not exactly a comforting sort of air to the place," Jack said.

"Film crews suffered a rash of unexplained deaths, a wing caught fire in the seventies and burned some no-name actress," Sanford said. "After the fire, the estate came looking for investors, and they contacted me." He grinned, walking to the windows. Outside, a swimming pool full of dead branches and a foot or so of stinking sewer-tinged water glowed with oily life. "I knew right away what had gone on here."

Something to rend the Black so thoroughly it was a dead vortex across all his senses. Jack tried to keep his expression neutral. Sanford didn't have a talent, was nothing more than a groupie. What he actually knew about magic would probably be a wild guess, at best.

"Locke didn't just collect esoteric shit," Sanford said. "He found something much better. Something tangible." He pressed his palms against the glass. "He found a way to pass through just like light through a window."

Jack and Sanford turned as one when the front doors swung open again and a shadow rolled across the foyer, causing the light bulb to explode.

"Don't sugarcoat it," Abbadon said, standing in the doorway. "It sounds so much better when you just say it out loud."

Jack could scream all he wanted inside his own head, that Sanford had fucked him and that Abbadon was going to take what he wanted out of his hide. Reacting, though, wasn't going to do any good. He could always go through the window, if he didn't mind shedding a little blood, but then where the fuck would he go? Miles from anywhere, in terrain he didn't know, he might as well smear himself in marinade and leave himself for the coyotes.

Sanford's jaw ticked when Abbadon approached. "Took you long enough," he said.

Abbadon shrugged. "Jackie-boy isn't going anywhere. He loves his little sperm receptacle too much to misbehave." He reached out and patted Jack on the cheek. "That someone like you could actually love something, even a useless whore like that, is kind of sweet. Almost gives you faith in humanity or some shit."

"Can we please get this moving?" Sanford said. "Tell him what needs to happen and get a move on."

Abbadon sighed and gave Jack a conspiratorial look. "Humans. Always got their dicks out, waving them around. Fucking pain in the ass, am I right?"

"I'd like to know," Jack said. "Since I'm apparently to be terrorized into helping you with whatever it is."

"Like Bill Shakespeare over there was saying," Abbadon said. "Old Basil Locke found a way to pass between the veils. Not just from Black to daylight— any stupid fuck can do that if they've got a little talent or are tripping hard enough. He found a way to cross back and forth." Abbadon grinned at Jack, showing his full row of teeth. "Basil Locke found a portal to Hell."

CHAPTER 23

Jack felt his lip curl. "You're pulling my bloody leg."

Abbadon shrugged. "Believe it or not. I do." He looked to Sanford. "He does." He approached Jack and put a finger under his chin. "And you do too. Deep down in that rotten little human soul of yours."

Jack slapped the hand away. "I do believe I can do without you feeling me up."

"Touchy." Abbadon held up his hands. "I'll make this simple. Locke *did* find a way to open a gate between Hell and here, but he could never manage it. The spirit and the flesh and all that crap. But I'm not human. I'm going to do it, and you're going to help me."

"And why, pray tell," Jack said, "would I ever help you with something like that? I have to live in this world, mate. I don't fancy a giant gaping maw into Mordor in the middle of southern California."

"Because you don't give a fuck about this world." Abbadon drew close. "But you do give a fuck about sweet little Petunia, and as I believe Harlan here has already stated, we're all prepared to take turns doing unspeakable things to her if you don't follow what I'm about to tell you to the letter."

Abbadon knew he had him—this was just twisting the knife in. Making him say the words, to know they'd bent Jack over properly. "Pete doesn't have anything to do with this," he said. "Of course I'll do what you want. You know I will."

"You're wrong about that, you know," Sanford said. He snapped his fingers at Gator. "Go get the bags." He faced Jack again. "Petunia isn't some poor little waif caught up in all this. She made that deal with Belial. She's the one who caught the eye of the Hecate. Hell, Jack, if it wasn't for her, you'd be dead in some tip with a needle still dangling out of your arm, and the world would be a better place."

Jack shrugged. "Probably. But then who would be around to listen to you jabber on?"

Sanford grinned. "In this town, you can pay people to listen to you. What I need from you is a little more complicated. Abbadon and I have been chatting—have been ever since I had that crime scene tranced when I heard you were in town sniffing around the old murders, so you're right—I did lie to you, shine you on when you came to me with your grand plan to spy on the fuck mages, and for that I apologize. But it was a lie of necessity, for the greater good. Not that you'd understand."

Gator returned with a leather case, dropped it, and retreated to the corner of the room. Sanford opened it and gestured Jack over. "Locke's ritual is pretty complete. But to open a gate, you need a key. A blood key, and it can't just be any old blood." He grinned. "Demon blood. And there's one particular demon that's very attached to you. When you fell into my lap, and brought Don with you, it was perfect. I couldn't have pitched a better serve."

Belial. Of course. That collector bullshit would be a fine cover to trap and use your very own demon. If you were stupid enough to open a portal to Hell, you were certainly the type who'd think a demon would sit still for a flaying.

"Let me ask you a question," Jack said. "What exactly do you think is going to happen when you drain Belial and open this Hell-hole, and about ten thousand of his closest friends come pouring out to make sushi from your liver?"

"They're not going to do shit," Abbadon said. "I belong in Hell, and Hell is where I stay. The Princes won't stand against me when they see what I've become."

"Become a great twat, you mean," Jack muttered.

Sanford thrust chalk into his hands. "Belial comes when you call. Get him here and we'll consider your part in this done."

"We'll even overlook that little stunt you pulled at the ranch," Abbadon said. "And you can go on to have babies, get old, and die, secure in the knowledge that you helped put right one of the greatest travesties of this age or any other."

Jack knelt and started to chalk a circle into the floor. Sanford would just hand him over to Abbadon if he didn't, and Abbadon would just find new and inventive ways to torture him. "Let me ask you a question," he said to Abbadon. "You ever get tired of the sound of your own voice?"

"It was all I had for so long," Abbadon said. "Can't be too picky."

The marks to summon a demon weren't particularly different from the marks to call anything—a ghost, a hex, whatever you wanted. Jack let his hands work the familiar symbols while he devoted his brainpower to thinking over the clusterfuck he'd walked into. Pete wasn't who Sanford and Abbadon were really interested in—she was leverage, and they'd leave her be until Jack kicked up a fuss about doing what they needed done. Basil Locke's door into Hell sounded like a fairy tale on the surface, but all good fairy tales had a grain of truth.

If Abbadon did open a doorway into Hell from the daylight world, what would spill out? He was insane to think he could stand against the Princes and all of their legions, but there were more than a few citizens of Hell who'd welcome the chance to turn the world into their own private resort.

Sanford checked his watch. "You almost done there? I heard you were supposed to be good at this."

"D'you want it fast, or d'you want it right?" Jack sat back on his heels, chalk dust gritty on his fingertips.

Abbadon sniffed. "Quit stalling, Winter. What do you care if Belial bites it, anyway? He did to you

exactly what he did to me—locked you away in
Hell and put his claws into you so deep you can
never escape."

The freak had a point, even if Jack was loath
to admit it. Belial was a snake. A different breed
of snake than Abbadon, but they shared common
blood. Wasn't it Belial's fault he was in this situation? *Or Pete's fault.*

Pete had done what she'd done out of desperation. Belial had taken advantage of her. Snakes
were good at finding the vulnerable underbelly.

Of course, if Pete hadn't been trying to keep him
out of Hell in the first place, she'd never have had
to make a deal with a demon. *So it's all your fault,
Winter. As usual.*

He stood and tossed the chalk away. "There. Can
I go now, headmaster?"

"Stay," Abbadon purred. "Stay and see what's
going to happen. Trust me, Jack—you're going to
want to be able to say 'I was there.'" He put his
hand on Jack's shoulder, nails digging through the
leather. "Do it."

Jack felt a tremor run through him, the same
heart-stopping cold that had gripped him when
he'd killed Parker, but he shook it off. "Belial," he
said. "Demon of Hell. I call upon you to appear."

The words weren't really important, but Jack
figured it couldn't hurt to give Abbadon a show.
For a long moment, nothing happened at all. The
Black remained a void. Jack didn't know if his talent would even work in this place, this dead spot
that sucked all the magic around it in like a hungry,

dying star, but then he felt the slithering of a presence shifting into his sensory plane, the velvety sensation of a demon's talent against his sight.

Belial didn't shimmer or appear in a puff of smoke—you blinked and there he was. He caught sight of Abbadon and lowered his head. "Fuck me."

Abbadon clapped his hands together. "Haven't even started yet. Trust me, when I fuck you—you know it."

Belial looked over at Jack. "Did I tell you, crow-mage, or did I tell you?"

"You did," Jack agreed. "Fact is, I don't owe you shit. You were never going to let Pete out of that bargain she made, and you're never going to leave us be."

Belial shook his head. "Ye of little faith, Jack. Have I ever welshed on a deal? Have I ever tried to bend you over?" His voice rose. "No. Because I'm not like that *thing* over there. I'm not an animal."

Abbadon stepped to Belial, mindful of the chalk, and cracked him across the face. "That's enough out of you, shit for brains."

Belial ran his tongue over his bloody teeth, and spat. "So what's the plan, dogfuck? Going to poke me with sticks and feel better about your sorry-arse lot in life?"

"Better," Abbadon said, and snapped his fingers at Sanford and Jack. "Get it down."

Sanford went to a pulley system anchored in the wall and unhooked the rope, snarling at Jack. "Help me."

Jack gripped the rope. He was close enough. He

could throw a hex on Sanford and be out of here before anyone had time to get across the room to him. Except Abbadon didn't need to touch him to fuck him up. And running now would only help him, not Pete and not the kid. Nor Kim, and Kim's spawn. Abbadon still needed a new body.

He watched the iron chandelier lower to just above waist height, one of those flat black affairs shaped like a wagon wheel. Small pyramid points rose from the iron rods, and chains dangled from between the spaces for candles.

Abbadon grabbed Belial by the back of the neck. "See that, demon? Get a good look, because that's your final resting place."

"It's cute how you think this is actually going to all work out for you," Belial said. "Like you won't get torn apart by the dogs of Hell the moment I get out of here."

"That's where you're wrong." Abbadon pushed Belial down, face first onto the metal rack. Jack couldn't help wincing when he heard the iron spikes bite into flesh. Belial let out a soft grunt, but that was all. Tough bastard, Jack thought. Were it him, he'd be screaming.

"Lift," Abbadon said. "Hang 'im high."

"Great flick," Sanford said. "Gary Cooper is the man."

"Harlan, shut the fuck up," Abbadon said. "Nobody cares, nobody's interested. Just shut up and hoist this fucker."

Sanford muttered, but he tugged at the rope, and Jack helped him raise Belial back to ceiling height.

The demon didn't make a sound, just stared impassively as his blood droplets painted a mosaic on the floor.

Why didn't he fight? Jack shot Belial a sidelong glance. Why didn't he break out, throw down with Abbadon, whip it out and see who was bigger once and for all?

This place was poison for magic. Maybe it was poison for demons as well. That had been Basil Locke's big secret—turning a patch of ground into a dead zone for creatures that could rip his face off, and use it to build his doorway.

He had to hand it to Locke, smart bastard. Not that it was going to help him, or Belial, one fucking ounce.

Abbadon stepped back and looked to Sanford. "Now we wait for the piggy to bleed out, and then we knock on Hell's back door and see who's home."

"I know that," Sanford said, spine straightening. "I'm the one who found Locke's work, after all."

" 'Course you did," Abbadon said. He pointed at Gator. "Your boy there is looking a little green. Need to send him to the nurse's office?"

"Ignore him," Sanford said. "He's a pussy without his big boyfriend around."

Abbadon knelt and smeared Belial's blood into a rough circle. There was a lot of it, more than a human could lose and still be walking and talking. "It's all physics," Abbadon told Belial. "You think you're floating in a soap bubble, impenetrable by anyone except your filthy blood. But all you have to do is twist the magic, use it to tether yourself to Hell. And then you can pass straight through, you and anyone else. Locke was a genius, when you think about it."

"He was a crazy bastard," Belial said. His voice was soft, softer than Jack had ever heard it, and there was a definite knife edge of pain. "If you could open a doorway, don't you think he'd have done? What, he just left this precious gift for you shiftless gits?" He gritted his teeth as more blood poured out. "You can bleed me dry, Abbadon, but in the end you're going back to Hell, and back to the same spot we put you, because that's the way of things. The natural order has moved on. You're a relic, and you're . . ."

He gave a scream as Abbadon dipped his finger into the demon's blood. It fizzed and boiled, and Belial's skin rippled with boils before quieting. Pink foam leaked from his nose and the corners of his mouth.

"Tell me what I am again," Abbadon said. "I dare you, fuckstick."

"Enough," Sanford said. "Now that we have the circle there come the words, and then the key to open the door." He gestured. "Gator, get over here."

Jack perked up. Finally, an opening. Sanford was smart, but his hard men weren't, and nothing was more dangerous than a dumb, pissed-off thug. "Wouldn't do it," he said.

Abbadon and Sanford both glared at him. "Shut up," Sanford said. "You've done your bit. You be a good boy and maybe I'll drive you home with your virtue intact."

"Really, mate," Jack continued, locking eyes with

Gator. "You didn't seriously think that you were going to skip out of here with all your fingers and toes. Not once the men started appearing from thin air and the blood magic began."

Gator looked at him, back to Sanford. "You don't know what you're talking about."

"Think about it. Key? That's human sacrifice, mate. That's *you*." Jack folded his arms. "You're not leaving here alive, Gator. Neither of us are."

"Be quiet," Abbadon hissed. "It doesn't matter. What's he going to do, shoot me?"

Gator's mouth dropped open, revealing a plethora of cavities behind his gold grin. "You motherfuckers!" he spat. "After everything I done for you. All the shit that I cleaned up for you, Harlan . . ."

"Oh, good lord," Sanford said. "You're replaceable, Gator. Parker was the one I was upset over losing. You're an overweight kiddie-fiddler with delusions of Satanism from Assrape, Louisiana. You think I can't find another one of you—a dozen— any time I wanted?"

Gator pulled his gun, which was all the distraction Jack had hoped for. Gator was panicked, and his shots went wide, picking holes out of the wall of windows, but he turned tail and ran, still shooting, shots spanging wildly off the plaster and tile, until his gun clicked empty and he simply fled.

Sanford stared after him. "Well, shit," he said.

"No matter," Abbadon said. He looked at Jack. "What exactly did you hope to accomplish with that, Jackie?" He raised a hand. "Never mind. I didn't have my heart set on that fat fuck." Abbadon looked at Sanford, and Jack thought that really, a man as smart as Harlan Sanford should have seen this coming.

Still, he screamed and tried to run, just like they all did. Abbadon grabbed him, shoved him over the line of the blood circle, and thrust a fist into his back. Sanford choked, a little blood sprayed from between his lips, and his eyes bulged. Abbadon let him drop, the gaping wound in his back wide as a cannon shot.

"Now," Abbadon said. "Now the veil is lifted. Now I return to my rightful place, and leave this stinking world behind. By the blood of my enemies, I open the doorway between the two worlds, the way back to the land of my birth and my blood."

Abbadon held up his own wrist, and a void appeared, dribbling his own blood into the circle. "The doorway opens. I am released."

"You forgot something," Jack told him. He knelt on the floor, smearing the small spot into a symbol. The demon blood caused feedback all through his body, into his sight, but he ignored it.

"What's that?" Abbadon said.

Jack licked the crimson spots from his fingers and stood. "You're not the only clever bastard who can do blood magic."

Banishment was much more difficult than summoning. To call something to you was simple—demons wanted to be called, wanted you to be desperate enough to need them. Getting rid of them once they had a foothold was much harder. Something like Abbadon, vastly powerful and strong-willed, would be impossible with his own blood, but with Belial's, it was like hitting the bastard with a tank.

Abbadon screamed, just once, and then vanished, leaving only a pop of air in his place. Belial grinned down at Jack. "If I ever had doubts about you, boy . . . no longer." He flexed his wrists, starting a fresh spatter of blood. "Care to get me down from here?"

"Piss off," Jack told him. "You can rot there for all I care."

"You should care," Belial said.

Jack stopped on his way out and looked back. Belial was grinning. Somebody in his position, demon or not, shouldn't grin. It meant he knew something Jack didn't, which was never the situation he wanted to be in. "Yeah?" he said. "Why? Out of the goodness of my heart?"

"Please," Belial said. "You've got less goodness in that shriveled lump of coal than I have appreciation for the music of Hall and Oates. No, Jack, you should care because that Sanford bloke wasn't talking bollocks." He shifted, trying to extricate himself from the spikes, and then grimaced. "Come on, get me down. Even I can't poof my way out of a cold iron torture rack."

"Poof being the operative word," Jack muttered. He could keep walking and leave Belial to think about things, or he could cut him down and have a demon in his debt. Not a difficult choice.

The chandelier was heavy, and Belial crashed to the ground. "Fuck me," he said, extricating himself from the spikes. "You're not much of a big strong sort, are you?"

His white shirt was stained with continents of blood, and his natty suit was shredded across the thighs, arms, and chest. The demon straightened his tie. "Obliged, Jack. You always were a stand-up sort in a pinch." He gestured at the circle. "You mind? I am rather indisposed at the moment."

Jack scuffed his boot across the chalk and blood, and Belial stepped out, letting out a long breath. "Can't wait to see the back of this place. Let's go."

"Wait," Jack told him. He bent down beside Sanford, who was still sucking air despite the hole in his guts. "Where is she?" he asked.

Sanford wheezed, what might have been a laugh before Abbadon had rearranged his innards. "Really? She's . . . all you want?"

Jack plunged his hand into Sanford's wound, grabbed a handful of something soft and warm, and squeezed it. Sanford howled, body jerking. "Where's Pete?" Jack said. "You're on the way out, mate. You don't get to make the rules."

"No," Sanford croaked. "I know where I'm going. Same place you are. See you around . . ." He gurgled, and died, without further comment.

"Shit." Jack straightened up and swiped Sanford's blood and guts onto his denim. "They still have her," he told Belial.

"I'm sure this is a cause for alarm in your small rodent brain," Belial said. "But Abbadon is going to come roaring back here like a freight train any moment, and he's not going to be in a charming mood. Might I suggest we not be here?"

"Fine," Jack said. "Do your *Star Trek* trick, then, and shift us out."

Belial coughed and swiped at his mouth with the back of his hand. "When I'm healthy, moving through space-time isn't easy with a human in tow. I'm barely standing, you git. I'm not going to perform tricks."

Jack sighed. "There's a car outside, but I can't drive and that bloke I ran off had the keys."

"Capital." Belial coughed again. "What do humans do in this situation, then? Call for a taxi?"

"I usually call Pete," Jack said. "But Sanford has her. And now that he's dead, fuck knows what'll happen." Couldn't think about that now. Had to stay calm, had to stay clever, if he ever wanted to see her again.

"She's a lot smarter than you," Belial said. "I wouldn't be overly concerned."

The night outside was warm, and a wind brushed across Jack's face and moved the trees along the drive. Belial inhaled. "I'm not going to last much longer up here. Unless you want a dead demon on your hands, Jack—and before you ask, yes, I can kick just like your kind can—then we need to be gone from this place."

Jack spread his arms. "And where do you suggest we go?"

Belial smiled. "Where poor little lost Abbadon wants to go. Home."

CHAPTER 24

He had to be mad, Jack decided. That was the only explanation for allowing Belial to talk him into going back to the place he'd tried with everything he had to avoid, had agreed to let the Morrigan change him to escape.

He was changed. That was a fact he couldn't ignore anymore. The scene with Parker proved it, and more than that, the new life he felt crawling under his skin. The Morrigan had what she wanted. She had him, body and soul, because he owed her his life. If it wasn't for her, he'd still be languishing in Hell.

His vision cleared, like coming back from a sharp blow to the head, and he saw that he and Belial stood in a street, slimy cobbles under their feet and orange gaslights spitting pollution into the air.

"Where are we?" he said.

"Hell, of course," Belial said, and coughed up a few droplets of black blood onto his rumpled shirt.

"Not any part of Hell I've seen," Jack muttered. "Looks more like Sweeney Todd's back garden."

"You don't let the prisoners walk into the warden's sitting room and put their boots on his furniture," Belial said. "The souls in Hell are in torment, Jack. The demons live here."

He mounted the steps to a narrow stone house with a door shaped like a keyhole that swung open at his approach. "Well, come in," he said. "You stand out there on the street, you're liable to end up as an attraction at the next Carnival of Souls."

Jack followed Belial up the steps. If he'd been told that he'd be following a demon into his nest, that the demon would be the one inviting him in, he'd have laughed in the teller's face, and then probably hit them for good measure, to knock some sense back into them.

"All of you live in snug little houses, then?" Jack said. Belial mounted the stairs and Jack followed. The house inside was done in shades of black and red, all very smooth and masculine, the sort of flat a banker or a lawyer in the City would own.

"Some live in houses," Belial said. "Some live in abbatoirs and some prefer to float in a void of nothing, listening to the screams of souls when they're in their private space." He shrugged. "Takes all kinds." He opened a wardrobe and took out a clean shirt and tie, shedding the ruined pair.

Jack wandered to the window, looking over the chimney pots of the street to the great black towers of Hell, billowing smoke in the distance. The Princes lived there, was the rumor, watched over their domain of ruined souls, high and inscrutable, just like the fictional God Jack's mum had tried to frighten him with.

He watched Belial, too, in the reflection. The demon had twin black marks down his back, curved like scythe blades, but the wounds he'd suffered at Abbadon's hands had already faded. "This isn't my real body," Belial said. "I figured I shouldn't overload you with all the sights at once."

"Didn't think you'd choose a pasty little midget voluntarily," Jack said. Belial put on his fresh shirt and twitched his cuffs.

"They aren't wings, either." He turned to Jack and showed his pointed teeth. "Saw you peeking."

"I wouldn't care if they were," Jack said.

"No angels," Belial said. "No God."

"Amen," Jack said.

"I'm one of the Named," Belial said. "We all have the mark on us, the mark of creation. Given by that bastard Abbadon, in point of fact, but that's all it is."

"Got to sting," Jack said. "Bloke who made you, who you fucked up the arse and locked away, is free and waving the bird in your faces."

"Abbadon isn't going to be free for long," Belial said softly. He tied his tie and went to a black lacquer box on the chest, pulling out a ruby stickpin and affixing it. "That's better," he said with a sigh. "Now, let's see if we can't do something about you."

"Me?" Jack shied away when Belial reached for him. "Fuck off. 'M not your makeover project."

"If you're going to an audience at the Triumverate," Belial said, "then you need to be dressed as something other than a hobo."

Jack felt his eyebrows go up, while his guts dropped through Belial's posh blood-colored carpet. "Excuse me?"

Belial slapped him on the shoulder. "You're a lucky man, Jack Winter. You're going to be the first living bloke in over five hundred years to meet the Princes of Hell."

CHAPTER 25

The Hell that Belial led Jack through was nothing
like the dreams he'd had. This Hell was a mass of
corridors made of stone and iron, veiled in steam.
Machines clanked from far below his feet, and noxious yellow smoke poured from crooked chimneys
that bent in over the street like arthritic fingers.

"Can I ask you something?" Jack stopped, patting himself down and finding that his fags had
made the journey along with the rest of him.

"You can ask," Belial said, pushing open an iron
gate and leading them down an alley. "Can't promise I'll answer."

Jack lit his fag with the tip of his finger. His talent,
at least part of it, was still at work. That was good.
If he had to shoot his way out, his guns were still
loaded. "This isn't some black hole deal, right? Go
to Narnia and come back a hundred years later?"

Belial laughed. "When you go to Narnia, time in

the real world stays exactly the same, first off," he said. "You're thinking of fairyland or some rot. Second, no. You're not going to walk out of Hell and find everyone zipping about on jetpacks."

"So why keep me here?" Jack said. "You're looking back to your usual reptilian self. You don't need me."

"I don't think you understand the unique position you've put yourself in," Belial said. "First, you slag off the four ancients who've escaped from Hell into your plane, and then you get mixed up with the one human bastard crazy enough to help them open Locke's door back down to the Pit. Nobody in Hell is taking their eyes off you, Jack. Not for a second. Where this ride stops, not even the Princes know."

He led them up a staircase into a long square, lined with more of the noxious gas lamps, which ended in a long flight up steps going into the tallest of the towers Jack had seen from his flat. The square was deserted, piles of ash lighter than snow blowing to and fro across the cobbles.

"You can't expect me to believe that a bloke who made terrible movies and got his jollies with Nazis actually found a way to cross back and forth from Hell," Jack said. "Bit of a complex way to get a laugh."

"Wasn't for a laugh," Belial said. "Now, when you go before the Triumverate, let me do the talking. I know it's hard for you to keep that great gob shut, but trust me, if you want to continue to be alive when you leave Hell this time, do it."

"Trust you?" Jack said. "There's a laugh."

Belial shot him an irate glare. "Have I done one thing since those fuckwits grabbed me to make you think you can't trust me? The enemy of my enemy, Jack. That's you. Now move your arse, they're waiting."

Jack followed Belial to a set of metal doors, the kind you'd find in a mental hospital or a prison. A demon sat in front of it at a metal desk, tapping his fingers against a clipboard. A red phone sat at his elbow, the sort you could use to summon Batman. A single light blinked atop it.

The demon himself was a bat-eared horror, long teeth pressing his black lips into a distorted shape. He wore a black uniform and peaked cap, and looked up at Belial's approach. "General," he said. "You're expected."

"I know that," Belial said. The demon looked Jack over.

"Go in," he said, and then spat on the floor beside Jack's boot, an acidic gob that sizzled when it hit the lino. "They've been waiting for you."

"Scavenger," Belial muttered as he pushed open the door. "One of Azeroth's boys. Disgusting little shits. They roost all over the City and crap on everything."

The demon picked up the red phone as the doors shut and barked something in a hissing, screeching language that caused Jack's eye to twitch. Mercifully, the doors slammed, and he found himself in a low room, light tubes flickering overhead.

"This is the Triumverate?" he said.

Belial straightened his tie and made sure his cuf-flinks were perfectly aligned. "You were expecting Lucifer's golden throne?"

"Well, no, but . . ." Jack looked down at the cracked lino, the brick walls painted a dozen times, bubbling with paint the color of pus. "This looks like the dole office my mum's boyfriend used to drag me into to con the case worker out of extra fag money."

"Just stand there and try not to say anything stupid," Belial muttered. "Even if that is a practi-cally impossible task for you."

The tubes at the far end of the room snapped to life, and Jack saw a long low table, and behind it three figures. The one in the center gestured. "Step forward."

Belial jabbed Jack in the small of his back, and he moved. There was no Black here, no way to get a read on what was sitting in front of him. He'd just have to smile and hope for the best.

"Jack Winter." Belial cleared his throat. "The Triumverate, the Princes of Hell—Beelzebub, Azrael, and Baal. Gentlemen, this is . . ."

"We know the crow-mage, Belial," the one on the left snapped. Jack guessed that was Beelzebub. Belial ducked his head.

"Of course, sir."

"I suppose you think you're very clever." Azra-el's voice sounded like bodies being dragged over gravel. The Princes' faces were in shadow, which didn't lessen the feeling that Jack was being weighed, judged, and readied for his sentence.

"Most of the time, yeah," he said. "I get by."

Belial choked slightly beside him. "For fuck's sake, shut up," he grunted.

"You were tasked by Belial to return the four prisoners to their catacomb," said the last. Baal was a tall, thin shadow, wearing an all-black suit in contrast to Belial's snappy white number. "You failed."

"My fault," said Belial. "I asked the crow-mage for assistance and I expected too much of him. He's only human."

"We're aware of what he is," Azrael snapped. "Doesn't change the fact that you're a fuck-up and a miserable little snake, Belial."

"Calm down," Baal said. "Nothing to be gained by shouting."

"This has gone on too long already," Beelzebub snarled. "The ancients have found Locke's books. They came close enough thanks to your stupidity, and I'll have assurances they won't come so close again one way or the other."

"I can put it right," Belial said. "I know things that Abbadon doesn't. He doesn't understand humans the way I do."

"If you knew so much," Azrael grunted, "he never would have broken from the catacombs in the first place."

"That's not fair, sir," Belial started. "Nergal . . ."

"Nergal is not your concern at this time," said Baal. "You fucked up, Belial. You spend far too much time in the daylight world, among the human meat, and it's affected your perceptions. You're fat and slow. Your obsession with the crow-mage has brought you here, and it's time for consequences."

Jack looked to Belial, and he saw a bead of moisture work its way down the demon's temple. Belial was pissing himself in fear. That could be bad or good for Jack. Jack looked back at the Triumverate. They leaned in, shadowed heads bowed, and then Azrael stood up.

"Crow-mage, stay. Belial, you are relieved."

"No," Belial cried. "No, sir, give me a chance . . ."

The doors banged open, and a pair of demons wearing the same black uniforms and jackboots as the one in the hall came in. These were tall, with bulging foreheads and chests their black tunics barely contained. Fenris. Jack had seen them before. They were the big, hungry bastards of the demon world, hunters and trackers that would just as soon leave teethmarks on your tibia as look at you.

"Shit," Belial muttered. "Shit, shit, shit."

"Things not going as you expected, snake?" Jack muttered.

"Does this bloody look like it's going well?" Belial hissed. "You don't get a warning in your file, Jack. The Princes are going to liquidate me. I got one chance to bring Abbadon back and thanks to you and your insistence that you know better it's fucked backward and sideways."

The Fenris gripped Belial by the arms, their crimson lips pulling back to reveal rows of fangs.

"Wait," Jack said to the Princes.

Beelzebub tapped one finger on the table. His

nails were pure white, curved like a cat's claws. "You're speaking for yourself now, crow-mage?"

"Way I see it," Jack said. "You lot got egg on your faces when Nick Naughton got as far as calling up Nergal. It was so important that he stayed under wraps, you'd make sure of it. Same with Basil Locke and his ruddy portal or whatever it is. *You* three think you're untouchable, and now somebody's shown you you're not. Got to sting the ego, just a bit."

Azrael leaned over the table, and Jack saw white eyes, a long pale face, the sort of face that belonged to a thing that had lived in the dark for a long while, navigating by touch and sound. "Do you want to die today, crow-mage?"

"If you want to get the Morrigan and her kind down on your arse, then be my guest." Jack folded his arms. His stomach was quavering and his heart was thudding hard against his ribs, hard enough that the fat veins in his neck throbbed. He didn't know if the threat of the Morrigan was enough to dissuade the Princes from turning him into a wall ornament, but it had been enough for Belial to void their bargain for his soul, so it had to count for something. Just what the something was, he wouldn't let himself think about until he was someplace other than Hell.

"Belial's not wrong," Jack kept on. Azrael listened, flat nostrils flaring away from his skeletal face. Jack looked at the Fenris, standing implacable behind them. He'd never tangled with a Fenris.

Run the fuck away from one, sure. But taken one in a stand-up fight? He'd be shredded.

"Belial has failed," Baal said. "He's no longer of any use to us."

"I think you're wrong there," Jack said. "Because Abbadon still needs a demon to open Locke's doorway, and you know what they say." He spread his hands. "Better the devil you know."

Azrael cocked his head. "What are you proposing, crow-mage? You may be the Morrigan's pet, but a pet can still be a nuisance." He smiled, revealing a toothless mouth with a long, serpentine blue tongue. "Choose your next words very, very carefully."

"Let us go back upstairs," Jack said. "Abbadon will come after Belial, you get Abbadon and his backup singers, and then you can do whatever you want with the lot of them."

"And I suppose in exchange for this, you go free," Beelzebub said. "We're not idiots, Winter. Idiots don't stay in these seats while all below them are scheming for their heads."

"Never said you were, darling," Jack said. The room was cold but he was as soaked as Belial was, his T-shirt sticking to his skin like cold, clammy hands.

"So what do you want?" Azrael rasped. "Nothing is free, crow-mage. What's your bargain?"

"Leave me and Pete and our kid the fuck alone from now on," Jack said. "No demons sniffing around. No Belial trying to collect on whatever debts he thinks we owe. Point of fact, if I see one fucking bloke stinking of sulfur darkening my doorway from now until the day I die, I'm walking out right now and I'll see you all when you're roasting on Abbadon's victory fire with a spit shoved up your arse."

Baal started to laugh. It wasn't a pleasant sound. It was the sound, Jack decided, of several small animals in excruciating pain. "Oh, I like him," he purred. "He's got some swinging brass ones, doesn't he?"

"You'd be better off showing some of that," Azrael told Belial. "Why should we think that you can send Abbadon back from whence he came, crow-mage, when a Named demon of Hell can't manage the task?"

"Put Nergal's lights out, didn't I?" Jack said. "And from what I've heard, Abbadon is a fluffy pup in comparison. A veritable ray of fuckin' sunshine." He wasn't, but the only chance for Pete was for Jack to get out of Hell, and the only way he was doing that was by talking. Talking was the one thing he was always good at—he could talk that dole woman out of extra cash, his friends out of their shitty drugs, girls he fancied out of their knickers. Talking was the only skill he could always rely on, the source of and solution to most of his problems.

He waited, watching the Princes, feeling his blood flow in and out of the chambers of his heart. If these were the last moments of his life, they were shit. He wasn't sentimental. There wasn't anything he wished he'd said, but he would've liked to see Pete again, to know that she was safe from Abbadon and from everyone else.

The Princes separated their heads and stared at Jack, three sets of black snake eyes, measuring the weight of his soul. "He's got a point," Beelzebub told his companions. "None of ours have managed anything better. We could waste legions chasing this fuckwit."

"If you do this and *if* you and the moron here survive the task," Baal said, "then your debt with Hell will be considered void, crow-mage. We'll gladly leave you to your fate. But only if."

"And Pete, and the baby," Jack reminded them. "They're out. Out of the life for good."

"If you insist," Beelzebub sighed. "I'll never understand your attachment to other humans, but so be it. We have no interest in your whore or your spawn."

"And watch your language, while you're at it," Jack said. "Before I come over that table and knock your teeth back a step."

"For fuck's sake," Belial muttered. "Always have to push it, don't you?"

Beelzebub stood to his full height, which Jack had to admit was impressive. "I'm a Prince of Hell, boy," he rumbled. "And you'd do well to remember that. While you're at it, you leave this place at my whim, because it amuses me to watch you struggle through the shit and mud of the human world. Now go, and do as you've promised, or you'll be standing in front of me again and I'll take every one of those ill-considered words out of your miserable, clammy hide."

"Got it," Jack said. The Fenris moved back as he turned, pulling Belial with him, and made for the door.

"Are you insane?" Belial asked when they were in the hall.

"You know, a 'Thanks, Jack, for saving my arse when you didn't have to' would be in order here," Jack said.

"What do I have to thank you for?" Belial snapped. "You're planning to offer me up to Abbadon on a plate."

"Like you didn't do the same to me just a day ago," Jack said. "Don't play wounded hero with me, demon. You'd bend me over soon as you got the chance in there."

Belial curled his fists, and then uncurled them, taking a deep breath. "Fucking Azrael," he said. "He's been trying to shove me out for centuries, get me booted to some backwater like the Well of Sorrows. Can't stand that I bring in more soul traffic than his little legions of dead men."

"I get it, he's not on your Christmas card list," Jack said. "Now are you going to take us topside or not?"

"Not like I have a choice," Belial snarled.

"Nope," Jack told him. "How are you liking that shoe on the other foot, by the way?"

"I'm going to pull your intestines out through your arse for this," Belial muttered.

"You won't," Jack said, "because I saved your arse, and now, for once, you owe me something." He snapped his fingers in the demon's face. He wouldn't be able to get away with that much longer, and he was going to savor it while he still held something over Belial's head. "Fetch, boy. Go bring me a monster."

CHAPTER 26

The air of Los Angeles was almost palatable after the constant burnt-hair stink of Hell, and Jack inhaled deeply. "Good to be back, eh?" he said.

Belial sat on the curb and scrubbed the heels of his hands across his eyes. "Centuries of devotion, of bringing them souls, and they hang me out to dry. Those fucking bastards."

Jack sat down next to him, lit a fag, and offered one to the demon. Belial took it and sucked on it viciously, until the cherry flared bright orange. "Cheer up," Jack said. "All you have to do is lock Abbadon back up and you're in their good graces."

"You don't understand," Belial said. "Abbadon and his kind are a threat to the Princes, and a threat to the Princes means scorched earth. Anyone responsible for their breakout is going to be a cinder when this is over, including me."

"Fuck me, you're a cheerful one, aren't you?"

Jack said. He'd never come across a maudlin demon and decided he definitely didn't like it. Seeing Belial slumped like a City trader who'd just been sacked wasn't right. It was like seeing a wolf who'd been hit by a car—you could discern the shape of the predator it had once been, but it was as broken and bloody as the next sad thing lying in the gutter.

"Abbadon's been free too long," Belial said. "Always knew if he ever broke out, there was no putting him back."

"This might be an odd thought for your sort," Jack said. "But why not try giving him the old sorry we fucked up, here's a patch of Hell and a lovely potted palm to make amends?"

"Because Abbadon doesn't understand peace," Belial snapped. "He thinks Hell is his to rule, and after he's done burning it down he'll move on to the Black and everything outside it." He blew a long stream of smoke into the air. "Abbadon is the closest you'll come to Armageddon, Jack. He's the end. The end of me, the end of people like you, the end of a world balanced on a knife-edge. It's a hard balance, and sometimes it cuts you, but we've all been able to coexist since the beginning. Abbadon and his ilk have no interest in coexisting. They just want to consume, and make the world their own. He's the metaphysical cockroach. Whatever we throw at him, he'll survive."

"You can step on a roach with a great bloody boot," Jack said. "That works for me."

"Azrael was right about one thing," Belial said. "I do wish I was human sometimes. That endless optimism and idiotic hope, even when things are clearly fucked. I like it."

"So glad you approve," Jack said. "And might I remind you, you had some grand secret plan to get Abbadon back where he belongs. If we can't squash him, we can at least put him back in his roach motel. That's got to be better than moaning about how it's the end of all things."

"The doorway ritual isn't complete," Belial said. "I got a good look when that great pig's arse Sanford had me hanging like a decorative mobile. Wouldn't have worked even if he'd bled me dry. That means Locke left something out of his notes, and I have an idea of where that bit might be."

Jack felt himself start to smile. Basil Locke hadn't been such a fuckwit after all. Fascist, quite possibly, but not an idiot. If Jack had carved a back door into Hell, he sure as fuck would have hidden the specs where nobody could get clever and decide to recreate his work. "Do share this wisdom," he told Belial.

"Locke was obsessed with an actress named Lucinda Lanchester," he said. "Nobody you've ever heard of. She played nightclub singers, gangsters' molls, the sister in the farces who takes the pratfalls."

"You're starting to sound like Sanford," Jack told him. "So old Basil had a hard-on for a no-name actress. Wouldn't be the first."

"Lucinda Lanchester happened to sell her soul to me in exchange for being in pictures," Belial said. "Sad for her, she didn't specify what pictures, and she never climbed off the B-roll. Locke wooed her, bought her extravagant presents, practically bankrupted himself. Then he knocked her up and she and the baby both kicked it during the birth. That was when he went to Germany and made friends with Himmler. Who wouldn't have had any talent for magic if it had crawled up his arse and fallen asleep, by the by."

"So you think Locke told this Lucinda girl whatever his great secret was," Jack said.

"I checked in with her from time to time, as I do with all my bargains," Belial said. "The last time she wasn't making any sense—well, less sense than she usually did. She had a love for little white pills of all varieties, poor thing. But she was ranting how she wasn't afraid of me, how she had a secret that would make her the mistress of any demon who tried for her soul. Obviously it was bollocks, as I collected not two months later, but now I wonder. I wonder what Locke told her to put her in such a state."

"Unless you have a hand for necromancy, I don't think we're finding out," Jack said. Belial grinned, and it was the familiar grin Jack knew, the sign the demon knew something the rest of the world at large did not. He'd always hated that look.

"I don't need a bone-rattler to recall a soul that I own," he said. "Although I don't fancy going down to the catacombs of Hell just now. No, all we need is her corpse, and I wager we'll have our answer."

"And I suppose you know right where she's buried," Jack said.

"Haven't the faintest," Belial said. "I don't care

what happens to the body once I have my property. I leave the flesh and bone to the necrophiliacs."

"Movie star dies tragically, gotta be something on where they put her bones down," Jack said. "Got a mobile? We can check online."

"She's something of a cult figure since she died," Belial said. "Vandals dug her body up twice in the sixties and stole bits, so they moved her and now the grave's unmarked. No idea where she's at now."

"Good job you have me," Jack said. "Otherwise you'd be lost."

"Don't tell me *you* know where Lucinda finally rested herself," Belial scoffed. "You barely know what day of the week it is, Winter."

"It's Thursday," Jack said. "And I don't, but I know someone who will."

CHAPTER 27

The shop was locked and shuttered when Jack and Belial climbed out of the taxi, but Jack banged on the grate until a light came on. The dark-haired, death-tinged shop girl appeared, glaring out at them, holding an old-fashioned shotgun in her fists. "What do you want?" she mouthed through the door.

"Sorry to bother you, luv," Jack said. "Need to ask you something."

She unlocked the door and pointed the shotgun toward Belial's chest. "You can come in. The *diablo* waits outside."

Belial bared his teeth at her. "Trust me, sweetheart—I am far from the worst thing in this miserable little hole of yours."

"Fuck you, *pendejo*," she snapped, and tugged Jack inside. "Why are you mixing it up with demons?" she demanded. "Sliver told me you were al right."

"I'm not mixing anything," Jack said. "I need him, and for the moment, he needs me. And we both need something from you."

"Oh yeah?" She propped the shotgun behind the counter and led Jack through the beaded curtain into a snug back room. A small flat telly blasted Spanish-language news and a glass of tequila sat on the arm of a ratty vinyl overstuffed chair. "Ask," the girl said, and offered Jack an empty jelly glass and a tequila bottle.

He poured a stiff shot. The tequila was fire mixed with turpentine, and it burned on the way down, spreading the fire through his guts and numbing his tongue. "Need to know where an old-timey sorceress is buried. Figured you'd be in the know."

The girl shrugged. "Maybe, what's her name?"

"Lucinda Lanchester," Jack said. The tequila was steadying everything, bringing it back into focus. He wondered when he'd last slept. He couldn't remember. The world vibrated at the edges—nothing to do with his sight, but with the throbbing in his skull. More tequila. That'd help.

"I'm supposed to know about some white bitch who kicked the bucket sixty years ago?" The girl snorted. "No way, man. You want my advice, leave the dead where they are and stop having demons for your homies. That'll make your life a lot easier."

Jack set the glass down. "Please," he said. "This isn't for my own amusement. Sliver told me you knew things. And I know what you are. We can both tell that Death is coming, that the Black is out of order. If you really don't know Lucinda, I'll turn and walk out. But don't brush me off and play like we don't both know what you are."

The girl sighed, and then clicked off the television and pointed through a curtain made from a faded floral bed sheet. "Go in there. Don't touch anything."

Jack ducked through the curtain. He was expecting a workroom or a sex dungeon, but not a tiny backroom crowded almost to bursting with an altar. Candle wax had congealed to stalagmites down the front and sides, and bowls of candy, bullets, and rosary beads were arranged at the foot of a statue of skeletal creature. More bottles of tequila crowded her feet, bourbon, every kind of liquor you could pick up cheaply and by the quart at the local market.

"They call her *La Flaca,*" the girl said at his shoulder. "The skinny girl." She kissed her fingertips and pressed them to the statue's feet.

"Santa Muerte," Jack said. "Ran into some of your lot down in Mexico City about ten years ago. Not very friendly."

"Not to nosy outsiders, no," the girl said. She folded her arms and looked at him, eyes boring in. Jack dropped his eyes to the beads around her neck and the crucifix riding between her cleavage. She had a gimlet stare, even for an avatar of Death. Her eyes were the Morrigan's eyes, black and animal and ancient. "Don't let me down, man," *La Flaca* said. "I know you follow Death. Might be the Eurotrash white-boy version of Death, but we're headed to the same place. Down the dark highway. That's the only reason I'm considering this."

Jack pulled back his sleeve and showed her the markings. "I've been involved with my own skinny bitch for quite some time," he said. "So yeah, I know what you're on about."

La Flaca pointed at the altar. "Give something to Santa Muerte. Ask your question, but unless you have an offering, I don't answer."

"Seriously?" Jack said. He looked into the face of the skeleton icon. It was cheap plaster, the features blurred and painted crookedly. Santa Muerte's robes were polyester, singed at the edges from the dozens of candles that cast the room's only pools of light. He looked back at her living counterpart. "What do you want from me, a kiss? A lock of my hair?"

The girl smacked him in the back of the head. "A little respect, for starters. Santa Muerte answers all requests. You just have to know how to ask her."

Jack looked into the girl's black eyes, back to the statue's crooked plaster face. "I don't have anything to offer you. Or anyone."

The girl took out a pocket knife and offered it to Jack. "You have what we all have." A small clay bowl between Santa Muerte's toes held a sticky red-black liquid, evidence of who'd come here before Jack.

"I never got your name," he told the girl as he took the knife and folded the blade open.

"I have a lot of them," she said. "Ana's good as any, and you're Jack Winter, the crow-mage."

"That obvious, is it?" The knife didn't hurt much—he'd cut himself enough times on purpose to know you just squeezed your fist around the blade and tugged a bit. If the steel was sharp, it would do the job for you.

The dribble became a rivulet, and Jack worked his fist a few times, sending a stream of droplets into the bowl to combine with the other blood. La Flaca folded her hands.

"Pray with me," she said.

Jack swiped his cut palm against his jeans. "Not much for praying. You got a plaster?"

The girl sighed and passed him a rag draped over the only piece of furniture in the room, an old kitchen chair. "You're not going to make this easy on me, are you?"

Jack started to reply, but out of the corner of his eye, the statue moved. He blinked and looked again, putting it down to the flickering flames all around the edges of his vision, but no. The skinny girl's arm, holding its long scythe, was definitely lifting, and the cheap robes wrapping the plaster were ruffling in a breeze.

The candle flames flickered and went out wholesale, filling the room with cloying beeswax smoke. Jack coughed and waved it away from his face. In the blur, the girl and the statue became one, the girl's face growing and skeletonizing, the statue beginning to move, to take on skin and flesh and life.

You want something? The statue was grinning at him, the painted mouth slipping crookedly off the plaster hunks. There was no way the thing was moving and yet it was, pointing and talking at him.

"As a matter of fact," Jack said. "Yeah, there's something you can tell me."

Nothing's free, crow-mage, the statue hissed. *What you got for me?*

"I gave you blood," Jack said. "That's enough."

Can't live by blood alone, the statue said, and coughed a laugh. *Got something else I want, crow-mage?*

"Might as well ask, then," Jack said. The statue was changing, growing details, the limbs moving as the skeletal feet picked their way delicately over the bowls and candle wax.

Got any smokes? The statue grinned at him.

Jack fished in his pocket and brought out his half-squashed pack of Parliaments. "Need a light?"

Nope. The cherry flared and the skeleton sucked in smoke. It billowed out from between her ribs, and she sighed. *That's the good shit.*

Jack had seen stranger things than a cheap Mexican saint statue sit up and cadge a fag, but the smoke was getting thicker, making him dizzy, and he sat hard in the scarred kitchen chair. "You feel like answering a question for me?"

You can always ask La Flaca, the statue hissed. *But you might not like what she has to spit back at you.*

"I'll take my chances," Jack said. Things crawled in the shadow behind the statue, things with snakes' bodies and women's faces, and they leered at Jack in the low light.

Then shoot, brother, said the statue. *A friend of the Hag's is a friend of mine, you know.*

One of the snakes wound its way around Jack's wrist, pushing his sleeve back and exposing the Morrigan's marks.

"I need to know where Lucinda Lanchester is buried," Jack said. "Her body was moved and it's apparently a big secret now."

Poor little lost Lucy, the statue purred. *Rolled the bone dice with a bad man and came up snake-eyes.*

"It's important," Jack said. "If we don't find her I can promise your city isn't going to be around much longer."

What do you care about the living? the statue asked. *You're one of the dead, crow-mage. The walking dead, but dead all the same.*

"None of your business, you hollowed-out bitch," Jack said. "How about that?"

You think once the four are back underground that everything will come up roses? the statue said. *You think you'll save the world and stand in the sun?*

"Don't care about that," Jack said. "I care about a self-righteous prick not getting to play with the entire world like he's having a tantrum in a sandbox."

You can keep fooling yourself, amigo, said the statue. *But sooner or later you're going to see it. You have death inside you. It's in your bones and it's in your blood, and sooner or later death will take you for her own. You can't fight death. We're the end of all lines, the last stop on that dark high-*

way, and sooner or later you'll take that exit, crow-mage. Your kind always do.

"If you're not going to help me you can save the bullshit for some gang-banger who's impressed with it," Jack said. "I know what the Morrigan wants from me. It's the same thing she's always wanted, and my answer is the same, too: you death-cunts can fuck off. The lot of you."

The snakes were thick around his ankles now, worming their way up his legs, spilling over the altar. The statue cackled, plaster teeth clacking and raining dust down on the heaving backs of her serpents.

I can see why she chose you, Jack. She dropped the end of the cigarette and went back to her repose on the altar. *Little lost Lucy is buried behind Paramount, looking at the lake.*

The statue froze again, and Jack came back to himself. He wasn't sitting, but on the floor, and the girl crouched beside him, wearing human skin once again. "What did you see?" she said.

"Snakes," Jack muttered. The scent of incense and the taste of tequila in his throat mixed, and he retched, bile running in rivulets across the dirty, wax-covered floor. "You put something in my fucking drink."

"It's nothing I wouldn't give my grandmother," Ana said. "Just a little encouragement to help you see. You're a stubborn boy. You wouldn't look unless you had help taking the ride."

"That wasn't a ride," Jack said. He sat up, swiping at his mouth with the back of his hand. His tongue and throat still burned. "That was dragged behind a fucking lorry. What was that shit?"

"It'll wear off soon," Ana said. "What did she say to you? *La Flaca*?"

"A lot of bollocks," Jack muttered. "Riddles, just like the bitch I usually deal with. What is it about death that makes you such a cryptic slag?"

"This body and *La Flaca* aren't exactly talking," the girl said. "Santa Muerte lives in all of us. Once, this body was a girl named Ana from Juarez. But I've been living here for a while. It's comfortable. There's a lot of death here, a lot of souls drifting on the Santa Anas." She smoothed her hands over her skirt. "Anyway, I've seen her movies. Lucinda. They're shit. What do you want with her?"

" 'Lucy is buried behind Paramount, looking at the lake,' " Jack grumbled. "How is that in any way useful? I ask you."

Ana, or the thing that had once been Ana, cocked an eyebrow. "Paramount, the studio? In Hollywood?"

"Dunno," Jack muttered. "Guess so."

"There's a cemetery behind Paramount," Ana said. "The Hollywood Forever. And there's a big man-made lake inside, which is usually full of garbage and goose shit. It stinks. Douglas Fairbanks has a huge crypt on this island in the middle. Bigger than this fucking apartment."

"This town seriously has a boneyard calling itself 'Hollywood Forever'?" Jack said. Standing was a risky proposition, but he managed, by clawing hand over hand along the faded wallpaper.

"Hey, man," Ana said. "This is LA."

"Thanks," Jack said. "I sincerely hope I never see you or Little Miss Skeletor again, but I suppose that'd be too much to ask."

"You can avoid her," Ana said. "But she's waiting for you at the end of the road. For all of us. Sooner or later you're gonna take that last ride."

"Cheers, luv," Jack said, and ducked through the twin sets of curtains to the front of the shop. The last thing he saw before the door swung shut was Santa Muerte, grinning her frozen grin.

CHAPTER 28

"Took you bloody long enough," Belial said. "You're going to cost me my weight in car fare." He examined Jack under the dome light of the taxi. "You look like shit."

"Just drive." Jack ignored him. He felt like shit—hammered, flattened shit. His head throbbed, and all of the bumps and blows he'd taken in the past days were catching up with him. He needed a drink, some sleep, or preferably a hit of smack. But that wasn't an option, not until they'd found Abbadon, and by extension found Pete, so he told the cabbie to take them to Hollywood and put his head back against the seat, watching the neon and palm trees and faces pass by.

Hollywood Forever sat on a quiet stretch of Santa Monica, nearly deserted after dark. The cemetery was closed, but Belial walked straight ahead, across the car park and past the chapel.

In the dark, the cemetery was full of stone spirits, white mausoleums and graves scattered across flawless green lawns. Cemeteries in London were wild, overgrown, crowded to the brim with the dead. Too little land and too many bodies. Here, the dead went on forever.

"By the pond," Jack told Belial. He smelled it before he saw it—goose shit and algae, just as Ana had said. The Fairbanks mausoleum loomed over the water, reflecting its own ghost into the dank water.

Belial walked from tomb to tomb until he stopped at a small flat-roofed Egyptian box, then kicked his foot against the iron door. "This one."

Jack examined the unassuming tomb. The grass was mowed, but all of the flowers placed on the steps were dead, and somebody had graffitied the ironwork on the doors. "You sure? I don't really fancy getting pinched for cracking open some random bird's final rest."

"Haven Carstairs." Belial pointed at the brass nameplate bolted to the granite, rust rivulets running down the face of the tomb. "One of her characters. Gangster boyfriend shoots her to death after she finds Jesus behind the settee or some rot. On-screen death scene. Decent stuff."

"Great." Jack rattled the doors. "Locked, too."

"Your particular talent, isn't it?" Belial said. "I'm a demon, not a petty thief."

"You lot are useless, you know that?" Jack said. "Amazed you don't just get flattened by a bus."

"I've been walking this earth a lot longer than

you and I'll be walking it often," said Belial. "Open the fucking tomb, will you? I haven't got all night."

Jack placed his hand over the lock and let his talent flow into it. After his time in Hell and in the void of Locke's mansion, it felt like cool water filling the space behind his eyes to feel the Black again. It was strong here, a dark vein of power running under the cemetery, fed by both the restless dead and the living of Los Angeles.

The lock popped open and Jack shoved the door wide.

Lucinda's coffin was encased in cement, which had cracked across the top. Cobwebs drifted back and forth in the draft from the door, but otherwise the tomb was undisturbed. Belial pushed a chunk of concrete off the coffin with a clatter and swiped the dust from the nameplate with his sleeve.

Lucinda Carpenter
Beloved Daughter
1919–1939

"Lanchester was a stage name," Belial said. "She was from Waukegan. Not really surprised she cut a deal. Miserable place."

"I have seen *Bride of Frankenstein*," Jack said. " 'M not a complete tit."

Belial grabbed one end of the coffin by its pall-bearer handle and tugged. "Come on, Winter. Help me get this dead bitch out and about."

The coffin was heavy, in the way that old things

were heavy, and landed on the floor of the tomb with a crash. Jack felt something spasm in his back and let his end go. "Try not to alert the entire city, yeah? I can't exactly nip back to the Pit when the cops show up."

"You're a great nanny," Belial said. "I remember the days when you had balls." He grinned, and Jack could see the gleam of his teeth as the demon went about prying open the coffin. "The dad-to-be bit softened you up, has it? Made you all gooey on the inside? I tell you, the thought of a little Winter toddling about got me excited, rightly enough. Imagining what your blood and the Weir's will do together is one of my favorite daydreams."

Jack moved without thinking, moved because the cold was in his blood again, and slammed Belial into the broken concrete, holding him there with fingers clasped around his windpipe. "You shut your fucking mouth or it'll be the last thing you live to regret saying," he whispered. On the backs of his hands, the Morrigan's marks writhed, and where he touched Belial, the demon's skin went pasty and blue, like he'd contracted a bad case of frostbite.

"You need a good wank, mate," Belial croaked. "You are wound *way* too tightly for your own good."

"You and I have our thing," Jack said. "But you leave Pete out of it." He let go of Belial and shook off the cold. It was what he imagined being possessed felt like—an alien presence inside his skin, moving and talking for him.

"What you have is an unhealthy obsession with

that woman," Belial said. He straightened out his suit and rubbed his neck. "She's not a saint, you know."

"She's as close as I'm ever going to get," Jack said. "So if you want my help, stay fucking quiet."

"Fine," Belial said. "You talk too much anyway."

Jack ignored him. Belial was only doing what he did best—getting under a man's skin and prodding all of his weak spots. It was the instinct of all demons. He just wished Belial wasn't so fucking good at it.

The coffin was old, not airtight, and the lid wasn't hard to break off. Lucinda Lanchester was little more than a skeleton with brown leather skin stretched over it, nibbled by rodents. Belial wrinkled his nose.

"At least she's old enough that she doesn't stink. Small mercies."

Jack lifted up the remnants of the silk dress Lucinda had been buried in, which came apart in his hands. He felt under the skeleton, through the dust of the flowers that had been laid in the coffin, and felt nothing. He looked back at Belial. "Any time you want to jump in here, mate. Any time."

"You're doing a splendid job," Belial said. "Really."

Jack patted down the lining of the coffin, which had been pink at one point, but was now faded to a sad urine color. If he hadn't been prodding he would have missed it—a small crackle against the wooden side of the coffin. He ripped it away and saw a single square of paper folded and taped to the side.

Belial snatched it before Jack could get a look.

"Oi," he said. "Didn't anyone teach you not to be grabby?"

"Likely the same person who failed to teach you," Belial said. He unfolded the paper carefully, mindful of his pointed nails, and then grinned. "Oh, this is a laugh."

Jack yanked the paper back. A sigil took up the center, of the page. None he'd seen before but not head-twistingly complicated, the sigil was surrounded by numbers and symbols. Jack had quit going to school long before he learned any of them. Math was never his shining glory.

"What the fuck was Locke on about?" he said. Belial chuckled.

"Abbadon said it was physics, didn't he? Magical math. Expressing the door to Hell in numbers and sigils. That's clever, that is." He held out his hand. "Give it here. For safekeeping."

"Fuck off," Jack said. "I give you this and you're going to skip straight back to the Princes and act like the good little scent hound."

"I'm not that predictable." Belial snatched for the paper again. "Come on now, Winter. Don't be a cock."

Jack folded the paper and tucked it inside his jacket. "Or maybe I was wrong," he said to Belial. "Maybe you'll hold on to it and use it with the Princes to leverage yourself. Get yourself a room in that tower and a nice little legion of your own to command."

Belial's lip curled. "Now you're thinking like a demon, Winter. Always said you had it in you."

"Either way," Jack said. "We're holding on to this until Abbadon and his merry band shows."

Belial stepped out of the tomb, onto the grass, and folded his arms. "You really think I couldn't take it from you if I wanted it?"

"You really think I know you wouldn't have already tried if you could?" Jack said. "The Princes hung you out, mate. You're not on your home turf, and you're pissing yourself because Abbadon can play footie with your head as long as we're in the daylight world. So just simmer down."

Belial set his jaw, but he sat down on the steps of Lucinda's tomb and looked at the lake. "This place is a laugh," he said. "You'd think Roman emperors were lying in state."

"Close," Jack said. "Film stars. Rock stars. Basically the same thing in America."

"You wouldn't believe how many bargains I've wrought with the stiffs in this place," Belial said. "Me and others."

"I would," Jack said. "Would explain most of cinema for the past twenty years."

"Isn't that the truth," Belial said. "I used to try to bargain with the ones who actually had some talent, but there's only so many Connerys. The rest are Luncindas and Lockes."

Jack watched the lamplight on the lake. If Abbadon came, he couldn't rely on Belial. To defend Locke's secret, yes. Him, no. He was expendable, and Belial would probably enjoy watching him twitch while Abbadon ripped his guts out.

"This is your fault, you know," Belial said. Jack turned on him.

"Yeah? How is possible Hell wrought on earth *my* fault, exactly?"

"If I had never made that bargain with you, back when you were lying there bleeding out lo these many years ago, then we wouldn't be here." Belial sighed. "What can I say? It seemed like a good idea at the time."

"You fucking stoned?" Jack said. "I wasn't exactly specific. I was dying, and I was looking for anyone. You just happened to be in the neighborhood."

"No," Belial said quietly. "I wasn't."

Jack felt a cold in him that had nothing to do with his talent or his tattoos. He hadn't called any one demon, that day fourteen years earlier. Hadn't even expected it to work. It was a last gasp. He was dying, he'd drawn a summoning mark in his own blood, sent out the call to any bottom-feeder who bargained souls from the boot of his car. And instead Belial had come, one of the Named, and cut him a sweetheart deal. Thirteen years of life in exchange for his soul. Of course, he hadn't mentioned that a decade of that would be spent in a smack haze, sleeping on floors and hustling for cash, but demons weren't famous for specifics. He'd lived, and Belial had saved him. That was all it was.

"So what?" Jack said at last. He lit a fag, the one thing that could reliably calm tremors in his hands and disguise fear as something else. "You just hung around waiting for some ghost to rip my lungs out during an exorcism and swooped in for the kill?"

"Think it through, Winter," Belial said. He shoved a hand through his hair, and in the low light the lines of his face were stark. The demon looked tired, if such a thing were possible, and worn down in the way of long-term addicts on the arse end of a bender. "A Named demon doesn't show his face because you scribble something in your own blood and flop about like a fish, calling down every elemental and scum-sucker in the greater London area."

"Just spit it out." Jack blew smoke. "Whatever you're alluding too, quit the foreplay and plunge it in."

"I had my eye on you," Belial said. "It was like a gift. The crow-mage, dying and begging for my help. Taking a favored son from that bitch of a Hag, well. That's a thing most of us soul-traders dream of."

"Didn't manage to keep me for long," Jack said. "Bet your bosses loved that one."

"You're always going to be in Hell, Winter," Belial said. "One way or the other. You're bound to Death as surely as you're bound to your own skin. You'll be back. It's just a matter of time."

"It's over, remember?" Jack snapped. "Nergal's gone. The war is over. The Morrigan doesn't have a claim on me any more than you do."

Belial barked a laugh. "Boy, look at yourself. That cunt's fingerprints are all over you. And if you think Nergal was her last volley, you're a fucking idiot. That was an opening salvo. The Morrigan will never stop trying to bring her armies to the daylight world. She's the endless cycle—war, birth, and death. You can't stop those things, Jack, any more than you can stop the sun from rising."

"So what?" Jack said. "I'm supposed to be scared about something that might go on, decades from now? I think I'll save myself for Abbadon."

"I'm saying that when the Hag comes back for you," Belial said, "Hell might not be such a bad alternative after all." He grinned. "We'd love to have you."

"Isn't that sweet?" Abbadon purred from behind Jack, close enough to feel his breath. "You two kissed and made up."

Jack threw himself down the steps just ahead of Abbadon, rolling to the side as the beast's foot came down. He didn't appear any larger than he had at Locke's ranch, but his psychic presence was infinitely larger, and Jack felt the power suck the air from his lungs.

"Heya, Belial," Abbadon said. "Boy, you clean up nice. You have to tell me where you get those suits."

"Just you?" Belial said. He was pale and sweating, but he stood ramrod straight. "Where's your brood? You leave the kids at home?"

"Oh, don't worry," Abbadon said. "They're amusing themselves with Jack's baby mama. I figured I could handle two of the three Stooges on my own."

Jack lifted his head. There was blood in his mouth from where he'd bitten down, tasting like acid and pennies. "Pete?"

"Her." Abbadon nodded. "Although we've got to think up a new name for her. *Pete* is just confusing."

Jack hauled himself to his feet. The cold didn't come this time, just the rage, hot and blood-pounding and familiar. "I swear, if you've touched her . . ."

"Oh, save it," Abbadon said. "We're not going to use your little crumpet to re-enact *Last House on the Left*. What good is a body if it's fucked up beyond repair?"

Belial stood, then came at Abbadon from behind, but Abbadon turned, and the shadow of his power moved, and Belial went flying into the lake. He landed with a shallow crunch, then lay still amid the sloshing reeds.

"So, Jack," Abbadon said. "My offer stands. Quit being a bitch about all this and we'll make sure you're taken care of." He put his hand on Jack's shoulder. "We could use a fucked-up critter like you. You and those freaky death powers will be real useful once things are different around here."

Jack smacked the hand off his shoulder. "Where's Pete?"

Abbadon wagged a finger under Jack's nose. "That'd be telling. Say you'll help and I might give you a clue. It'll be a little fun for us. Or, you know, I could torture you into a pile of meat to tell me how you really open Locke's gateway."

Jack pulled the paper from his jacket. In that moment, if he were honest, he didn't give a fuck what Abbadon did with it. Didn't care if the hot, dry wind swept up from Locke's doorway and blew away the entire world. It was a mad feeling, the sort that made people smash their cars into bridge abutments, beat their wives to death, or douse their children in kerosene and light a match. All that mattered was Pete.

"Here." He threw it in the grass between them. "Have fun in Hell, you piece of shit. Now tell me where Pete is."

Abbadon grinned at him. "Not the deal. You want to set the terms, you should have held out a little longer." He bent to pluck the paper square from the grass, and Jack lifted his boot and drove the steel toe hard as he could into Abbadon's gut. The body Abbadon had picked out wasn't big as far as things went, and he folded around Jack's foot, spitting out a mouthful of blood.

"So it's like that."

"Yeah." Jack snatched the paper back up and shoved it in his jacket. "You can try to do whatever you want to me, Abbadon, but you're not getting this. Where's Pete?"

Abbadon got to his feet, brushing grass and dirt from his front. "I told you. Safe and sound and with my kind. I have to say, she's way too good for you. Regulation hottie, too. How did you manage that?"

Jack called up the leg-locker hex silently, and when Abbadon went down, banged his forehead into the steps of Lucinda Lanchester's tomb. "I was in a band."

Abbadon started to laugh, the blood dribbling down his forehead and across his mangled nose like dark fingers. "All right, Jack. All right, we'll do it your way." He shoved Jack off and stood. Jack hit the ground and realized that this might be the last shit plan he didn't think through. He hadn't gotten beyond pissing Abbadon off, making him tell where Pete was, and then kicking the blue hell out of him in return.

Abbadon's shoe pressed into his chest, and Jack felt a rib creak and then give. He didn't have enough air to make any sound, so that was a blessing. It was difficult to feel hard when Hellspawn was crushing your ribcage. "You fucked up," Abbadon told him. "I wanted to be friends, but now I'm just going to pull out your spine and shove it up your ass. You're a worm, like all the rest."

He moved his foot, but Jack did not make measurable progress toward sitting up. His chest was on fire, and his body had given his commands up for a bad job. Clearly, he didn't have their best interest in mind, and he was no longer in charge.

Jack stared as Abbadon grew large, eclipsing the lamppost, the Fairbanks mausoleum, everything. He lengthened and his eyes went black, his teeth grew and his hands formed into scaly masses, tipped with claws.

"*You wanted to see, Jack,*" Abbadon hissed. "*So behold the dragon.*"

"Fuck me," Jack whispered, because it was all he had the air for. "You do love the sound of your own fucking voice."

Abbadon's body curled between the tombs, and he leaned down so that Jack could smell the fetid breath pouring from between his underslung jaws.

"You cost me a good body. I'm going to take yours apart slowly, now."

A claw lanced into his arm, down to the bone, and Jack ground his teeth together. Even if he could scream, he wouldn't give Abbadon the satisfaction of hearing.

Abbadon held him down with his claws and ran a long, black tongue across Jack's face. *"This is my real face,"* he hissed. *"What do you think of it, Jack?"*

"I think your mum beat you every day with the ugly stick, and then kicked you down the stairs," Jack grunted.

Abbadon snarled and snapped his jaws. *"Funny man to the last, eh? See how funny you think it is when I make you eat your own guts."*

Jack saw a shadow rise behind Abbadon, and the creature screamed as something latched on to his back. Jack sailed through the air as Abbadon's claw slipped from his flesh, then landed with a crash against the gates of Lucinda's tomb.

The thing striking at Abbadon wasn't as large, but it was lithe and black, a wingspan behind it blotting out the sky. Black smoke roiled around the body, obscuring the details, and Jack smelled the scent of Hell, the burnt ash crowding his throat and sucking out what little breath he could draw.

"You may have come first," Belial snarled. "But you never grew beyond a petulant child, and it's time somebody showed you where you belonged."

"Finally, you grow some balls," Abbadon said. He and Belial circled each other, the ground shaking

under Jack's feet. He heard Belial scream as Abbadon turned on him, wrapping him in serpentine coils, snapping at his exposed neck.

Belial's form shimmered and writhed in Abbadon's grip. Abbadon put his claws through Belial's wing, tearing at the membranes, causing a spray of oily black liquid. Jack winced as he heard a bone crack, and Belial crumpled.

"*We should have gotten it on a long time ago, demon,*" Abbadon said. "*In a stand-up fight, you'd never break me, and you knew it.*"

"Fuck you," Belial gasped, as Abbadon dug his talons into Belial's belly. Jack saw the meaty sheen of intestines, then rolled onto his back.

Stand up, Winter. You're dead if you don't get your arse up.

Belial's blood stank of sulfur, and Jack felt the memory of the hot wind of Hell race across his senses.

"*Oh, we'll get to that,*" Abbadon purred. "*Because now you're going to be* my *bitch, demon, and you're going to know exactly what it felt like for all that time, alone in the dark with ghosts for company.*"

Jack levered himself up on the smooth marble of Lucinda's tomb. He didn't owe Belial shite. He could creep away now and hopefully find Pete before the rest of Abbadon's kind killed her or worse. Or he could never find her. Abbadon alone had nearly turned him into paste. The other three would swat him like a bug.

The memory of standing at the edge of the

chasm, of hearing the faintest whisper, came back strong amid the screams and the smell of blood. Abbadon's family had marked him, had marked him while he was in Hell.

Hello, Jack. Teddy's voice, or perhaps Levi's. It didn't matter. When they'd gone free, they'd told Abbadon about him, and Abbadon had known the crow-mage would be the one to use for his mad schemes.

He was a game piece, just like he was to Belial. And he was fucking sick of it, Jack decided, sick to the core. Belial, at least, had always been upfront that he was using Jack. And having a demon who owed you one would go a long way toward taking the edge off Abbadon's brood. Having a demon who owed him might be what saved Pete's life.

Jack cast around. His talent was useless against Abbadon, that much was clear. He should have wised up and punched the bastard in the nose ages ago. The front of Lucinda's tomb was destroyed, the stained glass in the door shattered, and the iron gate hung akimbo.

Belial screamed again, and Abbadon laughed. He had his snout in the wound now, and Jack heard the snap of teeth. Good. He'd be distracted.

Jack kicked at the gate until it came loose. The panel was about five feet tall but narrow, sharp latticework at the top covered over with green corrosion. He hefted it. It wasn't ideal, but it would do.

Abbadon didn't look up as he approached, which was probably a check in the plus column, since Jack couldn't be certain he was walking a straight line.

Once this was over, he decided passing out face down in the nice, soft grass would be the ideal finale to the evening.

Jack raised the gate and stepped to the side, aiming it for Abbadon's soft underbelly. He drove the latticework in far as it would go, jerked the iron back and forth, twisted. He wanted the bastard's guts to rain down, to cover the ground with blood and make it so nothing would ever grow there again.

Abbadon reared back, and his swipe narrowly missed taking off the top of Jack's skull. The wound around the iron began to corrode, black spreading across Abbadon's flesh, lemon-colored pus dripping out. Abbadon convulsed once, shrieked, and then Belial reached up and twisted Abbadon's scaly neck halfway round.

The snap resounded off the marble tombs, and Abbadon slumped, unmoving.

"Fuck, he's heavy," Belial grunted. "Get him off me, will you?"

Jack gripped Belial's arm and eased him out from under Abbadon's unmoving bulk. "Got some bad news for you, mate," he said, looking into Belial's pointed face, shredded wings spread underneath him. "You're ugly as fuck."

Belial bared his teeth. "Told you that you couldn't handle the sight of me."

Jack took quick stock. Belial's wings were a wreck, and blood was dribbling from his mouth and ears. Abbadon had torn a chunk out of his guts, and Jack caught the stench of a rent bowel.

"I'll be all right," Belial said. "Eventually. But I have to go, Jack."

"Oh no," Jack said. "You owe me now, you bastard. You'd be a big pile of demon meat if I hadn't stabbed that bastard." He looked at Abbadon's corpse. "He is dead, right?"

"Dead as I can make him," Belial gritted. "If I stay here, I'm going the same way."

"Pete . . ." Jack started.

"Pete is an arrow in your heel," Belial cut him off. "Sooner or later, Jack, that woman is going to be the end of you. Drop your losses and move on."

Jack let Belial's head down. That was a demon. Do everything right and they still found a way to fuck you. "That'll be it for me, then," he said. "But it's not going to happen today, and Abbadon doesn't get to keep her."

Belial laughed, though it turned to a phlegmy cough that caused a fresh flow of blood from his lips. "You're an idiot, Jack Winter. Good luck."

"Yeah," Jack said. "Fuck you, too. Thanks for your help."

"I've helped you more than you know, Winter," Belial said. "Not my fault you don't want to hear the truth."

"Telling you," Jack said. "Never had much use for the truth, me."

"That's why you're going to see me again," Belial whispered. "And why you'll never really be free of Hell."

"Today I am," Jack said. "So shove it up your arse, mate. I've got three more Hellspawn to kill tonight."

CHAPTER 29

Walking was the hardest thing in the world. His ribs screamed with every step, and his arm was a free-flowing canyon of blood and missing flesh. Jack tore off his shirt and wrapped the wound as tight as he could stand. Stanching the blood helped a little, but he was still the walking dead.

He managed to flag down a taxi on Santa Monica, managed to mumble out the address of Sliver's pub in Venice, and then mercifully passed out.

The dream boiled up at him, and this time it was as vivid as a memory. He stood barefoot on glass sand that pierced his flesh and left crimson footprints as he and Belial walked across an endless desert under a white sky. The City was far behind, and the only interruptions on the horizon were the black skeletons of dead trees. From each tree hung a bottle, blue glass, clinking gently in the endless wind. Inside each bottle was a wisp of white smoke.

"Souls," Belial said. "Souls so corrupted they don't even have bodies any more."

Jack was naked, and the sand blew and swirled around him, digging into the flayed spots on his flesh, turning the blood on his face sticky, and stinging his eyes. "You bring me out here for this?" he said. His voice was little more than another whisper of air. Screaming for hours didn't leave you with much lung power.

"No," Belial said. He pointed to where the world dropped away, and Jack went to the edge of a canyon, iron sides held together with rivets the size of his fist.

He heard the screaming, from far below. Heard the bellowing of a massive body in unbearable pain. The sides of the canyon quivered, flakes of rust coming loose and falling into the void.

"You think you're here forever?" Belial said. "I'm showing you it could be much worse."

It was hard to think how. Belial's torments were endless and creative. Jack didn't understand how his body could keep taking punishment. The small bit of his mind that hadn't shut down told him that he'd go completely around the bend soon, and then he'd belong to Belial. He'd forget his own name, that he'd ever been alive, and everything about his life before. Pete, everything.

Had she buried him? Was she even still thinking of him?

"Prince Azrael tortures these four endlessly," Belial said. "As punishment for daring to stand against the demons. You don't always have to be this pathetic smear of shit you are now, Jack."

Jack turned his head with effort. Below his feet, the ground shook and the screaming reached a fever pitch. "What?"

"Eventually, you'll give up on what you remember of your life," Belial said. "And then you might be useful to Hell, Jack. Nobody would own you here. Not the smack, not your sight, and not the Morrigan."

"No," Jack mumbled. "Just you."

Belial's claws grazed the back of his neck. "For now. But someday, I have a feeling you and I could be great friends."

That small part of Jack that had recognized he was sliding downhill fast spoke. "I'd rather be down in that pit with Azrael."

Belial's lip twisted down. "So be it," he said. "You'll break, Winter. Sooner or later they all do."

Something cold and wet hit him in the face and slithered down his throat. Jack choked and swiped at his lips.

"Jeez, man," Sliver said. "You scared the hell out of me."

He knelt beside Jack, holding an empty pitcher with a few ice cubes lingering in the bottom. Jack watched rivulets of pink trickle across the white tile floor and slip away down a drain. He was soaked from chest to head, but he was awake. "You should see the other bloke," he said.

Sliver set the pitcher aside and sat him up. "Funny. You want to tell me why you fall out of a cab in front of my bar, mumbling crazy shit, and then pass out on me in my back room?"

"Long story," Jack said. "Someday I'll tell you all about it, and you'll be amazed." He tried to stand, but his feet went out from under him, and he fell back to the tile.

"Dude," Sliver said. "You need to settle. You're fucked up."

"I'll be all right," Jack said. "Just need to rest for a moment . . ."

He wasn't all right. Blood loss had made a black border around his vision, and his ribs were on fire.

"I'll get somebody," Sliver said. "Just hang in there, all right?"

He left, and Jack passed in and out of consciousness for what could have been hours or weeks. The single bare bulb in the pub's back room swung back and forth, light and dark. Usually, this was when the Morrigan would show her face, when he was in the shadow land between the daylight world and the Land of the Dead. But she knew she had him now. There was no reason to attend his last hours when he'd be delivered to her at the end.

He couldn't help Pete. He couldn't even help himself.

"Shit," somebody said. "This guy is hamburger. Why the hell didn't you take him to a hospital?"

"Like I could explain this to somebody in a hospital," Sliver snapped. "I thought you said you could help him."

"Look," the second voice said, "this guy is beyond help." Chubby fingers gouged against Jack's neck. "His pulse is barely even there."

"Do what you can." A desperate edge crept into Sliver's voice. "I can't have a dead fucking body in my bar, Mayhew."

"Really, you of all people are more equipped to deal with a corpse than most," Mayhew said.

"Fuck you," Sliver said. "Are you going to help me or not?"

"Clear my tab, and I'll see if I can keep him breathing," Mayhew said.

"Are you shitting me? You owe me four hundred bucks."

Mayhew's fingers went away. "Hey, you want to put this fucker out with the trash after last call, you can argue with me. You want my help and expertise, clear my fucking tab."

"Fine." Shiver sighed. "I think his ribs are busted. He keeps making these wheezes when he tries to breathe."

A cold stethoscope pressed against Jack's chest, and Mayhew made a disapproving sound. "He's got fluid in his lungs. Probably internal bleeding." Jack's leather was stripped away, and a bandage went around his ribs. The pain intensified tenfold, and he cried out.

"Good sign," Mayhew said. He peeled back Jack's eyelid and Jack was blinded by a pocket torch. "Hello in there," Mayhew said, and Jack swiped at the light.

"Fuck off."

"Listen," Mayhew said. "You've got cracked ribs and a nasty head wound. Probably a concussion too. I'm going to give you something for the pain, but you need to stay still, all right?"

"No needles," Jack said. "No drugs."

Mayhew ignored him, fitting a sterile needle onto a syringe and drawing from a bottle of clear liquid that proclaimed SALINAS VET SUPPLY across the label in broad letters.

"No . . ." Jack tried. If he was doped, he had no chance. Pete would die, the baby would die. Hell, he'd probably die in the bargain, since Mayhew seemed to have learned first aid while drunk and standing on his head.

The needle slid in, small and cold, and the cold soon spread across all his limbs. Jack felt his heartbeat slow down, and he drifted on the opiate tide, the familiar fuzzy sensation of the high unfurling its wings and lifting him toward the ceiling.

He looked down, at the top of Sliver's head and Mayhew's orange Hawaiian shirt.

"I think you gave him too much," Sliver said. Mayhew zipped up his case and shoved the rest of his supplies back into a duffel bag.

"You want to do this?"

Sliver shook his head. Mayhew stood up and brushed off his knees. "I'll hang out in the front. Call me if anything changes."

"Don't you dare drink all the good shit," Sliver called after him, and then crouched beside Jack's body again. From this vantage, he really did look like shit. His face was gray, and the dried blood and the cut on his forehead made him look like some kind of film zombie. His bare chest, wrapped in bandages, was covered in old bruises and new cuts from where Abbadon had flung him into the tomb.

He'd come close to dying before—and had, when Belial took him. He knew the detachment, the gentle untethering of soul from flesh. But he couldn't die, not now. Pete needed him. More importantly, he needed her. The only kindness if he kicked now would be to the kid. Better to have a dead father you could idolize than a living one who was shit.

"*You don't have to let it end like this, you know.*"

Jack looked up at the shadows near the ceiling, cast by the swaying bulb. "Oh," he said. "Now you show up." He wasn't sure if he was really speaking, or just echoing his thoughts, but the crow woman glided down from the ceiling and put her hands on either side of his face.

"*You have the ability to make this stop right now, Jack. You have the means to help the little Weir. If you really want to.*"

Jack looked down at his body. "Don't know if you've noticed, but I'm already dead. We're just waiting out the formalities now."

The Morrigan dug her claws into his cheeks. She could be extraordinarily beautiful, pale skin and eyes like drowning pools, long hair drifting on spectral wind, body encased in a diaphanous black shroud. And then her face could change, could become the face of the crow woman, or the Hag, and she was the most terrifying thing he'd ever clapped eyes on.

"*I gave you the gift, Jack. I pulled you back from the Bleak Gates, and all you've done is deny me. I'm getting very tired of it, Jack. I won't save you this time. Either you save yourself and use what I gave you, or you'll never see your little Weir again.*"

She pressed her lips against his, and her teeth sliced into his lip, their blood mingling. "*You're mine, Jack. You can lie to yourself, but you can't lie to me. Now do what you know you want to. Take control of this.*"

She retreated, and Jack had to wonder if she'd ever been there. It wouldn't be even close to the first time he'd hallucinated the Morrigan. Bad enough when she actually did visit him.

He felt the cold, even from the vantage point of his stoned dream. It started in his hands again, and as he watched his body he saw his tattoos begin to writhe. He could try to hold it back, try to deny that the Morrigan had changed him, made him into what he'd tried not to be ever since he'd seen her the first time, back when she was just the lady in black who dogged his dreams night after night, when he finally drifted off after his mum and Kevin had stopped fighting or fucking in the other room.

He could try, but he didn't want to any more. He wasn't going to let Pete die. He wasn't going to let Abbadon steal her. And if that meant giving in to the Morrigan, than so be it. She'd changed him.

Without her he'd be dead. Whatever he dealt with later, well. He'd cross that bridge when he got there.

He didn't fight the cold this time, like he had when he'd killed Parker. He embraced it, let it rush through him like a freight train, and felt the Black spasm as his soul reeled back from the Land of the Dead.

Waking up felt like knives, or like he'd just been smacked with a defibrillator. He bolted upright, the cold expelling from his lungs in a rush of air, and then he promptly vomited, even though there was nothing in his stomach except a little bile.

"Fuck!" Sliver bellowed. "What the fuck, man!"

Jack felt himself jerked sharply to one side as his ribs snapped back into place. Vague, dull pain in his guts told him that whatever blood had been leaking was sealed. Even his forehead was smooth when he touched it.

His tattoos came to rest in a new configuration, no longer aimless swirls but feathers, boldly up each arm and reaching across his back and chest. Sliver stared, unblinking. "You, uh . . . you okay, man?"

Jack stood. The painkiller was gone along with the pain, but he had a new sense of detachment now, and it was nothing to do with the Morrigan or the Black or anything except the fact that Abbadon, that bastard, had taken Pete. "Never better," he said to Sliver. He grabbed a T-shirt off a shelf, advertising the pub, and shrugged into it. It was too large by half, but it covered him and that was all that mattered.

Jack banged the door to the pub open, garnering a stare from everyone in the place. Sliver's tinny sound system, pumping out the Marshall Tucker Band, was the only sound. Jack walked over to Mayhew, took away the whiskey bottle the fat arse was cradling like a baby, and took a long pull. The whiskey felt good, warmed him up a bit, and Jack slammed the bottle back down and pointed his finger in Mayhew's face.

"You need to get me a gun."

CHAPTER 30

Mayhew's gun wasn't nearly as large or penislike as Jack would have expected. It was a small Sig-Sauer, or so Mayhew told him. Jack had never found much use for guns. That was Pete's department. She was the one who could take aim and shoot.

"You know how to use one of these?" Mayhew asked. Jack took it, ejected the clip, checked the chamber, and then slid the clip home again and flipped the safety off. Pete had made him learn that much. Almost like she'd known one day he'd be on the other end of the rescue, being the knight on the steed. He'd already slain a dragon. How difficult could this be?

"Guess you do," Mayhew said. "You got any idea where she is?"

"That's your department, isn't it?" Jack said. "Come on, Mayhew. Prove you're something more than a sad old drunk."

Mayhew shook his head immediately. "Oh no. I don't mess with this shit. Scrying for what tagged you is going to get me a melted brain and a bed at Cedars."

"County nuthouse, is more like it," Sliver muttered. Mayhew flushed, but he still shook his head. "This is your mess, man."

"Listen," Jack said. "It's been ten years. The thing that killed Mrs. Case and stole her baby to ride in its skin is *right here*, and his friends have got Pete. You brought her here—you owe her, even if you don't give a fuck about me. And you owe the Cases, and the Herreras, and all the other dozens of unfortunate souls who got in Abbadon's way."

Mayhew drummed his fingers on the bar, then poured himself a shot of something clear and knocked it back. "Fine. I'm going to need something of hers."

Jack sent Sliver to retrieve Pete's Stiff Little Fingers shirt from her bag, then handed it to Mayhew. "It's her favorite," he said. "Don't ruin it."

Mayhew spread the shirt out on the bar, took another shot.

"Oi," Jack said. "Don't get pissed. We need you able to perform."

"Being hammered is *how* I perform," Mayhew said. "So shut the fuck up and let me do this, all right?"

Jack watched Mayhew pass his hands back and forth across the shirt, watched his eyes roll back in his head. Seeing somebody in a trance was always a bit unnerving—their eyes went white, and they tended to twitch and drool. It was why Jack had never put himself under in front of an audience. Simply wasn't dignified.

Mayhew's eyes crawled with black, and a tendril, then a second, of black smoke leaked from his mouth and nostrils. He exhaled, and the smoke formed a miasma above his head, drifting in lazy circles.

"I see her . . ." Mayhew rasped, and more smoke trickled from his mouth.

"Okay, that is just weird," Sliver said. "And I say that as a wraith *and* a bartender."

"Shut it," Jack said, as Mayhew shoved back from the bar and walked stiff-legged for the door. "He got that beast of a car still?"

"Far as I know," Sliver said. Jack snatched Mayhew's keys and tossed them to Sliver.

"Then you're driving."

The old him, the him who didn't have the marks, who hadn't healed himself and been through the fight with Abbadon, would have doubted himself and the wisdom of following Mayhew into the jaws of the beast, but he didn't. Abbadon could be as cryptic as he liked, but there was only one place in the daylight world where his brood would feel really safe.

Jack had strength now, had focus, had the tunnel vision that would mow down anything that got in his way. He realized, in the same small part of his brain that had known he was on the way out, that he was dangerous. Off the track, spinning toward a confrontation he had no hope of winning.

"Where is he going?" Sliver asked as they left the bar.

"Drive," Jack told him, climbing into the passenger side of Mayhew's car. "He'll tell us where to go."

Mayhew guided them onto the freeway with guttural grunts, and they headed north of downtown. Like Jack thought, there was only one place they could be going.

The journey toward Abbadon's ranch passed by in slices of headlamp illuminating road signs leading to places Jack had never heard of. Folsom. Lodi. Barstow. Desolate names for desolate towns, off the map of where he had to go tonight.

Mayhew came back to himself by degrees and sat up, choking. "The ranch . . ." he rasped. "The dead . . ."

"It's all right, mate," Jack said. "We got the gist."

Sliver turned to look at them in the light of the dash. "No offense, but I'm not toeing off against whatever it is that has you two spooked. I'll be the getaway driver, but you're on your own."

"No," Jack said, trying to settle back against the seat. His skin was vibrating, and his mind was as clear as if he'd just taken a hit of pure crystal. "These bastards are mine."

"Listen," Mayhew said after a time, when the radio had faded to nothing but static, country music, and late-night preachers telling them how the world would end, "I know you and I haven't always seen eye to eye . . ."

"You tried your best to fuck me," Jack said.

"But don't worry, Benji. I'm not going to test your manhood tonight."

The turn for the ranch loomed up in the cone of the Buick's headlights and Jack tapped Sliver on the arm. "Just there. Park on this side of the ridge and stay out of sight."

Mayhew leaned out his window as Jack walked away, boots crunching on the gravel. "What are you going to do?"

A single window was lit in the ranch house, and Jack saw the blue glow of a television through the tattered curtains. He lifted the Sig from his waistband and felt the weight in his hand. It was solid and real, probably the last piece of iron he'd ever touch.

"I'm going to kill every one of those sons of bitches," he said, then started toward the ranch house.

The void in the Black still existed, but it didn't cause a spike in his brain. That was Jack before, the Jack who was weak, who felt things and wanted heroin and wished for all of the sights and sounds of the Black to just stop from time to time, so he could rest. This Jack knew there could be no rest until he'd done what he came for.

If he couldn't use his talent, he'd gamble that Levi and the others couldn't either. Abbadon was clearly the bright bulb of the group. The others were simply insects attracted to the light.

He mounted the steps, mindful of the loose boards. This part had to go just right, because there were no second chances, and plenty of regrets waiting if he fucked up.

Trying the door, he found the knob locked tight.

He leaned back against the porch rail, bracing himself. Levi would be by the television, and he was too much of a fat fuck to move quickly. Teddy was immobile. That left the little girl as his primary problem—not that he was discounting her. Not that she was actually a little girl.

Jack swung his boot at the door, smashing it so that it banged against the farmhouse wall and tore a chunk from the rotting plaster.

"Hello, you bastards!" he bellowed. "Daddy's come home at last!"

There was no sound, only the burble of a TV game show from Levi's room. Jack lifted the Sig and fired a shot into the ceiling, causing more plaster to rain down. "Come on!" he screamed. "You wanted it, so let's get dirty! Show your ugly fucking faces, cunts!"

A shadow appeared at the top step, and resolved itself into the little girl. She'd traded in her shorts and tee for a dress, blue with small pink sprigs of flowers. Blood streaked the front. Whatever little girl had originally worn that dress was long gone. "Will you keep it down?" she said. "Some of us are trying to get our rest."

Jack raised the pistol, drew a bead, and fired. His shot went far wide and shattered an old-style lamp bolted to the wall of the upstairs hallway. He was a crap shot, but he didn't let it bother him. The gun served its purpose.

The little girl didn't even flinch. "Abbadon said you'd come. With or without him. He told us what to do."

"Did he, now?" Jack said. The old him would be pissing himself. This him was calculating lines and angles, force and velocity. The Morrigan's marks didn't change the fact he was a shit shot, but they were keeping his panic at bay. "Did he happen to tell you to let me have my girlfriend and walk out of here?"

"He said if he didn't come home we were to kill whoever walked through that door," the girl said. "Bad luck for you, nasty man."

She launched herself at Jack, knifelike claws and teeth bared, the black hair she'd kept braided into a rope at her back turning into a riot of bodies, tiny mouths and sharp, lava-glass blades. Jack brought the gun up, swiped it across the side of her head, and knocked her into the banister and then to the hall floor.

She snapped at him, and he whipped her with the gun barrel again, causing a trio of her black blade teeth to fly free.

The girl cowered, howling, and then launched at him again. Jack slipped his hand inside his leather and used it to wrap his fist around her living, writhing hair. He yanked. The girl screamed.

"Doesn't feel good, does it?" Jack said. "Perhaps if you were a bit nicer, we wouldn't have to go through this."

"What are you going to do to me?" she whined. "I'm only a baby. Compared to the rest, I haven't even done anything really terrible. I'm just a child, and I like to play with things. Live things." She blinked at him. "Is that so wrong?"

"I'm not going to debate with you, luv," Jack said. "If it makes you feel better, chalk it up to wrong place, wrong time." He mimicked Belial's move at the graveyard and jerked her head to the left by her braid. It was a clean break, quick and fast, her neck going just a bit too far and the gleam of bloodlust fading from her eyes. She wouldn't wake up quickly here, not on this ground that twisted and corrupted talent and the Black almost beyond recognition.

Jack picked up the pistol and stepped over the body, into the back room.

Levi looked up at him, docile face quivering around the edges. "You."

"Not the fucking tooth fairy," Jack agreed. "Where's Pete?"

Levi narrowed his eyes. "This isn't over, you know. You can't kill things like us. You can't kill your future, Jack. Sooner or later your little world is going to get devoured, just like the one before it and the one before that. I'm the one doing the devouring. I am the leviathan, and I eat the world."

Jack put the pistol barrel against Levi's temple and pressed it in just a bit, until it left a depression in his fatty flesh. "You know what the problem is with all of you ancient types? All the gods and demons and whatever the fuck you are?"

Levi's labored breathing increased, sounding a bit like a small saw inside his chest. "You can't kill me. You can't . . ."

"The problem is you talk too fucking much," Jack said, then squeezed the trigger.

There wasn't as much gore as films had led him

to believe. A little blood and a few bits of skull and brain covered the fuzzy telly screen, but the rest matted in Levi's hair as he slumped sideways in his scooter chair.

Jack left him there and stepped down the hall. Only Teddy left. The best and the worst of the four. Something that could get inside your head didn't leave you with a lot of options. You couldn't shoot something that could convince you that you were holding a teddy bear rather than a pistol. You couldn't reason with something that wanted more than anything to live.

He pushed the door open gently. A child's mobile lamp sat in the corner, projecting images of carousel horses and clowns onto the stained walls. Teddy still hung in state, hooked up to his IVs and machines.

Pete crouched at his feet, and she looked up at him. He wasn't the cold Jack in that moment, the Jack who had it all figured out. He dropped the pistol and crouched beside her, cupping her face in his hands. "Have they hurt you?"

Pete shook her head mutely. Her face was streaked with grime and twin rivulets where tears had cut through, but her eyes were dry. "I feel so fucking stupid," she muttered. "Didn't even see the bastards who snatched me."

Jack wrapped his arms around her. She let him, pressing her face against his leather. "You're all right," he said.

"I am," Pete said. She gave a small gasp, just an intake of air. "The baby . . ."

Jack felt the cold grow in him again. Of course. The baby. The fucking baby. How could he not have seen it? Kim had never been Abbadon's real plan, not since he and Pete had landed on their patch.

"What did they do to the baby?" he said.

Nothing yet. Teddy's voice sliced into him, and it still hurt. It bypassed his sight and cut straight to the part of his brain where his talent lived, hollowed it out and echoed there. *Abbadon had plans, though. Great plans, and they're in motion, and you can't stop them.* A thin giggle punctuated the sentence.

Jack looked up at Teddy. "Don't think I won't waste you in just a moment, you piece of shit."

"Abbadon said . . ." Pete sucked in a breath and steadied her voice. "He said that the baby was his now . . . that he'd done something . . . to me." She dug her fingers into Jack's wrists. "I can feel it. I can feel what he put in my kid, Jack. It's going to be his. I'm going to be just like those stupid cows that he sliced apart."

She's right, you know, Teddy purred. *Don never was happy with that raggedy meat bag he was riding. He had big plans. Big plans to live forever in that brave new world he was gonna open up.*

Kim hadn't been carrying a body for Teddy. Pete hadn't been snatched as leverage. Sanford had never intended to give her back. He'd traded Pete to Abbadon in exchange for his help with Locke's doorway. A brand new infant body, with talented blood pumping through it to sustain Abbadon's power. A body that wouldn't burn out like a regular meatbag, as Teddy had put it. A body that he could ride forever, while he ushered the fires of Hell into downtown LA.

"I've got some news for you," Jack told Teddy. "Abbadon is dead. He's gone. This baby isn't his and it isn't going to be."

He's not dead, Teddy said. *You know how many times Azrael did him in, down there in the Pit? Only for the fun of it? Thousands. We can't cease to exist, Jack. Not forever. We're the beginning and the end.*

"Yeah, yeah," Jack said. "The Alpha and the fucking Omega. He's still not getting my kid."

"He already has," Pete whispered. She wasn't crying, wasn't even shaking. The world could end and Pete would hold it together. "I can feel it, Jack. We were alone a long time, and he put his mark on the baby, the same as he did those other poor children, who got turned into things like . . ." She pointed at Teddy, gulping back a sob. "Like him."

There's a process. Teddy chuckled. *A seed to be planted. The child will be Abbadon. Poetic, if you think about it. The phoenix and the ashes.*

"You shut up," Jack told him. He pulled Pete to her feet. "They didn't touch you, yeah? Didn't hurt you?"

"Oh for fuck's sake, Jack, no," Pete said. "Nobody molested me, and honestly, when they snatched me that was the least of my worries." She laced her hands across her stomach. "That thing is right. He did a ritual, and his magic was so strong. When this

kid is born, it's going to become Abbadon. There's
no help for it." Her tears did start then, and she bit
her lip savagely, causing a trickle of blood. "You're
going to have to do it. I don't think I can."

Jack stared at Pete. Her stomach was barely
showing—he thought she might have put on a
stone, at worst. In all of his ramblings about the
kid, he'd never imagined there not being a kid at all.
*Head so far up your own arse you never even real-
ized what Abbadon really wanted,* the new Jack
whispered. That Jack was pragmatic. He saw the
whole picture. Abbadon couldn't be allowed near
the daylight world, never again. Pete was resilient.
She could have more children, when she was ready,
with someone who wouldn't be a complete cock-up
as a parent. And he'd keep the first evil the universe
had known at bay for a bit longer, and could go
through life knowing he hadn't contributed to anyone else's fucking up.

It made sense. In every way that mattered.

Jack dropped his hands to his side. He was hot
now, the air in Teddy's room stuffy and stinking
of a hospital ward, and massively tired. He could
curl up between the IV stands and sleep for a
week.

"I can't."

Pete let out a single, desperate sob. "You have
to . . ."

"No," Jack said. "No, we're going to make this
right, all right?" He grabbed Pete's shoulders, and
squeezed hard enough that she whimpered. "All
right?"

She licked the blood from her lip, and finally met his eyes. *Don't be scared,* he prayed. He needed one of them to not be scared, because the new Jack had deserted him, along with the cold singlemindedness, and he was only himself again, shit plans and shit luck and all.

"All right," Pete said softly. "Fuck him, anyway. Who the hell does he think he is?"

Jack pulled her against him, felt the hard swell of her stomach against his torso, and nothing else mattered. "A bastard," he said in her ear.

"The worst sort of cunt," Pete said. "I fucking hate this, Jack. It's never going to be over, is it? This kid is like a beacon for all the shit and evil of the Black, and it's all going to come down on the poor thing."

Jack pressed his face into Pete's neck, into the curve behind her ear. "Worry about it when you need to worry, luv. I won't let anything happen to you." He brushed his lips over her forehead, tasted the sweat there. "Either of you."

Pete's mouth curled down. "Promise?"

"On my fucking life," Jack said.

This is all very touching, Teddy said. *But you're not leaving here.*

"No," Jack told him. He pulled the paper he'd taken from Lucinda's coffin from his pocket. It was wrinkled and smeared in blood, but legible. "You are," Jack said.

From the next room, he heard stirring and skittering through the walls. Levi and the girl were awake. He turned to Pete. "We don't have a lot of time. No time, really."

She nodded. "What do you need from me?"

Jack handed her the gun. It was a relief to get rid of the thing, if he was honest. "Shoot anything that comes through that door right in the fucking face, and that includes adorable little girls."

"Right," Pete said. Jack pulled out his knife and she cocked her eyebrow. "And what are you going to do?"

She gave a small gasp when Jack jammed the knife into Teddy's neck. It wasn't demon blood, but it would do.

Teddy screamed. *This isn't going to save you, Jack. Not you or your whore or your brat.*

"Let me tell you something," Jack said. "She is not a whore. She's a good woman and I don't deserve her, and that attitude of yours is exactly why you're hanging from a wall in this shit-trap." He twisted the knife in deep, and felt Teddy's heart give its last misshapen tremble. "Try to be less of a twat in your next life, yeah?"

He drew Locke's sigil in the blood pooling on the warped floorboards. He stood in the center of it and recited the words that Sanford had intoned, although he liked to think he sounded like less of a pretentious gobshite while doing it. As a last thought, he picked up a discarded bottle of cheap Mexican beer—probably Levi's doing—and tucked it inside his jacket.

He'd thought a portal straight to Hell would be

more dramatic, but instead a thin line of white smoke rose from the circle, and the sigil fell away. The real world started to ash away little by little as the physical laws of space bent, burned up, and blew away.

Jack grabbed Pete by the hand and pulled her into the circle. The Black here was strong. He *was* the Black, inside Locke's doorway, atoms spread from one end of the universe to the other. Pete's Weir talent flowed through him, except this time it wasn't an onrushing storm, a flood that could drown him. Here they were two halves, and they fit together. Weir and mage, floating on the time stream of magic, outside the realm of anything usual.

Jack put one hand on Pete's stomach, used the Weir to widen his sight. His skull didn't hurt—it merely felt as if the top had come off and an avalanche of foreign sensation had poured in.

The child was vague—not really thoughts so much as impulses, impulses of hunger and curiosity and fright. It wasn't formed yet, didn't really exist in the psychic space.

Abbadon's magic rode it like a caul over its psychic presence, like an oil spill in cool water. He'd slipped inside Pete's talent, inside her physical body, and planted a seed amid the psychic DNA of his child so that when it formed, it would form in his image.

Jack drew the darkness out, drew out the spark of Abbadon that still lived, inside Pete.

He saw the glass sands of Hell and smelled the hot wind. It wasn't a dream, now. He was here, could taste the ashes, hear the screams and the clink of the soul bottles, smell the acrid roast of human flesh borne on the air.

Pete stared, turning in a slow circle. "This is Hell."

"You are smart, luv," Jack said. "I do love that about you."

Pete pointed over his shoulder. "Another time, Jack."

Abbadon stood there. He wasn't the dragon that Jack had faced in the graveyard, not the slick-faced human. He was a shadow, all teeth and screams. "You think you're so fucking smart," he snarled.

"Smarter than you," Jack said. "You decided to use my fucking child as your next ride into the daylight world. Not your brightest move, mate. Not even on a slow day."

"You think you put me in Hell and I'll stay?" Abbadon snapped. "I got out of this place once, Jack. I can do it again."

"About that," Jack said. "See, I don't peg old Nergal as the generous sort. He may have weakened the bars, but I think you had help crawling out the first time. Whether it was a general, or one of the Princes, or a rat you trained to gnaw through the bars—it doesn't matter. Belial knows your tricks now. I think this time, you'll stay right where I put you."

He pulled the bottle from his coat and held it up to Abbadon. "You're bound, by the laws of Hell and by my will, Abbadon. Bound to stay in this place, until Hell ends or you do. So fuck off, and leave us alone."

Abbadon's shadow flickered once, twice, like faulty film, and then he disappeared, a curl of black smoke at the bottom of a manky bottle, sharing space with a half-centimeter of beer and two dead fag-ends.

Jack shook the bottle a bit, watched the smoke swirl. "Reckon he's very angry?"

"Who bloody cares?" Pete said. "Trying to get at my kid. Twat."

"You said it, luv," Jack said. He walked to where the world dropped off, at the edge of the iron ravine. "Oi!" he shouted. "The prodigal son returns. Enjoy it, you coldblooded sons of bitches."

Pete caught his arm. "Let me," she said. Jack handed her the bottle. Just a sad scrap of soul. Just like everyone, no matter how evil or how much they wanted to stay alive, ended up eventually.

"Go on," he said.

Pete cocked her arm back and flung the bottle hard as she could. It arced out over the ravine and flashed in the harsh white light before it fell from sight and disappeared.

She looked up at Jack. "That's done, then?"

Jack looked down into the ravine. "For now." Without Abbadon, Belial and his ilk would make short work of the other three. Jack stepped back, let go of the threads of Locke's gateway spell, and watched as the daylight world slowly blended back together, and the laws of physics righted themselves.

Pete grimaced. "Awful. Feel like I'm going to puke now."

"I'll join you," Jack said. Nothing else stirred in

the farmhouse. Teddy's corpse hung silently, blood-less and still. In the hallway, the little girl lay star-ing at the water-spot continents on the ceiling, unblinking.

Pete flinched. "Christ, she was creepy, wasn't she?"

Jack shivered. "Adorable ones usually are."

Outside, he saw a line of light on the horizon. It was nearly dawn. Pete sat down on the steps, in-haling a deep breath of air. "Don't suppose we've got a ride out of here."

"I came with that twat Mayhew and with Sliver," Jack said. "But I imagine after that light show, Sliver got smart and fucked off back to Angel City. And Mayhew is just fucking useless."

"He really was a twat," Pete said. "I'm sorry, you know. You told me it was bad business and I went anyway."

"Luv, if you lined up all the bad business I've followed up on in me life, you'd circle the earth," Jack said. "Possibly twice." He tapped a fag out of his pack and offered the last to Pete.

"I'm pregnant, you tit," she said. "What exactly am I supposed to do with that?"

Jack touched his finger to the end of the fag. It took a few tries, in this zone where the Black twisted back on itself, but he got the fag lit and took a long drag. "I have no idea what the fuck I'm doing, Pete," he said. Once it was out, it seemed silly he hadn't said it sooner. Nothing caught on fire. No one slapped him. The sun was up, and he heard some sort of wild bird scream, off in the brush.

"You think I do?" she said.

Jack watched the end of his fag, smoke curling. "I'm not going to be a decent sort of father," he said. "I'll try, yeah, but I'll cock up, and you were right. This kid has no idea what it's in for. Everyone will want it, both sides. And if it has a talent . . . I can't quit, Pete. I can try, but it'll always find me, so it's best if I just bow out now, because I can't be what you need or want."

"It's a girl," Pete said. "I had a new ultrasound right before we left the UK." She exhaled, as if she'd just confessed something. "So not an it. A girl."

"You didn't tell me," Jack said. Christ, a girl. This was going to be even worse than he'd imagined. He didn't know what the fuck he'd do with a baby girl.

"I didn't know if I should," Pete said. "Didn't think you'd be sticking around."

"About that," Jack said. "It's pretty fucking clear that I need to. For the kid."

"I don't want you to stick around because of some cockeyed obligation," Pete said. "I can stay with Lawrence, with Ian Mosswood. Hell, even with my mum and the fucking Order. They can keep her safe."

"Why not?" Jack snapped. Suddenly he was fed up. Through dancing. If he stepped on feet, so be it, but he was too tired to be subtle any longer. "Why can't I be obligated to stay around? 'S more than my fucking father ever offered."

"Because I don't want you to hate me," Pete said

softly. "Jack, I don't want you retired, but I don't want you gone, either. You were gone for so long, and when you were in Hell . . . but I won't trap you. I won't be that woman. I just fucking won't."

The sunrises in California were magnificent. Jack had heard somewhere that it was from all the pollution. A pink rind of cloud sat below the glowing half-orb, white flashes chasing away the velvety night sky, while the moon and stars clung, far off beyond the mountains.

"You're not," he said at last. He could be scared—could be fucking terrified—but that didn't mean he had to run. "I can't see hating you, luv," he said. "Thought I did, for a long while, but I don't, and I won't, and I won't be my fucking cunt of a father, either. I'll be there for the girl, until you won't have me."

Pete placed her hand over his knee, gave a squeeze. Her touch set off a series of aches and pains, and Jack grimaced.

"You all right?" Pete said.

"I'm old, luv," Jack said. "This baby is going to run me fucking ragged, I hope you know."

Pete leaned her head against his shoulder. "I think you'll manage. We will, somehow."

Jack sat quietly with Pete for some time, while the sun rose. He could tell her later about the Morrigan's marks, her visitation, the strange new thing living under his skin. About the Princes of Hell and how Belial had picked him, all those years ago, to be one of their legion. About how the slow fracture and dissolution of the Black hadn't stopped with Nergal, would never stop, and things back in London would likely never be all right for the crowmage and the Weir again. He could tell her all that later, Jack thought as he slipped his arm around Pete's thin shoulders.

He had the time.

REVELATION

"And his name that sat on him was Death, and Hell followed with him."

—Book of Revelation, 6:8

CHAPTER 31

He'd been back in London nearly a month, and Jack was beginning to feel almost right with things again. Aside from the occasional dirty look down the Lament pub or a dead bird nailed to his door, the magic sector of London had seemed to accept that he was back and he wasn't going anywhere.

Pete hadn't taken the news about the Morrigan well. He hadn't been able to tell her what it meant, furnish specifics that she could quantify and assess. Hell, *he* didn't know what it meant. Just that the Morrigan had her claws into him, at last, and she wasn't letting go.

At least Pete hadn't run off. Jack looked over to where she was sitting cross-legged on the sofa, tapping away at her laptop. He'd still been able to find jobs outside of London, mostly small villages without any local talent. The locals in big cities—Liverpool, Newcastle, Cardiff—all talked among themselves, and none of them were overly wel-coming.

Pete turned her eyes on him. "What?"

"Nothing," Jack said. He levered himself off the sofa and went into the loo. They talked, but not about anything below the surface. Jack didn't know if Pete was afraid of him. He was, if he was honest. The markings called up power he'd never even come close to touching. Human beings weren't meant to channel that much of the Black, and Jack had to wonder how long before his head popped off like a gasket.

Sleep was nonexistent, and he was still sporting bruises from the beating Abbadon had given him in LA. Pete had fed Shavers some poppycock story about cults and serial killers and he'd gotten himself in the paper and hadn't dug too deeply. Probably got a promotion out of it, the twat.

"Jesus, Winter," Jack muttered as he pissed and washed his hands. His reflection looked old, eyes bagged and face grey. "Pull it together."

"Talking to yourself again?"

Jack jerked and knocked the mug containing his and Pete's toothbrushes off the vanity. The ceramic smashed on the tile. "Fuck!"

Belial grinned at him in the mirror. "Jumpy. Perhaps you should cut out the caffeine."

Jack spun and jabbed his finger into the demon's face. "You don't get to show up in my flat and talk shit. You bloody left me."

"I saved your life, Winter, and you'll do well to

remember that," Belial said. "Anyway, I didn't just pop in for a chat."

Pete knocked on the door. "Jack? Who's in there with you?"

Jack opened the door and Pete locked eyes with Belial, then glared. "Oh," she said. "You."

"Me," Belial agreed. "Again. Aren't you positively glowing, little Petunia?"

"I'll put my fist through your fucking shark teeth, you cunt," Pete said. "Get the hell out of my loo."

"Relax." Belial held up his hands. "I'm just here to talk to your loving man." He inclined his head at Jack. "Is there somewhere . . ."

Jack shook his head. "Whatever you have to say to me, say it here."

"Fine," Belial said. "Azrael is out, mate. The Triumverate is short a member. Or was."

Jack stayed quiet. Azrael was one of the oldest names in most demonic grimoires. If Baal and Beelzebub had sent him the way of Abbadon, it meant very few things, none of them wholesome for the rest of the Black.

"Seems he and Abbadon got to talking all those millenia down in his pit," Belial said. "Seems that he became sympathetic to their cause, and when Nergal busted out that was the cover he needed."

Jack shrugged. "Can't say I'm surprised," he said. "What's this got to do with me?"

"I am a Prince of Hell now," Belial said. "And I've come to tell you that my offer still stands, Jack. Even with all that mess on your skin."

Pete looked between them, arms folded over the swell of her stomach. "What offer, Jack?"

"He didn't tell you. Shocking, that," Belial said. "But I will—I offered your boy here a chance to sit at my table, be at my side. He doesn't have to die and be reborn or anything tacky and Biblical of that sort. All he has to do is say yes." Belial grinned at Jack. "No lies. No tricks."

"But a bargain," Jack told him. "Another fucking axe to dangle above me neck."

"Not a bargain," Belial said. "An agreement. An alliance, between a general and a valued soldier. And what a soldier you'd make, Jack. You'd never have to worried about any of this . . ." he gestured through the bubbly glass of the loo window, out across the chimney pots and post-war box flats of Whitechapel. "None of the politics, none of the bullshit. Nobody coming after you because they fancy you're the cause of their little problems. You'd be protected."

"But he'd be in Hell," Pete said.

Belial cocked his head. "I would think you'd be in favor of this. You do have the baby to consider. This is a dangerous world for a child, Petunia. You of all people know that."

Pete curled her fists into tight knots. "Get out. Before I kick the shite out of you and make you eat it."

Belial turned back to Jack. "What do you say, Winter? Right hand of the devil. It really is the better choice. Better than anything the Hag is going to offer you." He put his hand on Jack's shoulder.

"Think it over. Don't say no just to be a cunt. I want you, Jack. Hell wants you. What do you say?"

Jack moved the demon's hand off him, along with the slimy essence that brushed against his sight. "I say . . ." Belial's offer made sense. The Morrigan would ask him to do something, sooner or later, even worse than to allow Nergal to be released into the world. And he honestly wasn't sure he could say no. But to be in Hell, voluntarily. To be a servant of Belial, willingly. That wasn't Jack—not before the bargain, not during his smack days, not now, and not fucking ever.

"You say yes, lad," Belial prompted. "Easiest word in the language."

"Jack . . ." Pete said, but he brushed against the back of her hand with his fingers and quieted her.

"Go fuck yourself," he told Belial. "And you can tell your two bum-buddies down there in the City I said the same."

Belial's mouth turned down. "Bad choice, Jackie. Bad, bad choice."

"But it is my choice," Jack said. "I did what you asked. I sent Abbadon and his freaks back to their prison. You've no claim on either of us any longer, so kindly get the fuck out."

Belial straightened his cuffs and stepped around Pete. "Fine. I'll see myself out. And Jack?" The demon pointed one black-tipped finger at him. "You're a bloody idiot."

Jack stayed still until the door slammed, then let out the breath he'd been holding until it burned. "Shit. I hate it when he does that."

Pete sat on the edge of the tub. "That was bad, wasn't it? Saying no to him?"

"Probably come back and bite my arse, yeah," Jack said. He sat next to her and put an arm around her shoulders. Pete was warm and smelled faintly of cocoa butter. He pressed his face against her hair.

"What if we fuck this up?" Pete murmured. "Like, beyond repair? What if the kid gets an ASBO and starts lighting people's pets on fire?"

"We won't," Jack said, feeling no conviction whatsoever.

"Maybe you should have said yes," Pete whispered. "It's the only way we could be sure . . ."

"No," Jack said. "Belial would find some way to put one over on me, and I'd end up even worse off."

"At least you're learning," Pete said.

"Trying," Jack said. "Not doing a fantastic job."

"It's all right," Pete said, and kissed his cheek before resuming her position. "We'll figure something out."

Jack let his eyes close, to just be still for one moment. Soon enough he'd have to move, find them a place to go where the local mages and sorcerers weren't howling for his blood and freaks weren't trying to sell their souls to ancient demons, while other freaks optioned the movie rights. Soon. But right now, he could be with Pete, and that was worth anything Belial could have offered him, true bargain or not.

"Yeah," he said to Pete. "I think we've sorted it."

"We'll move to the country, I'll get fat and pop

out six more kiddies, and you can take up sheep farming," Pete said.

"Or I could sit in front of the telly and shout at you the baby needs changing," Jack said. "And to fetch me another lager."

"Or I could smack you in the head," Pete said.

"All of the above?" Jack suggested. "Or none."

"I don't know," Pete said. "And that's all right, Jack. Really. I don't expect you to have it all sorted this second." She wrapped her arms around his waist. "I'm just glad you're not leaving."

"Not for anything," Jack said. "And I mean that, Pete."

"I know you do," Pete said softly. Jack pressed his lips against her hair.

"That's all that matters, then."